THE WORLD'S CLASSICS

AN OLD MAN'S LOVE

ANTHONY TROLLOPE (1815–82), the son of a failing
London barrister, was brought up an awkward and
unhappy youth amidst debt and privation. His mother
maintained the family by writing, but Anthony's own
first novel did not appear until 1847, when he had at
last established a successful Civil Service career in the
Post Office, from which he retired in 1867. After a slow
start, he achieved fame, with 47 novels and some 16
other books, and sales sometimes topping 100,000. He
was acclaimed an unsurpassed portraitist of the lives of
the professional and landed classes, especially in his
perennially popular *Chronicles of Barsetshire* (1855–67),
and his six brilliant Palliser novels (1865–80). His
fascinating *Autobiography* (1883) recounts his successes
with an enthusiasm darkened by memories of a miserable
youth. Throughout the 1870s he developed new styles of
fiction, but was losing critical favour by the time of his
death.

JOHN SUTHERLAND is professor of English at the
California Institute of Technology. He has edited
Trollope's *The Way We Live Now, Is he Popenjoy? He knew he
was Right*, and *Ralph the Heir*, Jack London's *John
Barleycorn* and Thackeray's *Vanity Fair* for the World's
Classics series.

THE WORLD'S CLASSICS

——

ANTHONY TROLLOPE
An Old Man's Love

——

Edited with an Introduction by
JOHN SUTHERLAND

Oxford   New York
OXFORD UNIVERSITY PRESS

Oxford University Press, Walton Street, Oxford OX2 6DP

Oxford New York Toronto
Delhi Bombay Calcutta Madras Karachi
Petaling Jaya Singapore Hong Kong Tokyo
Nairobi Dar es Salaam Cape Town
Melbourne Auckland

and associated companies in
Berlin Ibadan

Oxford is a trade mark of Oxford University Press

Introduction, Note on the Text, Select Bibliography, Appendices, Explanatory Notes
© John Sutherland 1991

Chronology of Anthony Trollope © N. John Hall 1991

First published posthumously 1884
First issued as a World's Classic paperback 1991
Reprinted 1992

British Library Cataloguing in Publication Data

Data available

Library of Congress Cataloging in Publication Data

Trollope, Anthony, 1815–1882.
An old man's love/Anthony Trollope: edited with an introduction
by John Sutherland.
p. cm.—(The world's classics)
I. Sutherland, John, 1938–.   II. Title.   III. Series.
PR5684.04   1991   823'.8—dc20   90-25615

ISBN 0-19-282646-8

Printed in Great Britain by
BPCC Hazells Ltd
Aylesbury, Bucks

CONTENTS

INTRODUCTION

*Readers who do not wish to learn details of the plot will
prefer to treat the Introduction as an Epilogue.*

An Old Man's Love is an older man's novel.
Trollope's hero—William Whittlestaff—is just 50
years old. Hale, Whittlestaff has never had a day's
illness and his only sign of decrepitude is a slightly
crooked finger. It may be gout and he has pru-
dently forsworn port for whisky-and-water, a tipple
that he anyway prefers and that is easier on his
pocket. Otherwise this 'old man' is as sound
as a nut. Trollope began writing the novel on
20 February and finished it on 9 May 1882. He was
67 years old and anything but hale. Since 1873 he
had been completely deaf in one ear. His eyesight
was poor. He was grossly overweight (sixteen
stone, on a medium frame). From 1879 onwards,
he had suffered from writer's cramp and was
obliged increasingly to dictate his books. In late
1881, Trollope went to his local Hampshire doctor
with chest pains. He received the dreadful news
that he had angina pectoris. 'I may drop dead at
any moment,' he glumly told a friend.[1] And he
informed his brother Tom that 'my heart is worn
out having been worked too hard'.[2]

[1] *Trollope: Interviews and Recollections*, ed. R. C. Terry (London,
1987), 232.
[2] *The Letters of Anthony Trollope*, ed. N. John Hall (2 vols., Stanford,
Calif., 1983), ii. 912.

In mid-January 1882 Trollope learned from a London specialist that he did not, after all, have angina. He wryly promised to 'walk up all the hills in the country' to celebrate his reprieve. In fact, he could barely move his bulk around a room. He had suffered a hernia and was obliged to wear a rupture truss, which effectively rendered him a semi-invalid. He also had severe asthma (cardiac asthma, as N. John Hall surmises), which further restricted his movements. His asthma was worsening fast in 1882. As Trollope told Cecilia Meetkerke in mid-April of that year (while writing the middle chapters of *An Old Man's Love*), 'there is only one way out of the trouble that I see'.[3] Not that Trollope shrank from death. He confided to his friend the poet Alfred Austin, a month before beginning *An Old Man's Love*: 'there is nothing to fear in death,—if you be wise. There is so much to fear in life, whether you be wise or foolish.'[4] More bleakly he informed his brother Tom that 'the time has come upon me of which I have often spoken to you, in which I should know that it were better that I were dead'. He did not have many months to wait.

At the head of Chapter 17 of *An Old Man's Love*'s manuscript, Trollope scrawled faintly in pencil 'not sick'. For most of the novel's composition one can assume that he was very sick. But he died as he had lived, working at full steam. After finishing *An Old Man's Love* in May 1882, he went straight on to his last novel, *The Landleaguers*. Incredibly, for a man in his terminal state, Trollope undertook two

---

[3] *Letters*, ii. 959.   [4] Ibid. 942.

trips to Ireland to research this story—the first on 15 May, just seven days after writing 'Finis' to *An Old Man's Love*. He did not win his race with the undertaker, and *The Landleaguers* was never finished. That it should have been even started is astonishing.

Six months after finishing *An Old Man's Love*, on 3 November 1882, Trollope suffered a catastrophic stroke while laughing at F. Anstey, reading aloud from his new comic novel, *Vice Versa*. Trollope lingered on paralysed and speechless (apparently an inarticulate 'No!' was all he could manage) before his body mercifully gave out on 6 December. Trollope was a much-loved public figure and bulletins on his health were issued for the English newspapers. The Queen's physician, Sir William Jenner, attended him in his last illness.

Trollope had no publisher lined up for *An Old Man's Love* and after his death the manuscript was laid in a drawer together with that of *An Autobiography*. The novel remained unpublished until March 1884, fifteen months after its author's death. He himself was uncertain whether it would appear in serial or volume form, and wrote with both possibilities in mind. The manuscript was prepared for press and proof was read by the novelist's son and literary executor, Henry Merivale Trollope.

As Trollope never tires of telling us, writing novels is hard work. Why should a man in such extreme pain as he was in 1882 persist in punishing himself? Trollope was not hard up (his estate was valued at a little under £26,000). And

anyway, his novels were not now earning him
much—even when he could find publishers to take
them. Two hundred pounds or so—which was
what *An Old Man's Love* was worth—was neither
here nor there. The vogue for Trollope's fiction had
long since passed. He was fondly remembered by
the novel-reading public, mainly for his Barsetshire
chronicles; but there was no overwhelming demand
for more of his wares than the two score or so
currently available in the circulating libraries.

Trollope's reason for working himself if not to
death then up to the moment of death was, it
seems, purely emotional. He needed to do it as
other compulsives need to drink or gamble. He
described the need to his son in December 1880: 'I
finished on Thursday the novel I was writing [*Kept
in the Dark*], and on Friday I began another [*The
Fixed Period*]. Nothing really frightens me but the
idea of enforced idleness. As long as I can write
books, even though they be not published, I think
that I can be happy.'[5] Trollope wrote to keep
'terror' at bay. There was much to terrify him in
1882 as he contemplated the inexorable decay of
his body.

In the grisly circumstances, *An Old Man's Love* is
a fine performance. Some Trollopeans, Michael
Sadleir for instance, rate the work highly. I do not
rank *An Old Man's Love* as quite among the author's
best things. Dictation, it seems to me, diffused a
faint cloudiness through Trollope's narrative.
(Those passages he wrote in his own hand are, I
believe, palpably sharper—see Appendix 1.) The

[5] Ibid. 886.

young-maiden-with-two-lovers dilemma, if not exactly stale, is perhaps too familiarly Trollopean. The novelist evidently dried up in the middle sections of the narrative, and dragged in sections of his 1878 travel book *South Africa*, as part of John Gordon's off-stage history (see Appendix 2). It's lively enough material, but argues a flagging invention.

The plot of *An Old Man's Love* also contains a weak link that one feels a younger Trollope would never have let stand. Some years before the action opens John Gordon and Mary Lawrie fell in love in Norwich. The affair came to nothing. Disgraced by the failure of his father's bank and scorned by Mary's haughty stepmother, Gordon left for the diamond fields of Kimberley. There was never any open word spoken of his love and only the enigmatic promise 'that if he returned he would come to Norwich'. Over the next eighteen months, Mary is orphaned and, penniless as we understand, is taken in by her father's old friend William Whittlestaff. Over the year and a half following, Whittlestaff's heart is won by his pretty, black-haired ward, who is half his age. Mary's heart remains true to Gordon. But she has heard nothing from him. There was no understanding between them as to engagement. He may well have found another—may even be married or dead—life is cheap in the diamond fields (women are easily bought, too, if like John Gordon you have a pocketful of diamonds). Out of gratitude to her guardian, Mary finally accepts his delicately offered proposal. Later that very day Gordon returns unannounced. He has struck it rich in South Africa and has come to claim Mary as his bride.

The coincidence of the two proposals strains credulity. But even more incredible is Gordon's silence over the three years of his absence and his strange failure to make any enquiry about Mary's circumstances while he was away. The mails between England and her colonies were fast and reliable, as none knew better than Anthony Trollope. One feels that at his most energetic, the novelist would have invented some plausible reason for Gordon's silence—an embarrassing entanglement with some other woman abroad (like Paul Montague's in *The Way We Live Now*, for instance) or the skulduggery of a rival. By way of explanation of Gordon's silence in *An Old Man's Love* Trollope merely tells us that 'It was the nature of the man.'

There are ample good things in *An Old Man's Love* to outweigh this improbability at its core. The depiction of Whittlestaff's character as he grapples with his love problem is vintage Trollope. Whittlestaff himself is fascinatingly cross-grained. Behind a pugnacious exterior (as Montagu Blake observes, he is a dog who will not easily give up his bone) Whittlestaff is morbidly sensitive to the passing blows of life that a genuinely robust man would easily shrug off. Whittlestaff has never recovered from a cluster of early disappointments in life. As a young man he fell out with his admiral-father, who wanted him to be a barrister. As a student at Oxford William failed to win the fellowship he yearned for. His youthful poems were scorned. Catherine Bailey, his first love, was stolen from him by his rival Compas, an Old Bailey lawyer with a 'cruelly sensuous face'. The libidinous Compas has over the years fathered ten children on Catherine. Had she accepted the gentler Whittle-staff 'there might perhaps have been less than ten children'. (Does Trollope mean that Whittlestaff would gallantly have used contraceptives, or that he would not have demanded his conjugal rights as remorselessly as Compas?)

A defeated 30-year-old Whittlestaff gave up any thought of a career and turned his back on life. He now never writes a line of verse. He does not even console himself with the pleasures of the hunt or angling. He has retreated to his Hampshire house, Croker's Hall, like some male Miss Havisham. There he lives comfortably, if uselessly, on the £1,000-a-year which his father has left him (also a disappointment; he expected twice as much). Whittlestaff is looked after by his housekeeper Mrs Baggett, another of love's refugees. Until Mary appears, Whittlestaff's principal pleasure in life is reading Horace in his garden. He is civil to his neighbours but habitually solitary in his social habits. His dearest wish is to be left alone. He accepts the responsibility of a young female ward reluctantly, and only out of painful duty to his dead friend.

Whittlestaff's behaviour in love is of a piece with everything else in his life. He has every reason to hold Mary to her promise to marry him. She gave him her word freely. Why should he surrender her to a rival who has no legitimate claim on her, who may well be disreputable, and whose one claim is that he is her own age? Have not other old men (so-called) taken young brides? Cannot a girl *learn* to love an older man who is good to her? But, inevitably, Whittlestaff gives in and gives up, as he has done at every crisis of his life. Because he loves, he sacrifices what he loves. 'I could not hold her to my bosom,' he declares, 'knowing that she would so much rather be in the arms of another man.' His renunciation is recorded in Chapter 20, 'Mr. Whittlestaff takes his journey' (the journey is to London, to tell John Gordon that he will surrender Mary). Trollope anatomizes the old man's emotions at this crisis with surgical precision:

When he came to the end of his journey, [Mr Whittlestaff] had himself driven to the hotel, and ordered his dinner, and ate it in solitude, still supported by the ecstasy of his thoughts. He knew that there was before him a sharp cruel punishment, and then a weary lonely life. There could be no happiness, no satisfaction, in store for him. He was aware that it must be so; but still for the present there was a joy to him in thinking that he would make her happy, and in that he was determined to take what immediate delight it would give him. He asked himself how long that delight could last; and he told himself that when John Gordon should have once taken her by the hand and claimed her as his own, the time of his misery would have come. (page 223)

As Whittlestaff clearly foresees while munching his lonely steak, he will experience a momentary gratification at doing the right thing followed by a lifetime's festering envy of the young man who has snatched away his prize. Trollope's coded language clearly suggests the sexual nature of Whittlestaff's disappointment. He is, one assumes, a virgin. It would be surprising if, among the rough and tumble of Kimberley, Gordon had contrived to keep his Temple pure. As his *louche* friend Tookey puts it 'at the Fields there isn't the same sort of prudish life which one is accustomed to in England'. It will be easy and natural for a sexually outgunned Whittlestaff to slip into the role of father and settle his fortune on Mary ('Are you not my daughter, my only child?'). It will also be easy and natural for Whittlestaff to give Mary away ceremonially, at her wedding. But what will the old man feel that same evening when, in a bedroom not too far away, Gordon 'claims Mary as his own' and the marriage is consummated? 'I shall never cease to regret all that I have lost' are Whittlestaff's last words in the novel, addressed to Mary Gordon (as she now is) in his bedroom, as she prepares to leave on 'her long wedding trip'. It is the last time he will see her as a virgin. Whittlestaff is that much-admired English thing, a good loser. Conscience and duty are satisfied by his giving up Mary Lawrie. But would not a real man have fought to hold what was rightfully his? The novel leaves us with the suspicion that after all Whittlestaff is *too* gentlemanly.

As recent biographers have shown, Trollope evidently shared much of Whittlestaff's inner hypersensitivity. To the outside world he was the monster that the American J. R. Lowell saw: 'a big, red-faced, rather underbred Englishman of the bald-with-spectacles type . . . A good roaring

positive fellow who deafened me.'[6] Julian
Hawthorne, another American, had much the
same reaction in 1879. Trollope was, he observed,
'a modernised Squire Western, nourished with beef
and ale, and roughly hewn out of the most robust
and least refined variety of human clay'.[7] Trollope
had developed a formidable bark (in both senses)
to protect himself. People who met him casually
thought him the quintessence of Victorian
masculinity. Friends who knew him well detected a
softer, almost feminine streak in Trollope's character. This streak is most clearly revealed in the
posthumously published *An Autobiography* (1883),
particularly the chapters dealing with his early
family life. As a child and as an adolescent,
Trollope had been painfully shy, solitary, tongue-
tied, and awkward—'hobbledehoyish', to use his
own favourite term. When he grew up, he learned
to mask his vulnerability by an exaggerated
heartiness. But the unhappy child was never
entirely exorcised from Trollope's personality. It
rendered him a profoundly paradoxical person, at
once bullyingly aggressive and morbidly sensitive.
Sadleir sees this dualism as the key to Trollope's
character: 'never in one man was greater contrast
between the manner and the spirit; between the
outward assurance and the actual tenderhearted-
ness; between the rough insensibility of gesture and
the delicate transparency of mind'.[8] This dualism
is evident in Trollope's creation, William Whittlestaff, a man whose first words in the novel are the

---

[6] *Interviews and Recollections*, 77.   [7] Ibid. 144.
[8] Michael Sadleir, *Trollope: A Commentary* (London, 1927), 385.

brutal 'I'll be whipped if I will have anything to do with her' and whose last act is to give up all his wealth to promote the happiness of Mary Lawrie, at the expense of his own.

There were two circumstances—one immediate and one in his past—that sharpened Trollope's treatment of Whittlestaff's dilemma and gave it what Sadleir calls 'an intimate significance'.[9] The immediate circumstance was the way in which he wrote the novel. Some of it was evidently done at his desk in his study, using his old-fashioned straight pen. But he did not have enough flexibility and strength in his hand for much autograph composition, certainly not for the page after page at 250 words every quarter of an hour which he had routinely churned out in his prime. Two stretches at least of *An Old Man's Love* Trollope scribbled in one of the public rooms of the Athenaeum. One knows this because he used club notepaper. I like to think that something of the club's atmosphere permeates those sections of the narrative (see notes to pages 206 and 257). But, in 1882, Trollope's visits to his beloved clubs must have been fairly rare. Most of *An Old Man's Love* was dictated to Trollope's favourite (and extremely competent) niece, Florence Nightingale Bland. One assumes that during these spells of dictation he was lying down, or semi-recumbent in an armchair, as his young amanuensis sat at the desk in his study at Harting.

Florence was the daughter of Rose Trollope's sister, Isabella Heseltine. At 8 years old Florence

[9] Ibid. 212.

was left a penniless orphan. Trollope and his wife took the little girl into their household in 1863. She won their hearts. As the biographer Richard Mullen puts it, 'Florence became the daughter that Trollope never had.'[10] We are told that on her part the girl grew up adoring her benefactor. As a young woman she was his inseparable companion. They would ride together in Hyde Park and go to dinners together. As Trollope advanced in years, and as his fingers stiffened, she became his secretary and his travelling companion. He left her £4,000 in his will. In 1882, she was an eligible 27 years old. According to Mullen, 'Trollope expected Florence to marry and yet feared that, when that happened, "I shall have a bad time of it".'[11]

One does not know what was the exact mixture of emotions Trollope had for his young helper. Obviously paternal benevolence prevailed. But there may also have been a sexual pang at the thought of her leaving him. It is not easy for fathers—however well-wishing—to contemplate giving up their daughters (or their foster-daughters) to lovers of their own age. One may suppose that *An Old Man's Love* plays out, in fiction, some of the 'bad time' that Trollope anticipated on surrendering Florence to her John Gordon, whoever that young man might be. Certainly it cannot have done the novel any harm to have been largely dictated by an old man to a young lady of whom he was inordinately fond.

Trollope created most of *An Old Man's Love* with

[10] Richard Mullen, *Anthony Trollope: A Victorian in his World* (London, 1990), 434.   [11] Ibid. 613–14.

Florence sitting in front of him. He may also have been conscious of another dear young woman as he framed the story, but one who was on the other side of the world. Trollope first met Kate Field in 1860, on a visit to his mother in Florence. She was then 22; he was 45. Kate was American, the daughter of a famous actor, vivacious, and a feminist. Despite Trollope's being fiercely opposed to the woman's movement he and Kate struck up a friendship that was, as he said in his *Autobiography*, 'one of the chief pleasures which has graced my later years. In the last fifteen years', he writes in 1875, 'she has been, out of my own family, my most chosen friend. She is a ray of light to me, from which I can always strike a spark by thinking of her.'[12] He had every reason to think of Kate in spring 1882 as he wrote *An Old Man's Love*. She had told him she was coming to England in May of that year. He probably realized that it would be the last time he would see this young woman who so stimulated him. Sadleir goes so far as to assert that Trollope wrote *An Old Man's Love* with 'Kate Field and himself in mind'.[13]

The nature of Trollope's relationship with Kate Field has been speculated about. It has been suggested—inevitably—that they were lovers, that she was his Ellen Ternan. (Trollope, incidentally, was related to Dickens's mistress by his brother Tom's second marriage.) It is an exciting idea but unfortunately not very likely. The most reliable commentators deny that there was anything

[12] Anthony Trollope, *An Autobiography* (1883, repr. Oxford, 1923), 288.   [13] *Trollope: A Commentary*, 211.

between Trollope and his young friend to worry Mrs Trollope (who also seems to have been fond of Anthony's Kate). But, in his innocent way, he loved her. Like Whittlestaff he may well have regretted that decency prevented him from being anything more than a flirtatious uncle to her. Richard Mullen sums up the connection judiciously:

Although there was never an 'affair' between Trollope and Kate Field, there was always a mildly flirtatious side to his friendship. He ended one letter in 1868, when he was miserable and lonely in a hot July in Washington: 'Give my kindest love to your mother. The same to yourself dear Kate—if I do not see you again,—with a kiss that shall be semi-paternal—one third brotherly, and as regards the small remainder, as loving as you please.' She undoubtedly filled certain emotional needs for Trollope.[14]

The portrayal of Mr Whittlestaff's agony of lover's conscience is the supremely good thing in *An Old Man's Love*. Particularly fine is the scene in which (with comically ill grace) Whittlestaff finally gives the great gift—Mary Lawrie—to John Gordon as they walk up and down the shady paths of Green Park. There is much else to recommend the novel. The bevy of eligible young ladies—the bubbling Hall girls and Kattie Forrester—are a delight with their prattle and good-natured sarcasms against the male sex, those natural enemies among whom they all expect to find their destined mates. Trollope's familiar duo, the squire

---

[14] *Anthony Trollope. A Victorian in his World*, 364.

and the parson, are well up to standard with the avuncularly selfish Mr Hall and the exquisitely fatuous Revd Montagu Blake. The portrait of Fitzwalker Tookey hints broadly that Trollope knew much more about Victorian delinquency than the proprieties of Victorian fiction allowed him to divulge. Mrs Baggett, Whittlestaff's aged and garrulous housekeeper, is also something to relish. Like Mary Lawrie, Mrs Baggett has a partner who returns unexpectedly from the past. In her case it is Sergeant Baggett, her drunken, idle, wooden-legged, red-nosed rogue of a spouse. Like Mary, Mrs Baggett sternly resolves to follow the dictates of 'dooty' and cleave to her disreputable mate, suffer though she will. 'Duty' means that Mary must live with Mr Whittlestaff—something she does not want to do. 'Dooty' means that Baggett must leave Mr Whittlestaff—something she equally does not want to do. Like Mary, Mrs Baggett is saved from the painful sacrifice of all personal comfort by the generosity of William Whittlestaff, who pensions the obstreperous Sergeant on condition that he stay away from Alresford for ever more. One is glad that he made the one trip to give the novel its comic sub-plot.

It is astonishing that a man suffering as Trollope was in 1882 can so have added to the gaiety of readers with the creation of characters like Timothy Baggett and Montagu Blake. But among the many amusements of *An Old Man's Love* a more sombre and thoughtful note is heard. It is evident from the frequent quotation that Trollope was reading Horace for consolation in the last year of his life.

The Latin poet's wisdom and mellow irony permeate this novel, which is certainly his most Horatian in tone. Particularly, Trollope seems to have been haunted by the opening poem from the fourth book of the *Odes*, in which the weary poet berates Venus for yet again, at the age of 50, making him fall in love (see note to page 181; I quote from Ben Jonson's translation):

> Venus, again thou mov'st a war
> Long intermitted: pray thee, pray thee, spare;
> I am not such as in the reign
> of the good Cinara I was; refrain,
> Sour mother of sweet loves, forbear
> To bend a man, now at his fiftieth year.

But Venus does not forbear. Love the weary poet must, for all his grey hairs. So too William Whittlestaff must play the lover's game to the bitter-sweet end. And Trollope will write about him to the end.

NOTE ON THE TEXT

TROLLOPE, as was habitual with him, made up a work calendar for *An Old Man's Love* before starting to write. His covering note indicates some uncertainty about the novel's title and form of publication:

> An Old Man's Love
> or
> Crocus Hall
> or
> Mary Lawrie
> One volume (or two)
>
> ———
>
> Begun 20 Feb. 1882
> Completed 9 May 1882

Although he here visualizes the work in volume(s) form, Trollope actually wrote it with magazine serialization also in mind. The story, he estimated, would run to eight instalments. Each instalment would be three chapters long, making twenty-four chapters in all.

Trollope wrote—or dictated—*An Old Man's Love* steadily and according to plan. He finished the novel's first number on 7 March (1). Others followed regularly: 17 March (2), 28 March (3), 5 April (4), 14 April (5), 23 April (6), 30 April (7), 9 May (8). Accompanying Trollope's calendar is a rough worksheet with estimates of the number of pages 'over' and 'under' quota. Richard Mullen plausibly suggests that Trollope was anxious, in his weakened physical state, about keeping up to his schedule.[1]

The manuscript of *An Old Man's Love* is held at Princeton University Library, to whom I am indebted for permission to inspect it. The manuscript comprises 329 handwritten quarto sheets. Each sheet is identified by three running-total numbers: the first indicating the serial part, the second indicating the chapter, the third indicating the page. This system of triple numeration was standard with Trollope. The manuscript was evidently a first and only draft and served as printer's copy.

Some 226 pages of *An Old Man's Love*'s manuscript are in the hand of Florence Bland; 103 are in Trollope's hand (see Appendix 1). Trollope's handwriting at this stage of his life is hard to read, and one might surmise that Florence was making fair copies of Trollope's drafts. She may indeed have done so in some places. But it is clear from her acoustic errors that she was most of the time taking dictation. For example, Florence evidently took down 'Crocus Hall' as 'Croker's Hall'. Trollope liked the change, which aptly reflects Whittlestaff's senile gloom, and retained it. She took down 'The Claimant's Arms' (a symbolic inn-name) as 'The Clayman's Arms'. Trollope did not like this, and corrected it. 'Hear' she erroneously took down as 'here' and 'through' for 'threw'. She very often omitted to start fresh paragraphs, evidently because Trollope in the flow of dictation didn't tell her to.

---

[1] *Anthony Trollope: A Victorian and his World* (London, 1990), 641.

These errors, which are sprinkled through Florence
Bland's sections of the manuscript, confirm that
she was taking down Trollope's spoken words.

Trollope looked over the passages Florence
wrote in her very clear hand and made occasional
corrections or improvements. Given the fact that
the manuscript has fewer inconsistencies as to
names and details of plot than those of Trollope's
other autograph manuscripts which I have seen,
I guess that she caught many of his verbal slips
before they reached paper. Florence resolutely
denied, however, that she at all helped Trollope in
the composition of his works.

Readers may like to see if they can detect any
difference in tone, rhythm, or 'feel' between the
passages Trollope wrote and those he dictated.
The only difference I detect is that when he was
himself writing Trollope handled swift exchanges
of dialogue better. And his sense of paragraph
structure seems to have been slightly unsettled by
dictation. But he was well practised in oral
composition by 1882. It is reasonable to suppose
that dictation helped more than hindered his flow.

Trollope did not habitually make extensive
plans or much revise his fiction, once written. The
manuscript of *An Old Man's Love* shows few changes
of direction or conception and no notes or forecasts
survive. William Whittlestaff was originally
'William Wainwright'. Mary Lawrie's and John
Gordon's home town was originally Exeter rather
than Norwich. These and a few other unimportant
details are all that one can find by way of changed
authorial mind. Trollope evidently worried a little

about chronology, and at the head of chapters would occasionally mark what day it was in the narrative. At the top of Chapter 17, for example, he wrote 'Sunday. 5 day,—not sick'; by which he meant that it was Sunday in the narrative, five days after John Gordon's return, and that he, Trollope, was feeling well.

Having arranged for the publication of *An Autobiography* with the Scottish firm of William Blackwood, Henry Trollope asked for £500 for *An Old Man's Love*. Blackwood declined. He could not see the novel doing well in *Blackwood's Magazine*. The publisher eventually gave £225 for the copyright. (I am indebted to N. John Hall for these facts.) It was a very low price, but Blackwood had recently lost money on publishing Trollope's *The Fixed Period* (1882), for which he gave £450.

Proofs of *An Old Man's Love* came at the end of January 1884, and were evidently corrected by Henry Trollope. He, or Blackwood's compositor, eliminated a minor blasphemy (see note to page 178) and probably let through some slips that his father would have picked up. Henry may also have supplied the felicitous title for Chapter 17 ('Mr Whittlestaff meditates a Journey'), which Trollope originally called 'Mr Whittlestaff intends to see a man upon Business'. Someone, whether Henry Trollope or the Blackwood printers, added a lot of commas to the text.

The novel appeared in two volumes in March 1884. The text was neatly divided between Chapters 12 and 13 with Squire Hall's 'I'll introduce you to my daughters and Miss Forrester.'

A lot of bulking out was required to make two decent-sized volumes. Generous leading (twenty-two lines a page) and huge margins enabled the short work to extend to 216 and 219 pages per volume. It retailed at twelve shillings.

An Old Man's Love was kindly received. The *Saturday Review* called it 'not an unfitting finale' to Trollope's career. C. E. Dawkins in the *Academy* found 'no falling off in the vigour and the sincerity of the style'. The *Athenaeum* declared the work to be 'interesting'. The most sympathetic notice was from *The Times*, which declared Mr Whittlestaff to be 'very nearly a masterpiece'. The reviewer (who may have been Mrs Humphry Ward) added 'we are glad to think that the last of Trollope's works should leave us with agreeable memories of its writer almost at his very best'.[2]

This World's Classics text follows the 1884 two-volume edition.

[2] For the full reviews, see Donald Smalley (ed.), *Trollope: The Critical Heritage* (London, 1969).

SELECT BIBLIOGRAPHY

THE corpus of books on Trollope is large and still growing. As biography, Richard Mullen's *Anthony Trollope: A Victorian and his World* (London, 1990) and R. H. Super's *The Chronicler of Barsetshire* (Ann Arbor, Mich., 1988) supersede Michael Sadleir's pioneering *Trollope: A Commentary* (London, 1927). Sadleir also put together *Trollope: A Bibliography* (London, 1928). A splendidly pictorial account of Trollope's life and Civil Service career is given in C. P. Snow's *Trollope: His Life and Art* (London, 1975). N. John Hall has edited *The Letters of Anthony Trollope*, 2 vols. (Stanford, Calif., 1983). R. C. Terry compiles an eye- and earwitness portrait of the novelist in *Trollope: Interviews and Recollections* (London, 1987). Terry has also compiled the useful *A Trollope Chronology* (London, 1989). Trollope's own *An Autobiography* (London, 1883; repr. in World's Classics, Oxford, 1923) remains the essential introduction to any reading of the fiction.

The best extended discussion of *An Old Man's Love* is to be found in Robert Tracy, *Trollope's Later Novels* (Berkeley, Calif., 1978). Tracy also discusses an important aspect of *An Old Man's Love* in his essay 'Lana Medicata Fuco, Trollope's Classicism', in John Halperin (ed.), *Trollope: Centenary Essays* (New York, 1982). Another sidelight to *An Old Man's Love* is found in Trollope's travel book *South Africa*, 2 vols. (London, 1878; repr. in 2 vols., Gloucester, 1987, with an introduction by Sheila Michell).

As a general introduction I would recommend James R. Kincaid, *The Novels of Anthony Trollope* (Oxford, 1977) and Ruth apRoberts's *Trollope, Artist and Moralist*

(London, 1971). Among other very informative and useful critical books are: Bradford A. Booth, *Anthony Trollope: Aspects of his Life and Art* (London, 1958); A. O. J. Cockshut, *Anthony Trollope: A Critical Study* (London, 1955); P. D. Edwards, *Anthony Trollope: His Art and Scope* (London, 1978); Geoffrey Harvey, *The Art of Anthony Trollope* (London, 1980); W. J. Overton, *The Unofficial Trollope* (London, 1982); Robert Polhemus, *The Changing World of Anthony Trollope* (Berkeley, Calif., 1968); A. Pollard, *Anthony Trollope* (London, 1978); R. C. Terry, *Anthony Trollope: The Artist in Hiding* (London, 1977); Stephen Wall, *Trollope and Character* (London, 1988); Andrew Wright, *Anthony Trollope: Dream and Art* (London, 1983).

For the critical reception of this and other Trollope fiction see: Donald Smalley (ed.), *Trollope: The Critical Heritage* (London, 1969), a selection of contemporary reviews; David Skilton, *Trollope and his Contemporaries* (London, 1972); J. C. Olmsted and J. E. Welch, *The Reputation of Trollope: An Annotated Bibliography 1925–75* (New York, 1978).

A CHRONOLOGY OF
ANTHONY TROLLOPE

Virtually all Trollope's fiction after *Framley Parsonage* (1860–1) appeared first in serial form, with book publication usually coming just prior to the final instalment of the serial.

1815   (24 Apr.) Born at 16 Keppel Street, Bloomsbury, the fourth son of Thomas and Frances Trollope. (Summer?) Family moves to Harrow-on-the-Hill.

1823   To Harrow School as a day-boy.

1825   To a private school at Sunbury.

1827   To school at Winchester College.

1830   Removed from Winchester and returned to Harrow.

1834   (Apr.) The family flees to Bruges to escape creditors.
(Nov.) Accepts a junior clerkship in the General Post Office, London.

1841   (Sept.) Made Postal Surveyor's Clerk at Banagher, King's County, Ireland.

1843   (mid-Sept.) Begins work on his first novel, *The Macdermots of Ballycloran*.

1844   (11 June) Marries Rose Heseltine.
(Aug.) Transferred to Clonmel, County Tipperary.

1846   (13 Mar.) Son, Henry Merivale Trollope, born.

1847   *The Macdermots of Ballycloran*, published in 3 vols. (Newby).

(27 Sept.) Son, Frederic James Anthony Trollope, born.

1848   *The Kellys and the O'Kellys; Or, Landlords and Tenants* 3 vols. (Colburn).
(Autumn) Moves to Mallow, County Cork.

1850   *La Vendée. An Historical Romance* 3 vols. (Colburn).
Writes *The Noble Jilt* (a play, published 1923).

1851   (1 Aug.) Sent to south-west of England on special postal mission.

1853   (29 July) Begins *The Warden* (the first of the Barsetshire novels).
(29 Aug.) Moves to Belfast as Acting Surveyor.

1854   (9 Oct.) Appointed Surveyor of Northern District of Ireland.

1855   *The Warden* 1 vol. (Longman).
Writes *The New Zealander*.
(June) Moves to Donnybrook, Dublin.

1857   *Barchester Towers* 3 vols. (Longman).

1858   *The Three Clerks* 3 vols. (Bentley).
Doctor Thorne 3 vols. (Chapman & Hall).
(Jan.) Departs for Egypt on Post Office business.
(Mar.) Visits Holy Land.
(Apr.–May) Returns via Malta, Gibraltar and Spain.
(May–Sept.) Visits Scotland and north of England on postal business.
(16 Nov.) Leaves for the West Indies on postal mission.

1859   *The Bertrams* 3 vols. (Chapman & Hall).
The West Indies and the Spanish Main 1 vol. (Chapman & Hall).
(3 July) Arrives home.
(Nov.) Leaves Ireland; settles at Waltham Cross,

Hertfordshire, after being appointed Surveyor of the Eastern District of England.

1860   *Castle Richmond* 3 vols. (Chapman & Hall).
First serialized fiction, *Framley Parsonage*, published in the *Cornhill Magazine*.
(Oct.) Visits, with his wife, his mother and brother in Florence; makes the acquaintance of Kate Field, a 22-year-old American for whom he forms a romantic attachment.

1861   *Framley Parsonage* 3 vols. (Smith, Elder).
Tales of All Countries 1 vol. (Chapman & Hall).
(24 Aug.) Leaves for America to write a travel book.

1862   *Orley Farm* 2 vols. (Chapman & Hall).
North America 2 vols. (Chapman & Hall).
The Struggles of Brown, Jones, and Robinson: By One of the Firm 1 vol. (New York, Harper—an American piracy; first English edition 1870, Smith, Elder).
(25 Mar.) Arrives home from America.
(5 Apr.) Elected to the Garrick Club.

1863   *Tales of All Countries*, Second Series, 1 vol. (Chapman & Hall).
Rachel Ray 2 vols. (Chapman & Hall).
(6 Oct.) Death of his mother, Mrs Frances Trollope.

1864   *The Small House at Allington* 2 vols. (Smith, Elder).
(12 Apr.) Elected a member of the Athenaeum Club.

1865   *Can You Forgive Her?* 2 vols. (Chapman & Hall).
Miss Mackenzie 1 vol. (Chapman & Hall).
Hunting Sketches 1 vol. (Chapman & Hall).

1866   *The Belton Estate* 3 vols. (Chapman & Hall).
Travelling Sketches 1 vol. (Chapman & Hall).

Clergymen of the Church of England 1 vol. (Chapman & Hall).

1867   *Nina Balatka* 2 vols. (Blackwood).
The Claverings 2 vols. (Smith, Elder).
The Last Chronicle of Barset 2 vols (Smith, Elder).
Lotta Schmidt and Other Stories 1 vol. (Strahan).
(1 Sept.) Resigns from the Post Office.
Assumes editorship of *Saint Pauls Magazine*.

1868   *Linda Tressel* 2 vols. (Blackwood).
(11 Apr.) Leaves London for the United States on postal mission.
(26 July) Returns from America.
(Nov.) Stands unsuccessfully as Liberal candidate for Beverley, Yorkshire.

1869   *Phineas Finn, The Irish Member* 2 vols. (Virtue & Co).
He Knew He was Right 2 vols. (Strahan).
Did He Steal It? A Comedy in Three Acts (a version of *The Last Chronicle of Barset*, privately printed by Virtue & Co).

1870   *The Vicar of Bullhampton* 1 vol. (Bradbury, Evans).
An Editor's Tales 1 vol. (Strahan).
The Commentaries of Caesar 1 vol. (Blackwood).
(Jan.–July) Eased out of *Saint Pauls Magazine*.

1871   *Sir Harry Hotspur of Humblethwaite* 1 vol. (Hurst & Blackett).
Ralph the Heir 3 vols. (Hurst & Blackett).
(Apr.) Gives up house at Waltham Cross.
(24 May) Sails to Australia to visit his son.
(27 July) arrives at Melbourne.

1872   *The Golden Lion of Granpere* 1 vol. (Tinsley).
(Jan.–Oct.) Travelling in Australia and New Zealand.
(Dec.) Returns via the United States.

1873   *The Eustace Diamonds* 3 vols. (Chapman & Hall).
       Australia and New Zealand 2 vols. (Chapman &
       Hall).
       (Apr.) Settles in Montagu Square, London.

1874   *Phineas Redux* 2 vols. (Chapman & Hall).
       Lady Anna 2 vols. (Chapman & Hall).
       *Harry Heathcote of Gangoil. A Tale of Australian Bush
       Life* 1 vol. (Sampson Low).

1875   *The Way We Live Now* 2 vols (Chapman & Hall).
       (1 Mar.) Leaves for Australia via Brindisi, the
       Suez Canal, and Ceylon.
       (4 May) Arrives in Australia.
       (Aug.–Oct.) Sailing homewards.
       (Oct.) Begins *An Autobiography*.

1876   *The Prime Minister* 4 vols. (Chapman & Hall).

1877   *The American Senator* 3 vols. (Chapman & Hall).
       (29 June) Leaves for South Africa.
       (11 Dec.) Sails for home.

1878   *South Africa* 2 vols. (Chapman & Hall).
       Is He Popenjoy? 3 vols. (Chapman & Hall).
       How the 'Mastiffs' Went to Iceland 1 vol. (privately
       printed, Virtue & Co).
       (June–July) Travels to Iceland in the yacht
       'Mastiff'.

1879   *An Eye for an Eye* 2 vols. (Chapman & Hall).
       Thackeray 1 vol. (Macmillan).
       John Caldigate 3 vols. (Chapman & Hall).
       Cousin Henry 2 vols. (Chapman & Hall).

1880   *The Duke's Children* 3 vols. (Chapman & Hall).
       The Life of Cicero 2 vols. (Chapman & Hall).
       (July) Settles at South Harting, Sussex, near
       Petersfield.

1881   *Dr Wortle's School* 2 vols. (Chapman & Hall).
       Ayala's Angel 3 vols. (Chapman & Hall).

1882 *Why Frau Frohmann Raised Her Prices; and Other
      Stories* 1 vol. (Isbister).
      The Fixed Period 2 vols. (Blackwood).
      Marion Fay 3 vols. (Chapman & Hall).
      Lord Palmerston 1 vol. (Isbister).
      Kept in the Dark 2 vols. (Chatto & Windus).
      (May) Visits Ireland to collect material for a new
      Irish novel.
      (Aug.) Returns to Ireland a second time.
      (2 Oct.) Takes rooms for the winter at Garlant's
      Hotel, Suffolk St., London.
      (3 Nov.) Suffers paralytic stroke.
      (6 Dec.) Dies in nursing home, 34 Welbeck St.,
      London.

1883 *Mr Scarborough's Family* 3 vols. (Chatto &
      Windus).
      The Landleaguers (unfinished) 3 vols. (Chatto &
      Windus).
      An Autobiography 2 vols. (Blackwood).

1884 *An Old Man's Love* 2 vols. (Blackwood).

1923 *The Noble Jilt* 1 vol. (Constable).

1927 *London Tradesmen* 1 vol. (Elkin Mathews and
      Marrat).

1972 *The New Zealander* 1 vol. (Oxford University
      Press).

An Old Man's Love

CONTENTS

xl CONTENTS

CHAPTER I

Mrs. Baggett

M^R. WILLIAM WHITTLESTAFF was strolling very slowly up and down the long walk at his country seat in Hampshire,* thinking of the contents of a letter which he held crushed up within his trousers' pocket. He always breakfasted exactly at nine, and the letters were supposed to be brought to him at a quarter past. The postman was really due at his hall-door at a quarter before nine; but though he had lived in the same house for above fifteen years, and though he was a man very anxious to get his letters, he had never yet learned the truth about them. He was satisfied in his ignorance with 9.15 A.M., but on this occasion the post-boy, as usual, was ten minutes after that time. Mr. Whittlestaff had got through his second cup of tea, and was stranded in his chair, having nothing to do, with the empty cup and plates before him for the space of two minutes; and, consequently, when he had sent some terrible message out to the post-boy, and then had read the one epistle which had arrived on this morning, he thus liberated his mind: 'I'll be whipped if I will have anything to do with her.' But this must not be taken as indicating the actual state of his mind; but simply the condition of anger to which he had been reduced by the post-boy. If any one were to explain to him afterwards that he had so expressed himself on a subject of such importance, he would have declared of himself that he certainly deserved to be whipped himself. In order that he might in truth make up his mind on the subject, he went out with his hat and stick into the long walk, and there thought out the matter to its conclusion. The letter which he held in his pocket ran as follows:—

'St. Tawell's, Norwich, *February* 18—.

'My dear Mr. Whittlestaff,—Poor Mrs. Lawrie has gone at last. She died this morning at seven o'clock, and poor Mary is altogether alone in the world. I have asked her to come in among us for a few days at any rate, till the funeral shall be over. But she has refused, knowing, I suppose, how crowded and how small our house is. What is she to do? You know all the circumstances much better than I do. She says herself that she had always been intended for a governess, and that she will, of course, follow out the intention which had been fixed on between her and her father before his death. But it is a most weary prospect, especially for one who has received no direct education for the purpose. She has devoted herself for the last twelve months to Mrs. Lawrie, as though she had been her mother. You did not like Mrs. Lawrie, nor did I; nor, indeed, did poor Mary love her very dearly. But she, at any rate, did her duty by her step-mother. I know that in regard to actual money you will be generous enough; but do turn the matter over in your mind, and endeavour to think of some future for the poor girl.—Yours very faithfully, Emma King.'

It was in answer to such a letter as this, that Mr. Whittlestaff had declared that 'He'd be

whipped if he'd have anything to do with her.'
But that expression, which*must not in truth be
accepted as meaning anything, must not be supposed to have had even that dim shadow of a
meaning which the words may be supposed to
bear. He had during the last three months been
asking himself the question as to what should be
Mary Lawrie's fate in life when her step-mother
should have gone, and had never quite solved
the question whether he could or would not bring
into his own house,* almost as a daughter, a
young woman who was in no way related to
him. He had always begun these exercises of
thought, by telling himself that the world was a
censorious old fool, and that he might do just as
he pleased as to making any girl his daughter.
But then, before dinner he had generally come
to the conclusion that Mrs. Baggett would not
approve. Mrs. Baggett was his housekeeper, and
was to him certainly a person of importance. He
had not even suggested the idea to Mrs. Baggett,
and was sure that Mrs. Baggett would not approve. As to sending Mary Lawrie out into the
world as a governess;—that plan he was quite
sure would not answer.

Two years ago had died his best beloved friend,
Captain Patrick Lawrie. With him we have not
anything to do, except to say that of all men he
was the most impecunious. Late in life he had
married a second wife,—a woman who was hard,
sharp, and possessed of an annuity. The future
condition of his only daughter had been a terrible
grief to him; but from Mr. Whittlestaff he had
received assurances which had somewhat comforted him. 'She shan't want. I can't say anything

further.' Such had been the comfort given by
Mr. Whittlestaff. And since his friend's death
Mr. Whittlestaff had been liberal with presents,
—which Mary had taken most unwillingly under
her step-mother's guidance. Such had been the
state of things when Mr. Whittlestaff received
the letter. When he had been walking up and
down the long walk for an extra hour, Mr.
Whittlestaff expressed aloud the conclusion to
which he had come. 'I don't care one straw for
Mrs. Baggett.' It should be understood as having
been uttered in direct opposition to the first
assurance made by him, that 'He'd be whipped
if he'd have anything to do with her.' In that
hour he had resolved that Mary Lawrie should
come to him, and be made, with all possible
honours of ownership, with all its privileges and
all its responsibilities, the mistress of his house.
And he made up his mind also that such had
ever been his determination. He was fifty and
Mary Lawrie was twenty-five. 'I can do just
what I please with her,' he said to himself, 'as
though she were my own girl.' By this he meant
to imply that he would not be expected to fall
in love with her, and that it was quite out of the
question that she should fall in love with him.
'Go and tell Mrs. Baggett that I'll be much
obliged to her if she'll put on her bonnet and
come out to me here.' This he said to a gardener's
boy, and the order was not at all an unusual one.
When he wanted to learn what Mrs. Baggett intended to give him for dinner, he would send
for the old housekeeper and take a walk with her
for twenty minutes. Habit had made Mrs. Baggett
quite accustomed to the proceeding, which upon

the whole she enjoyed. She now appeared with a bonnet, and a wadded cloak which her master had given her. 'It's about that letter, sir,' said Mrs. Baggett.

'How do you know?'

'Didn't I see the handwriting, and the black edges? Mrs. Lawrie ain't no more.'

'Mrs. Lawrie has gone to her long account.'

'I'm afeared, sir, she won't find it easy to settle the bill,' said Mrs. Baggett, who had a sharp, cynical way of expressing her disapprobation.

'Mrs. Baggett, judge not, lest you be judged.' Mrs. Baggett turned up her nose and snuffed the air. 'The woman has gone, and nothing shall be said against her here. The girl remains. Now, I'll tell you what I mean to do.'

'She isn't to come here, Mr. Whittlestaff?'

'Here she is to come, and here she is to remain, and here she is to have her part of everything as though she were my own daughter. And, as not the smallest portion of the good things that is to come to her, she is to have her share in your heart, Mrs. Baggett.'

'I don't know nothing about my heart, Mr. Whittlestaff. Them as finds their way to my heart has to work their way there. Who's Miss Lawrie, that I'm to be knocked about for a new comer?'

'She is just Mary Lawrie.'

'I'm that old that I don't feel like having a young missus put over me. And it ain't for your good, Mr. Whittlestaff. You ain't a young man —nor you ain't an old un; and she ain't no relations to you. That's the worst part of it. As sure as my name is Dorothy Baggett, you'll be falling in love with her.' Then Mrs. Baggett, with the sense of the audacity of what she had said, looked him full in the face and violently shook her head.

'Now go in,' he said, 'and pack my things up for three nights. I'm going to Norwich, and I shan't want any dinner. Tell John I shall want the cart, and he must be ready to go with me to the station at 2.15.'

'I ought to be ready to cut the tongue out of my head,' said Mrs. Baggett as she returned to the house, 'for I might have known it was the way to make him start at once.'

Not in three days, but before the end of the week, Mr. Whittlestaff returned home, bringing with him a dark-featured tall girl, clothed, of course, in deepest mourning from head to foot. To Mrs. Baggett she was an object of intense interest; because, although she had by no means assented to her master's proposal, made on behalf of the young lady, and did tell herself again and again during Mr. Whittlestaff's absence that she was quite sure that Mary Lawrie was a baggage, yet in her heart she knew it to be impossible that she could go on living in the house without loving one whom her master loved. With regard to most of those concerned in the household, she had her own way. Unless she would favour the groom, and the gardener, and the boy, and the girls who served below her, Mr. Whittlestaff would hardly be contented with those subordinates. He was the easiest master under whom a servant could live. But his favour had to be won through Mrs. Baggett's smiles. During the last two years, however, there had been enough of discussion about Mary Lawrie to convince Mrs. Baggett that, in regard to this 'interloper,' as Mrs. Baggett had once called her, Mr. Whittlestaff intended to have his own way. Such being the case, Mrs. Baggett was most anxious to know whether the young lady was such as she could love.

Strangely enough, when the young lady had come, Mrs. Baggett, for twelve months, could not quite make up her mind. The young lady was very different from what she had expected. Of interference in the house there was almost literally none. Mary had evidently heard much of Mrs. Baggett's virtues,—and infirmities,—and seemed to understand that she also had in many things to place herself under Mrs. Baggett's orders. 'Lord love you, Miss Mary,' she was heard to say; 'as if we did not all understand that you was to be missus of everything at Croker's Hall,'—for such was the name of Mr. Whittlestaff's house. But those who heard it knew that the words were spoken in supreme good humour, and judged from that, that Mrs. Baggett's heart had been won. But Mrs. Baggett still had her fears; and was not yet resolved but that it might be her duty to turn against Mary Lawrie with all the violence in her power. For the first month or two after the young lady's arrival, she had almost made up her mind that Mary Lawrie would never consent to become Mrs. Whittlestaff. An old gentleman will seldom fall in love without some encouragement; or at any rate, will not tell his love. Mary Lawrie was as cold to him as though he had been seventy-five instead of fifty. And she was also as dutiful,—by which she showed Mrs. Baggett more strongly even than by her coldness, that any idea of marriage was on her part out of the question.

This, strange to say, Mrs. Baggett resented. For though she certainly felt, as would do any ordinary Mrs. Baggett in her position, that a wife would be altogether detrimental to her interest in life, yet she could not endure to think that 'a little stuck-up minx, taken in from charity,' should run counter to any of her master's wishes. On one or two occasions she had spoken to Mr. Whittlestaff respecting the young lady, and had been cruelly snubbed. This certainly did not create good humour on her part, and she began to fancy herself angry in that the young lady was so ceremonious with her master. But as months ran by she felt that Mary was thawing, and that Mr. Whittlestaff was becoming more affectionate. Of course there were periods in which her mind veered round. But at the end of the year Mrs. Baggett certainly did wish that the young lady should marry her old master. 'I can go down to Portsmouth,' she said to the baker, who was a most respectable old man, and was nearer to Mrs. Baggett's confidence than any one else except her master, 'and weary out the rest on 'em there.' When she spoke of 'wearying out the rest on 'em,' her friend perfectly understood that she alluded to what years she might still have to live, and to the abject misery of her latter days, which would be the consequence of her resigning her present mode of life. Mrs. Baggett was supposed to have been born at Portsmouth, and, therefore, to allude to that one place which she knew in the world over and beyond the residences

in which her master and her master's family had
resided.

Before I go on to describe the characters of Mr.
Whittlestaff and Miss Lawrie, I must devote a
few words to the early life of Mrs. Baggett.
Dorothy Tedcaster had been born in the house
of Admiral Whittlestaff, the officer in command
at the Portsmouth dockyard. There her father
or her mother had family connections, to visit
whom Dorothy, when a young woman, had returned from the then abode of her loving mistress, Mrs. Whittlestaff. With Mrs. Whittlestaff
she had lived absolutely from the hour of her
birth, and of Mrs. Whittlestaff her mind was so
full, that she did conceive her to be superior, if
not absolutely in rank, at any rate in all the graces
and favours of life, to her Majesty and all the
royal family. Dorothy in an evil hour went back
to Portsmouth, and there encountered that worst
of military heroes, Sergeant Baggett. With many
lamentations, and confessions as to her own weakness, she wrote to her mistress, acknowledging
that she did intend to marry 'B.' Mrs. Whittlestaff could do nothing to prevent it, and Dorothy
did marry 'B.' Of the misery and ill-usage, of
the dirt and poverty, which poor Dorothy Baggett
endured during that year, it needs not here to
tell. That something had passed between her
and her old mistress when she returned to her,
must, I suppose, have been necessary. But of her
married life, in subsequent years, Mrs. Baggett
never spoke at all. Even the baker only knew
dimly that there had been a Sergeant Baggett in
existence. Years had passed since that bad quarter
of an hour in her life, before Mrs. Baggett had

been made over to her present master. And he, though he probably knew something of the abominable Sergeant, never found it necessary to mention his name. For this Mrs. Baggett was duly thankful, and would declare among all persons, the baker included, that 'for a gentleman to be a gentleman, no gentleman was such a gentleman' as her master.

It was now five-and-twenty years since the Admiral had died, and fifteen since his widow had followed him. During the latter period Mrs. Baggett had lived at Croker's Hall with Mr. Whittlestaff, and within that period something had leaked out as to the Sergeant. How it had come to pass that Mr. Whittlestaff's establishment had been mounted with less of the paraphernalia of wealth than that of his parents, shall be told in the next chapter; but it was the case that Mrs. Baggett, in her very heart of hearts, was deeply grieved at what she considered to be the poverty of her master. 'You're a stupid old fool, Mrs. Baggett,' her master would say, when in some private moments her regrets would be expressed. 'Haven't you got enough to eat, and a bed to lie on, and an old stocking full of money somewhere? What more do you want?'

'A stocking full of money!' she would say, wiping her eyes; 'there ain't no such thing. And as for eating, of course, I eats as much as I wants. I eats more than I wants, if you come to that.'

'Then you're very greedy.'

'But to think that you shouldn't have a man in a black coat to pour out a glass of wine for you, sir!'

'I never drink wine, Mrs. Baggett.'

'Well, whisky. I suppose a fellow like that wouldn't be above pouring out a glass of whisky for a gentleman;—though there's no knowing now what those fellows won't turn up their noses at. But it's a come-down in the world, Mr. Whittlestaff.'

'If you think I've come down in the world, you'd better keep it to yourself, and not tell me. I don't think that I've come down.'

'You bear up against it finely like a man, sir; but for a poor woman like me, I do feel it.' Such was Mrs. Baggett and the record of her life. But this little conversation took place before the coming of Mary Lawrie.

CHAPTER II

Mr. Whittlestaff

MR. WHITTLESTAFF had not been a fortunate man, as fortune is generally counted in the world. He had not succeeded in what he had attempted. He had, indeed, felt but little his want of success in regard to money, but he had encountered failure in one or two other matters which had touched him nearly. In some things his life had been successful; but these were matters in which the world does not write down a man his good luck* as being generally conducive to his happiness. He had never had a headache, rarely a cold, and not a touch of the gout. One little finger had become crooked, and he was recommended to drink whisky,* which he did willingly, —because it was cheap. He was now fifty, and as fit, bodily and mentally, for hard work as ever he had been. And he had a thousand a-year to spend, and spent it without ever feeling the necessity of saving a shilling. And then he hated no one, and those who came in contact with him always liked him. He trod on nobody's corns, and was, generally speaking, the most popular man in the parish. These traits are not generally reckoned as marks of good fortune; but they do tend to increase the amount of happiness which a man enjoys in this world. To tell of his misfortunes a somewhat longer chronicle of his life would be necessary. But the circumstances need only be indicated here. He had been opposed in everything to his father's views. His father, finding him to be a clever lad, had at first designed him for the Bar. But he, before he had left Oxford, utterly repudiated all legal pursuits. 'What the devil do you wish to be?' said his father, who at that time was supposed to be able to leave his son £2000 a-year. The son replied that he would work for a fellowship, and devote himself to literature. The old admiral sent literature to all the infernal gods, and told his son that he was a fool. But the lad did not succeed in getting his fellowship, and neither father nor mother ever knew the amount of suffering which he endured thereby. He became plaintive and wrote poetry, and spent his pocket-money in publishing it, which again caused him sorrow, not for the loss of his money, but by the obscurity of his poetry. He had to confess to himself that God had not conferred upon him the gift of writing poetry; and having acknowledged so much, he never again put two lines together. Of all this he said nothing; but the sense of failure made him sad at heart. And his father, when he was in those straits, only laughed at him, not at all believing the assurances of his son's misery, which from time to time were given to him by his wife.

Then the old admiral declared that, as his son would do nothing for himself, he must work for his son. And he took in his old age to going into the city and speculating in shares. Then the Admiral died. The shares came to nothing, and calls were made; and when Mrs. Whittlestaff followed her husband, her son, looking about him, bought Croker's Hall, reduced his establishment, and put down the man-servant whose departed glory was to Mrs. Baggett a matter of such deep regret.

But before this time Mr. Whittlestaff had encountered the greatest sorrow of his life. Even the lost fellowship, even the rejected poetry, had not caused him such misery as this. He had loved a young lady, and had been accepted;— and then the young lady had jilted him. At this time of his life he was about thirty; and as to the outside world, he was absolutely dumfounded by the catastrophe. Up to this period he had been a sportsman in a moderate degree, fishing a good deal, shooting a little, and devoted to hunting, to the extent of a single horse. But when the blow came, he never fished or shot, or hunted again. I think that the young lady would hardly have treated him so badly had she known what the effect would be. Her name was Catherine Bailey, and she married one Compas, who, as years went on, made a considerable reputation as an Old Bailey barrister. His friends feared at the time that Mr. Whittlestaff would do some injury either to himself or Mr. Compas. But no one dared to speak to him on the subject. His mother, indeed, did dare,—or half dared. But he so answered his mother that he stopped her before the speech was out of her mouth. 'Don't say a word, mother; I cannot bear it.' And he stalked out of the house, and was not seen for many hours.

There had then, in the bitter agony of his spirit, come upon him an idea of blood. He himself must go,—or the man. Then he remembered that she was the man's wife, and that it behoved him to spare the man for her sake. Then, when he came to think in earnest of self-destruction, he told himself that it was a coward's refuge. He took to his classics for consolation, and read the philosophy of Cicero, and the history of Livy, and the war chronicles of Cæsar. They did him good,—in the same way that the making of many shoes would have done him good had he been a shoemaker.* In catching fishes and riding after foxes he could not give his mind to the occupation, so as to abstract his thoughts. But Cicero's de Natura Deorum*was more effectual. Gradually he returned to a gentle cheerfulness of life, but he never burst out again into the violent exercise of shooting a pheasant. After that his mother died, and again he was called upon to endure a lasting sorrow. But on this occasion the sorrow was of that kind which is softened by having been expected. He rarely spoke of his mother,—had never, up to this period at which our tale finds him, mentioned his mother's name to any of those about him. Mrs. Baggett would speak of her, saying much in the praise of her old mistress. Mr. Whittlestaff would smile and seem pleased, and so the subject would pass away. There was something too reverend to him in his idea of his mother, to admit of his discussing her character with the servant. But he was well pleased to hear her thus described. Of the other woman, of Catherine Bailey, of her who had falsely given herself up to so poor a creature as Compas, after having received the poetry of his vows, he could endure no mention whatever; and though Mrs. Baggett knew probably well the whole story,* no attempt at naming the name was ever made.

Such had been the successes and the failures

of Mr. Whittlestaff's life when Mary Lawrie was added as one to his household. The same idea had occurred to him as to Mrs. Baggett. He was not a young man, because he was fifty; but he was not quite an old man, because he was only fifty. He had seen Mary Lawrie often enough, and had become sufficiently well acquainted with her to feel sure that if he could win her she would be a loving companion for the remainder of his life. He had turned it all over in his mind, and had been now eager about it and now bashful. On more than one occasion he had declared to himself that he would be whipped if he would have anything to do with her. Should he subject himself again to some such agony of despair as he had suffered in the matter of Catherine Bailey? It might not be an agony such as that; but to him to ask and to be denied would be a terrible pain. And as the girl did receive from his hands all that she had—her bread and meat, her bed, her very clothes—would it not be better for her that he should stand to her in the place of a father than a lover? She might come to accept it all and not think much of it, if he would take before himself the guise of an old man. But were he to appear before her as a suitor for her hand, would she refuse him? Looking forward, he could perceive that there was room for infinite grief if he should make the attempt and then things should not go well with him.

But the more he saw of her he was sure also that there was room for infinite joy. He compared her in his mind to Catherine Bailey, and could not but feel that in his youth he had been blind and fatuous. Catherine had been a fair-haired girl, and had now blossomed out into the anxious mother of ten fair-haired children. The anxiety had no doubt come from the evil courses of her husband. Had she been contented to be Mrs. Whittlestaff, there might have been no such look of care, and there might perhaps have been less than ten children; but she would still have been fair-haired, blowsy, and fat. Mr. Whittlestaff had with infinite trouble found an opportunity of seeing her and her flock, unseen by them, and a portion of his agony had subsided. But still there was the fact that she had promised to be his, and had become a thing sacred in his sight, and had then given herself up to the arms of Mr. Compas. But now if Mary Lawrie would but accept him, how blessed might be the evening of his life!

He had confessed to himself often enough how sad and dreary he was in his desolate life. He had told himself that it must be so for the remainder of all time to him, when Catherine Bailey had declared her purpose to him of marrying the successful young lawyer. He had at once made up his mind that his doom was fixed, and had not regarded his solitude as any deep aggravation of his sorrow. But he had come by degrees to find that a man should not give up his life because of a fickle girl, and especially when he found her to be the mother of ten flaxen haired infants. He had, too, as he declared to himself, waited long enough.

But Mary Lawrie was very different from Catherine Bailey. The Catherine he had known had been bright, and plump, and joyous, with a quick good-natured wit, and a rippling laughter,

which by its silvery sound had robbed him of his
heart. There was no plumpness, and no silver-
sounding laughter with Mary. She shall be
described in the next chapter. Let it suffice to
say here that she was somewhat staid in her demeanour, and not at all given to putting herself
forward in conversation. But every hour that he
passed in her company he became more and
more sure that, if any wife could now make
him happy, this was the woman who could
do so.

But of her manner to himself he doubted much.
She was gratitude itself for what he was prepared to do for her. But with her gratitude was
mingled respect, and almost veneration. She
treated him at first almost as a servant,—at any
rate with none of the familiarity of a friend, and
hardly with the reserve of a grown-up child.*
Gradually, in obedience to his evident wishes,
she did drop her reserve, and allowed herself to
converse with him; but it was always as a young
person might with all modesty converse with her
superior. He struggled hard to overcome her
reticence, and did at last succeed. But still there
was that respect, verging almost into veneration,
which seemed to crush him when he thought
that he might begin to play the lover.

He had got a pony carriage for her, which he
insisted that she should drive herself. 'But I never
have driven,' she had said, taking her place,
and doubtfully assuming the reins, while he sat
beside her. She had at this time been six months
at Croker's Hall.

'There must be a beginning for everything,
and you shall begin to drive now.' Then he took

great trouble with her, teaching her how to hold the reins, and how to use the whip, till at last something of familiarity was engendered. And he went out with her, day after day, showing her all those pretty haunts among the downs which are to be found in the neighbourhood of Alresford.

This did well for a time, and Mr. Whittlestaff thought that he was progressing. But he had not as yet quite made up his mind that the attempt should be made at all. If he can be imagined to have talked to a friend as he talked to himself, that friend would have averred that he spoke more frequently against marriage,—or rather against the young lady's marriage,*—than in favour of it. 'After all it will never do,' he would have said to this friend; 'I am an old man, and an old man shouldn't ask a young girl to sacrifice herself. Mrs. Baggett looks on it only as a question of butchers and bakers. There are, no doubt, circumstances in which butchers and bakers do come uppermost. But here the butchers and bakers are provided. I wouldn't have her marry me for that sake. Love, I fear, is out of the question. But for gratitude I would not have her do it.' It was thus that he would commonly have been found speaking to his friend. There were moments in which he roused himself to better hopes,—when he had drank his glass of whisky and water, and was somewhat elate with the consequences. 'I'll do it,' he would then have said to his friend; 'only I cannot exactly say when.' And so it went on, till at last he became afraid to speak out and tell her what he wanted.

Mr. Whittlestaff was a tall, thin man, not quite six feet, with a face which a judge of male beauty would hardly call handsome, but which all would say was impressive and interesting. We seldom think how much is told to us of the owner's character by the first or second glance of a man or woman's face. Is he a fool, or is he clever; is he reticent or outspoken; is he passionate or long-suffering;—nay, is he honest or the reverse; is he malicious or of a kindly nature? Of all these things we form a sudden judgment without any thought; and in most of our sudden judgments we are roughly correct. It is so, or seems to us to be so, as a matter of course,—that the man is a fool, or reticent, or malicious; and, without giving a thought to our own phrenological capacity, we pass on with the conviction. No one ever considered that Mr. Whittlestaff was a fool or malicious; but people did think that he was reticent and honest. The inner traits of his character were very difficult to be read. Even Mrs. Baggett had hardly read them all correctly. He was shamefaced to such a degree that Mrs. Baggett could not bring herself to understand it. And there was present to him a manner of speech which practice had now made habitual, but which he had originally adopted with the object of hiding his shamefacedness under the veil of a dashing manner. He would speak as though he were quite free with his thoughts, when, at the moment, he feared that thoughts should be read of which he certainly had no cause to be ashamed. His fellowship, his poetry, and his early love were all, to his thinking, causes of disgrace, which required to be buried deep within his own memory.

But the true humility with which he regarded them betokened a character for which he need not have blushed. But that he thought of those matters at all—that he thought of himself at all—was a matter to be buried deep within his own bosom.

Through his short dark-brown hair the grey locks were beginning to show themselves—signs indeed of age, but signs which were very becoming to him. At fifty he was a much better-looking man than he had been at thirty,—so that that foolish, fickle girl, Catherine Bailey, would not have rejected him for the cruelly sensuous face of Mr. Compas, had the handsome iron-grey tinge been then given to his countenance. He, as he looked at the glass, told himself that a grey-haired old fool, such as he was, had no right to burden the life of a young girl, simply because he found her in bread and meat. That he should think himself good-looking, was to his nature impossible. His eyes were rather small, but very bright; the eyebrows black and almost bushy; his nose was well-formed and somewhat long, but not so as to give that peculiar idea of length to his face which comes from great nasal prolongation. His upper lip was short, and his mouth large and manly. The strength of his character was better shown by his mouth than by any other feature. He wore hardly any beard, as beards go now,*—unless indeed a whisker can be called a beard, which came down, closely shorn, about half an inch below his ear. 'A very common sort of individual,' he said of himself, as he looked in the glass when Mary Lawrie had been already twelve months in the house; 'but then a man ought to be common. A man who is uncommon is either a dandy or a buffoon.'

His clothes were all made after one pattern and of one colour. He had, indeed, his morning clothes and his evening clothes. Those for the morning were very nearly black, whereas for the evening they were entirely so. He walked about the neighbourhood in a soft hat such as clergy-men now affect, and on Sundays he went to church with the old well-established respectable chimney-pot.* On Sundays, too, he carried an umbrella, whereas on week-days he always had a large stick; and it was observed that neither the umbrella nor the stick was adapted to the state of the weather.

Such was Mr. Whittlestaff of Croker's Hall, a small residence which stood half-way up on the way to the downs, about a mile from Alresford. He had come into the neighbourhood, having bought a small freehold property without the knowledge of any of the inhabitants. 'It was just as though he had come out of the sun,' said the old baker, forgetting that most men, or their an-cestors, must have come to their present residences after a similar fashion. And he had brought Mrs. Baggett with him, who had confided to the baker that she had felt herself that strange on her first arrival that she didn't know whether she was standing on her head or her heels.

Mrs. Baggett had since become very gracious with various of the neighbours. She had the pay-ing of Mr. Whittlestaff's bills, and the general disposal of his custom. From thence arose her popularity. But he, during the last fifteen years, had crept silently into the society of the place.

At first no one had known anything about him; and the neighbourhood had been shy. But by degrees the parsons and then the squires had taken him by the hand, so that the social endowments of the place were more than Mr. Whittlestaff even desired.

CHAPTER III

Mary Lawrie

THERE is nothing more difficult in the writing of a story than to describe adequately the person of a hero or a heroine, so as to place before the mind of the reader any clear picture of him or her who is described. A courtship is harder still—so hard that we may say generally that it is impossible. Southey's Lodore is supposed to have been effective;* but let any one with the words in his memory stand beside the waterfall and say whether it is such as the words have painted it. It rushes and it foams, as described by the poet, much more violently than does the real water; and so does everything described, unless in the hands of a wonderful master. But I have clear images on my brain of the characters of the persons introduced. I know with fair accuracy what was intended by the character as given of Amelia Booth, of Clarissa, of Di Vernon, and of Maggie Tulliver.* But as their persons have not been drawn with the pencil for me by the artists who themselves created them, I have no conception how they looked. Of Thackeray's Beatrix I have a vivid idea, because she was drawn for him by an artist under his own eye.* I have now to describe Mary Lawrie, but have no artist who will take the trouble to learn my thoughts and to reproduce them. Consequently I fear that no true idea of the young lady can be conveyed to the reader; and that I must leave him to entertain such a notion of her carriage and

demeanour as must come to him at the end
from the reading of the whole book.

But the attempt must be made, if only for
fashion sake, so that no adventitious help may be
wanting to him, or more probably to her, who
may care to form for herself a personification of
Mary Lawrie. She was a tall, thin, staid girl,
who never put herself forward in any of those
walks of life in which such a young lady as she
is called upon to show herself. She was silent and
reserved, and sometimes startled, even when
appealed to in a household so quiet as that of Mr.
Whittlestaff. Those who had seen her former
life had known that she had lived under the
dominion of her step-mother, and had so ac-
counted for her manner. And then, added to
this, was the sense of entire dependence on a
stranger, which, no doubt, helped to quell her
spirit. But Mr. Whittlestaff had eyes with which
to see and ears with which to hear, and was not
to be taken in by the outward appearance of the
young lady. He had perceived that under that
quiet guise and timid startled look there existed
a power of fighting a battle for herself or for a
friend, if an occasion should arise which should
appear to herself to be sufficient. He had known
her as one of her father's household, and of her
step-mother's; and had seen probably some little
instance of self-assertion, such as had not yet
made itself apparent to Mrs. Baggett.

A man who had met her once, and for a few
minutes only, would certainly not declare her to
be beautiful. She, too, like Mr. Whittlestaff, was
always contented to pass unobserved. But the
chance man, had he seen her for long, would

surely remark that Miss Lawrie was an attractive girl; and had he heard her talk freely on any
matter of interest, would have called her very
attractive. She would blaze up into sudden eloquence, and then would become shame-stricken,
and abashed, and dumfounded, so as to show
that she had for a moment forgotten her
audience, and then the audience,—the chance
man,—would surely set his wits to work and try
to reproduce in her a renewal of that intimacy to
which she had seemed to yield herself for the
moment.

But yet I am not describing her after the
accepted fashion. I should produce a catalogue
of features, and tell how every one of them was
formed. Her hair was dark, and worn very plain,
but with that graceful care which shows that the
owner has not slurred over her toilet with hurried
negligence. Of complexion it can hardly be said
that she had any; so little was the appearance of
her countenance diversified by a change of hue.
If I am bound to declare her colour, I must, in
truth, say that she was brown. There was none
even of that flying hue which is supposed to be
intended when a woman is called a brunette.
When she first came to Croker's Hall, health
produced no variation. Nor did any such come
quickly; though before she had lived there a year
and a half, now and again a slight tinge of dark
ruby would show itself on her cheek, and then
vanish almost quicker than it had come. Mr.
Whittlestaff, when he would see this, would be
almost beside himself in admiration.

Her eyes were deep blue, so deep that the
casual observer would not at first recognise their

colour. But when you had perceived that they were blue, and had brought the fact home to your knowledge, their blueness remained with you as a thing fixed for ever. And you would feel, if you yourself were thoughtful and contemplative, and much given to study a lady's eyes, that, such as they were, every lady would possess the like if only it were given to her to choose.

Her nose was slight and fine, and perhaps lent to her face, of all her features, its most special grace. Her lips, alas! were too thin for true female beauty, and lacked that round and luscious fulness which seems in many a girl's face to declare the purpose for which they were made. Through them her white teeth would occasionally be seen, and then her face was at its best, as, for instance, when she was smiling; but that was seldom; and at other moments it seemed as though she were too careful to keep her mouth closed.

But if her mouth was defective, the symmetry of her chin, carrying with it the oval of her cheek and jaws, was perfect. How many a face, otherwise lovely to look upon, is made mean and comparatively base, either by the lengthening or the shortening of the chin! That absolute perfection which Miss Lawrie owned, we do not, perhaps, often meet. But when found, I confess that nothing to me gives so sure an evidence of true blood and good-breeding.

Such is the catalogue of Mary Lawrie's features, drawn out with care by one who has delighted for many hours to sit and look at them. All the power of language which the writer possesses has been used in thus reproducing them. But now, when this portion of his work is done, he feels sure that no reader of his novel will have the slightest idea of what Mary Lawrie was like.

An incident must now be told of her early life, of which she never spoke to man, woman, or child. Her step-mother had known the circumstance, but had rarely spoken of it. There had come across her path in Norwich a young man who had stirred her heart, and had won her affections. But the young man had passed on, and there, as far as the present and the past were concerned, had been an end of it. The young man had been no favourite with her step-mother; and her father, who was almost on his death-bed, had heard what was going on almost without a remark. He had been told that the man was penniless, and as his daughter had been to him the dearest thing upon earth, he had been glad to save himself the pain of expressing disapproval. John Gordon had, however, been a gentleman, and was fit in all things to be the husband of such a girl as Mary Lawrie,—except that he was penniless, and she, also, had possessed nothing. He had passed on his way without speaking, and had gone—even Mary did not know whither. She had accepted her fate, and had never allowed the name of John Gordon to pass her lips.

The days passed very quickly at Croker's Hall, but not so quickly but that Mary knew well what was going on in Mr. Whittlestaff's mind. How is it that a girl understands to a certainty the state of a man's heart in regard to her,—or rather, not his heart, but his purpose? A girl may believe that a man loves her, and may be deceived; but she will not be deceived as to whether he wishes

to marry her. Gradually came the conviction
on Miss Lawrie's mind of Mr. Whittlestaff's purpose. And, as it did so, came the conviction also
that she could not do it. Of this he saw nothing;
but he was instigated by it to be more eager,—
and was at the same time additionally abashed
by something in her manner which made him
feel that the task before him was not an easy one.

Mrs. Baggett, who knew well all the symptoms
as her master displayed them,* became angry
with Mary Lawrie. Who was Mary Lawrie, that
she should take upon herself to deny Mr. Whittlestaff anything? No doubt it would, as she told
herself, be better for Mrs. Baggett in many respects
that her master should remain unmarried. She
assured herself that if a mistress were put over
her head, she must retire to Portsmouth,—which,
of all places for her, had the dreariest memories.
She could remain where she was very well, while
Mary Lawrie remained also where she was. But
it provoked her to think that the offer should be
made to the girl and should be refused. 'What
on earth it is they sees in 'em, is what I never can
understand. She ain't pretty,—not to say,—and
she looks as though butter wouldn't melt in her
mouth. But she's got it inside her, and some of
them days it'll come out.' Then Mrs. Baggett
determined that she would have a few words on
the subject with Mary Lawrie.

Mary had now been a year and four months
at Croker's Hall, and had, under pressure from
Mr. Whittlestaff, assumed something of the manner rather than of the airs of a mistress to Mrs.
Baggett. This the old woman did not at all resent,
because the reality of power was still in her

hands; but she could not endure that the idolatry of love should always be present in her master's face. If the young woman would only become Mrs. Whittlestaff, then the idolatry would pass away. At any rate, her master would not continue 'to make an ass of himself,' as Mrs. Baggett phrased it.

'Don't you think, Miss, as that Mr. Whittlestaff is looking very peeky?'

'Is he, Mrs. Baggett?'

''Deed and he is, to my thinking; and it's all along of you. He's got a fancy into his mind,— and why shouldn't he have his fancy?'

'I don't know, I'm sure.' But Mary did know. She did know what the fancy was, and why Mr. Whittlestaff shouldn't have it.

'I tell you fairly, Miss, there is nothing I hate so much as vagaries in young women.'

'I hope there are no vagaries to be hated in me, Mrs. Baggett.'

'Well, I'm not quite so sure. You do go as straightforward as most on 'em; but I ain't quite sure but that there are a few twists and twirls. What do you suppose he wants to be at?'

'How am I to say?' Then she bethought herself that were she to tell the truth, she could say very well.

'Do you mean as you don't know?' said the old woman.

'Am I bound to tell you if I do know?'

'If you wish to do the best for him, you are. What's the good of beating about the bush? Why don't you have him?'

Mary did not quite know whether it behoved her to be angry with the old servant, and if so, how she was to show her anger. 'You shouldn't talk such nonsense, Mrs. Baggett.'

'That's all very well. It is all nonsense; but nonsense has to be talked sometimes. Here's a gentleman as you owe everything to. If he wanted your head from your shoulders, you shouldn't make any scruple. What are you, that you shouldn't let a gentleman like him have his own way? Asking your pardon, but I don't mean it any way out of disrespect. Of course it would be all agin me. An old woman doesn't want to have a young mistress over her head, and if she's my sperrit, she wouldn't bear it. I won't, any way.'

'Then why do you ask me to do this thing?'

'Because a gentleman like him should have his own way. And an old hag like me shouldn't stand for anything. No more shouldn't a young woman like you who has had so much done for her. Now, Miss Mary, you see I've told you my mind freely.'

'But he has never asked me.'

'You just sit close up to him, and he'll ask you free enough. I shouldn't speak as I have done if there had been a morsel of doubt about it. Do you doubt it yourself, Miss?' To this Miss Lawrie did not find it necessary to return any answer.

When Mrs. Baggett had gone and Mary was left to herself, she could not but think over what the woman had said to her. In the first place, was she not bound to be angry with the woman, and to express her anger? Was it not impertinent, nay, almost indecent, that the woman should come to her and interrogate her on such a subject? The inmost, most secret feelings of her heart had been ruthlessly inquired into and probed by a menial servant, who had asked questions of her, and made suggestions to her, as though her part in the affair had been of no consequence. 'What are you, that you shouldn't let a gentleman like him have his own way?' Why was it not so much to her as to Mr. Whittlestaff? Was it not her all; the consummation or destruction of every hope; the making or unmaking of her joy or of her happiness? Could it be right that she should marry any man, merely because the man wanted her? Were there to be no questions raised as to her own life, her own contentment, her own ideas of what was proper? It was true that this woman knew nothing of John Gordon. But she must have known that there might be a John Gordon,—whom she, Mary Lawrie, was required to set on one side, merely because Mr. Whittlestaff 'wanted her.' Mrs. Baggett had been grossly impertinent in daring to talk to her of Mr. Whittlestaff's wants.

But then, as she walked slowly round the garden, she found herself bound to inquire of herself whether what the woman said had not been true. Did she not eat his bread; did she not wear his clothes; were not the very boots on her feet his property? And she was there in his house, without the slightest tie of blood or family connection. He had taken her from sheer charity, and had saved her from the terrible dependency of becoming a friendless governess. Looking out to the life which she had avoided, it seemed to her to be full of abject misery. And he had brought her to his own house, and had made her the mistress of everything. She knew that she had been undemonstrative in her manner, and that such was her nature. But her heart welled over with gratitude as she thought of the sweetness of the life which he had prepared for her. Was not the question true? 'What am I, that I should stand in the way and prevent such a man as that from having what he wants?'

And then she told herself that he personally was full of good gifts. How different might it have been with her had some elderly men 'wanted her,' such as she had seen about in the world! How much was there in this man that she knew that she could learn to love? And he was one of whom she need in no wise be ashamed. He was a gentleman, pleasant to look at, sweet in manner, comely and clean in appearance. Would not the world say of her how lucky she had been should it come to pass that she should become Mrs. Whittlestaff? Then there were thoughts of John Gordon, and she told herself that it was a mere dream. John Gordon had gone, and she knew not where he was; and John Gordon had never spoken a word to her of his love. After an hour's deliberation, she thought that she would marry Mr. Whittlestaff if he asked her, though she could not bring herself to say that she would 'sit close up to him' in order that he might do so.

CHAPTER IV

Mary Lawrie accepts Mr. Whittlestaff

BY the end of the week Mary Lawrie had changed her mind. She had thought it over, and had endeavoured to persuade herself that Mr. Whittlestaff did not care about it very much. Indeed there were moments during the week in which she flattered herself that if she would abstain from 'sitting close up to him,' he would say nothing about it. But she resolved altogether that she would not display her anger to Mrs. Baggett. Mrs. Baggett, after all, had done it for the best. And there was something in Mrs. Baggett's mode of argument on the subject which was not altogether unflattering to Mary. It was not as though Mrs. Baggett had told her that Mr. Whittlestaff could make himself quite happy with Mrs. Baggett herself, if Mary Lawrie would be good enough to go away. The suggestion had been made quite in the other way, and Mrs. Baggett was prepared altogether to obliterate herself. Mary did feel that Mr. Whittlestaff ought to be made a god, as long as another woman was willing to share in the worship with such absolute self-sacrifice.

At last the moment came, and the question was asked without a minute being allowed for consideration. It was in this wise. The two were sitting together after dinner on the lawn, and Mrs. Baggett had brought them their coffee. It was her wont to wait upon them with this delicacy, though she did not appear either at breakfast or at dinner, except on remarkable occasions. She now had some little word to say, meant to be conciliatory and comforting, and remarked that 'surely Miss Mary meant to get a colour in her cheeks at last.'

'Don't be foolish, Mrs. Baggett,' said Mary. But Mrs. Baggett's back was turned, and she did not care to reply.

'It is true, Mary,' said Mr. Whittlestaff, putting his hand on her shoulder, as he turned round to look in her face.

'Mrs. Lawrie used to tell me that I always blushed black, and I think that she was about right.'

'I do not know what colour you blush,' said Mr. Whittlestaff.

'I daresay not.'

'But when it does come I am conscious of the sweetest colour that ever came upon a lady's cheek. And I tell myself that another grace has been added to the face which of all faces in the world is to my eyes the most beautiful.' What was she to say in answer to a compliment so high-flown as this, to one from whose mouth compliments were so uncommon? She knew that he could not have so spoken without a purpose, declared at any rate to his own heart. He still held her by the arm, but did not once progress with his speech, while she sat silent by his side, and blushing with that dark ruby streak across her cheeks, which her step-mother had intended to vilify when she said that she had blushed black. 'Mary,' he continued after a pause, 'can you endure the thought of becoming my wife?' Now she drew her arm away, and turned her face, and compressed her lips, and sat without uttering a word. 'Of course I am an old man.'

'It is not that,' she muttered.

'But I think that I can love you as honestly and as firmly as a younger one. I think that if you could bring yourself to be my wife, you would find that you would not be treated badly.'

'Oh, no, no, no!' she exclaimed.

'Nothing, at any rate, would be kept from you. When I have a thought or a feeling, a hope or a fear, you shall share it. As to money——'

'Don't do that. There should be no talk of money from you to me.'

'Perhaps not. It would be best that I should be left to do as I may think most fitting for you. I have one incident in my life which I would wish to tell you. I loved a girl,—many years since,—and she ill-used me. I continued to love her long, but that image has passed from my mind.' He was thinking, as he said this, of Mrs. Compas and her large family. 'It will not be necessary that I should refer to this again, because the subject is very painful; but it was essential that I should tell you. And now, Mary, how shall it be?' he added, after a pause.

She sat listening to all that he had to say to her, but without speaking a word. He, too, had had his 'John Gordon'; but in his case the girl he had loved had treated him badly. She, Mary, had received no bad treatment. There had been love between them, ample love, love enough to break their hearts. At least she had found it so. But there had been no outspoken speech of love. Because of that, the wound made, now that it had been in some sort healed, had not with her been so cruel as with Mr. Whittlestaff. John Gordon had come to her on the eve of his going, and had told her that he was about to start for some distant land. There had been loud words between him and her step-mother, and Mrs. Lawrie had told him that he was a pauper, and was doing no good about the house; and Mary had heard the words spoken. She asked him whither he was going, but he did not reply. 'Your mother is right. I am at any rate doing no good here,' he had said, but had not answered her question further. Then Mary had given him her hand, and had whispered, 'Good-bye.' 'If I return,' he added, 'the first place I will come to shall be Norwich.' Then without further farewell ceremony he had gone. From that day to this she had had his form before her eyes; but now, if she accepted Mr. Whittlestaff, it must be banished. No one, at any rate, knew of her wound. She must tell him,—should she be moved at last to accept him. It might be that he would reject her after such telling. If so, it would be well. But, in that case, what would be her future? Would it not be necessary that she should return to that idea of a governess which had been so distasteful to her? 'Mary, can you say that it shall be so?' he asked quietly, after having remained silent for some ten minutes.

Could it be that all her fate must be resolved in so short a time? Since first the notion that Mr. Whittlestaff had asked her to be his wife had come upon her, she had thought of it day and night. But, as is so usual with the world at large, she had thought altogether of the past, and not of the future. The past was a valley of dreams, which could easily be surveyed, whereas the future was a high mountain which it would require much labour to climb. When we think that we will make our calculations as to the future, it is so easy to revel in our memories instead. Mary had, in truth, not thought of her answer, though she had said to herself over and over again why it should not be so.

'Have you no answer to give me?' he said.

'Oh, Mr. Whittlestaff, you have so startled me!' This was hardly true. He had not startled her, but had brought her to the necessity of knowing her own mind.

'If you wish to think of it, you shall take your own time.' Then it was decided that a week should be accorded to her. And during that week she passed much of her time in tears. And Mrs. Baggett would not leave her alone. To give Mrs. Baggett her due, it must be acknowledged that she acted as best she knew how for her master's interest, without thinking of herself. 'I shall go down to Portsmouth. I'm not worth thinking of, I ain't. There's them at Portsmouth as'll take care of me. You don't see why I should go. I daresay not; but I am older than you, and I see what you don't see. I've borne with you as a miss, because you've not been upsetting; but still, when I've lived with him for all those years without anything of the kind, it has set me hard sometimes. As married to him, I wouldn't put up with you; so I tell you fairly. But that don't signify. It ain't you as signifies or me as signifies. It's only him. You have got to bring yourself to think of that. What's the meaning of your duty to your neighbour, and doing unto others,

and all the rest of it? You ain't got to think just
of your own self; no more haven't I.'

Mary said to herself silently that it was John
Gordon of whom she had to think. She quite
recognised the truth of the lesson about selfishness; but love to her was more imperious than
gratitude.

'There's them at Portsmouth as'll take care
of me, no doubt. Don't you mind about me. I
ain't going to have a good time at Portsmouth,
but people ain't born to have good times of it.
You're going to have a good time. But it ain't
for that, but for what your duty tells you. You
that haven't a bit or a sup but what comes from
him, and you to stand shilly-shallying! I can't
abide the idea!'

It was thus that Mrs. Baggett taught her great
lesson,—the greatest lesson we may say which
a man or a woman can learn. And though she
taught it immoderately, fancying, as a woman,
that another woman should sacrifice everything
to a man, still she taught it with truth. She was
minded to go to Portsmouth, although Portsmouth to her in the present state of circumstances
was little better than a hell upon earth. But
Mary could not quite see Mr. Whittlestaff's claim
in the same light. The one point on which it did
seem to her that she had made up her mind was
Mr. Gordon's claim, which was paramount to
everything. Yes; he was gone, and might never
return. It might be that he was dead. It might
be even that he had taken some other wife, and
she was conscious that not a word had passed her
lips that could be taken as a promise. There had
not been even a hint of a promise. But it seemed

to her that this duty of which Mrs. Baggett spoke was due rather to John Gordon than to Mr. Whittlestaff.

She counted the days,—nay, she counted the hours, till the week had run by. And when the precise moment had come at which an answer must be given,—for in such matters Mr. Whittlestaff was very precise,—John Gordon was still the hero of her thoughts. 'Well, dear,' he said, putting his hand upon her arm, just as he had done on that former occasion. He said no more, but there was a world of entreaty in the tone of his voice as he uttered the words.

'Mr. Whittlestaff!'

'Well, dear.'

'I do not think I can. I do not think I ought. You never heard of——Mr. John Gordon.'

'Never.'

'He used to come to our house at Norwich, and—and—I loved him.'

'What became of him?' he asked, in a strangely altered voice. Was there to be a Mr. Compas here too to interfere with his happiness?

'He was poor, and he went away when my step-mother did not like him.'

'You had engaged yourself to him?'

'Oh, no! There had been nothing of that kind. You will understand that I should not speak to you on such a subject, were it not that I am bound to tell you my whole heart. But you will never repeat what you now hear.'

'There was no engagement?'

'There was no question of any such thing.'

'And he is gone?'

'Yes,' said Mary; 'he has gone.'

'And will not come back again?' Then she looked into his face,—oh! so wistfully. 'When did it happen?'

'When my father was on his death-bed. He had come sooner than that; but then it was that he went. I think, Mr. Whittlestaff, that I never ought to marry any one after that, and therefore it is that I have told you.'

'You are a good girl, Mary.'

'I don't know about that. I think that I ought to deceive you at least in nothing.'

'You should deceive no one.'

'No, Mr. Whittlestaff.' She answered him ever so meekly; but there was running in her mind a feeling that she had not deceived any one, and that she was somewhat hardly used by the advice given to her.

'He has gone altogether?' he asked again.

'I do not know where he is,—whether he be dead or alive.'

'But if he should come back?'

She only shook her head;—meaning him to understand that she could say nothing of his purposes should he come back. He had made her no offer. He had said that if he returned he would come first to Norwich. There had been something of a promise in this; but oh, so little! And she did not dare to tell him that hitherto she had lived upon that little.

'I do not think that you should remain single for ever on that account. How long is it now since Mr. Gordon went?'

There was something in the tone in which he mentioned Mr. Gordon's name which went against the grain with Mary. She felt that he was spoken of almost as an enemy. 'I think it is three years since he went.'

'Three years is a long time. Has he never written?'

'Not to me. How should he write? There was nothing for him to write about.'

'It has been a fancy.'

'Yes;—a fancy.' He had made this excuse for her, and she had none stronger to make for herself.

He certainly did not think the better of her in that she had indulged in such a fancy; but in truth his love was sharpened by the opposition which this fancy made. It had seemed to him that his possessing her would give a brightness to his life, and this brightness was not altogether obscured by the idea that she had ever thought that she had loved another person. As a woman she was as lovable as before, though perhaps less admirable. At any rate he wanted her, and now she seemed to be more within his reach than she had been. 'The week has passed by, Mary, and I suppose that now you can give me an answer.' Then she found that she was in his power. She had told him her story, as though with the understanding that if he would take her with her 'fancy,' she was ready to surrender herself. 'Am I not to have an answer now?'

'I suppose so.'

'What is it to be?'

'If you wish for me, I will be yours.'

'And you will cease to think of Mr. Gordon?'

'I shall think of him; but not in a way that you would begrudge me.'

'That will suffice. I know that you are honest, and I will not ask you to forget him altogether.

But there had better be no speaking of him. It is well that he should be banished from your mind. And now, dearest, dearest love, give me your hand.' She put her hand at once into his. 'And a kiss.' She just turned herself a little round, with her eyes bent upon the ground. 'Nay; there must be a kiss.' Then he bent over her, and just touched her cheek. 'Mary, you are now all my own.' Yes;—she was now all his own, and she would do for him the best in her power. He had not asked for her love, and she certainly had not given it. She knew well how impossible it would be that she should give him her love. 'I know you are disturbed,' he said, 'I wish also for a few minutes to think of it all.' Then he turned away from her, and went up the garden walk by himself.

She, slowly loitering, went into the house alone, and seated herself by the open window in her bed-chamber. As she sat there she could see him up the long walk, going and returning. As he went his hands were folded behind his back, and she thought that he appeared older than she had ever remarked him to be before. What did it signify? She had undertaken her business in life, and the duties she thought would be within her power. She was sure that she would be true to him, as far as truth to his material interests was concerned. His comforts in life should be her first care. If he trusted her at all, he should not become poorer by reason of his confidence. And she would be as tender to him as the circumstances would admit. She would not begrudge him kisses if he cared for them. They were his by all the rights of contract. He certainly had the best of the bargain, but he should never know how much the best of it he had. He had told her that there had better be no speaking of John Gordon. There certainly should be none on her part. She had told him that she must continue to think of him. There at any rate she had been honest. But he should not see that she thought of him.

Then she endeavoured to assure herself that this thinking would die out. Looking round the world, her small world, how many women there were who had not married the men they had loved first! How few, perhaps, had done so! Life was not good-natured enough for smoothness such as that. And yet did not they, as a rule, live well with their husbands? What right had she to expect anything better than their fate? Each poor insipid dame that she saw, toddling on with half-a-dozen children at her heels, might have had as good a John Gordon of her own as was hers. And each of them might have sat on a summer day, at an open window, looking out with something, oh, so far from love, at the punctual steps of him who was to be her husband.

Then her thoughts turned, would turn, could not be kept from turning, to John Gordon. He had been to her the personification of manliness. That which he resolved to do, he did with an iron will. But his manners to all women were soft, and to her seemed to have been suffused with special tenderness. But he was chary of his words,—as he had even been to her. He had been the son of a banker at Norwich; but, just as she had become acquainted with him, the bank had broke, and he had left Oxford to come home and find himself a ruined man. But he had never said a word to her of the family misfortune. He had been six feet high, with dark hair cut very short, somewhat full of sport of the roughest kind, which, however, he had abandoned instantly. 'Things have so turned out,' he had once said to Mary, 'that I must earn something to eat instead of riding after foxes.' She could not boast that he was handsome. 'What does it signify?' she had once said to her step-mother, who had declared him to be stiff, upsetting, and ugly. 'A man is not like a poor girl, who has nothing but the softness of her skin to depend upon.' Then Mrs. Lawrie had declared to him that 'he did no good coming about the house,'——and he went away.

Why had he not spoken to her? He had said that one word, promising that if he returned he would come to Norwich. She had lived three years since that, and he had not come back. And her house had been broken up, and she, though she would have been prepared to wait for another three years,—though she would have waited till she had grown grey with waiting,—she had now fallen into the hands of one who had a right to demand from her that she should obey him. 'And it is not that I hate him,' she said to herself. 'I do love him. He is all good. But I am glad that he has not bade me not to think of John Gordon.'

CHAPTER V

'*I suppose it was a Dream*'

IT seemed to her, as she sat there at the window, that she ought to tell Mrs. Baggett what had occurred. There had been that between them which, as she thought, made it incumbent on her to let Mrs. Baggett know the result of her interview with Mr. Whittlestaff. So she went downstairs, and found that invaluable old domestic interfering materially with the comfort of the two younger maidens. She was determined to let them 'know what was what,' as she expressed it.

'You oughtn't to be angry with me, because I've done nothing,' said Jane the housemaid, sobbing.

'That's just about it,' said Mrs. Baggett. 'And why haven't you done nothing? Do you suppose you come here to do nothing? Was it doing nothing when Eliza tied down them strawberries without putting in e'er a drop of brandy?* It drives me mortial mad to think what you young folks are coming to.'

'I ain't a-going anywhere, Mrs. Baggett, because of them strawberries being tied down which, if you untie them, as I always intended, will have the sperrits put on them as well now as ever. And as for your going mad, Mrs. Baggett, I hope it won't be along of me.'

'Drat your imperence.'

'I ain't imperence at all. Here's Miss Lawrie, and she shall say whether I'm imperence.'

'Mrs. Baggett, I want to speak to you, if you'll come into the other room,' said Mary.

'You are imperent, both of you. I can't say a word but I'm taken up that short that——. They've been and tied all the jam down, so that it'll all go that mouldy that nobody can touch it. And then, when I says a word, they turns upon me.' Then Mrs. Baggett walked out of the kitchen into her own small parlour, which opened upon the passage just opposite the kitchen door. 'They was a-going to be opened this very afternoon,' said Eliza, firing a parting shot after the departing enemy.

'Mrs. Baggett, I've got to tell you,' Mary began.

'Well!'

'He came to me for an answer, as he said he would.'

'Well!'

'And I told him it should be as he would have it.'

'Of course you would. I knew that.'

'You told me that it was your duty and mine to give him whatever he wanted.'

'I didn't say nothing of the kind, Miss.'

'Oh, Mrs. Baggett!'

'I didn't. I said, if he wanted your head, you was to let him take it. But if he wanted mine, you wasn't to give it to him.'

'He asked me to be his wife, and I said I would.'

'Then I may as well pack up and be off for Portsmouth.'

'No; not so. I have obeyed you, and I think that in these matters you should obey him too.'

'I daresay; but at my age I ain't so well able to obey. I daresay as them girls knew all about it, or they wouldn't have turned round upon me like that. It's just like the likes of them. When is it to be, Miss Lawrie?—because I won't stop in the house after you be the missus of it. That's flat. If you were to talk till you're deaf and dumb, I wouldn't do it. Oh, it don't matter what's to become of me! I know that.'

'But it will matter very much.'

'Not a ha'porth.'

'You ask him, Mrs. Baggett.'

'He's got his plaything. That's all he cares about. I've been with him and his family almost from a baby, and have grown old a-serving him, and it don't matter to him whether I goes into the hedges and ditches, or where I goes. They say that service is no heritage,* and they says true. I'm to go to—— But don't mind me. He won't, and why should you? Do you think you'll ever do half as much for him as I've done? He's got his troubles before him now;—that's the worst of it.'

This was very bad. Mrs. Baggett had been loud in laying down for her the line of duty which she should follow, and she, to the best of her ability, had done as Mrs. Baggett had told her. It was the case that Mrs. Baggett had prevailed with her, and now the woman turned against her! Was it true that he had 'his troubles before him,' because of her acceptance of his offer? If so, might it not yet be mended? Was it too late? Of what comfort could she be to him, seeing that she had been unable to give him her heart? Why should she interfere with the woman's

happiness? In a spirit of true humility she endeavoured to think how she might endeavour to
do the best. Of one thing she was quite, quite
sure,—that all the longings of her very soul were
fixed upon that other man. He was away;—
perhaps he had forgotten her; perhaps he was
married. Not a word had been spoken to her
on which she could found a fair hope. But she
had never been so certain of her love,—of her
love as a true, undoubted, and undoubtable fact
—of an unchangeable fact,—as she was now.
And why should this poor old woman, with her
many years of service, be disturbed? She went
again up to her bedroom, and sitting at her open
window and looking out, saw him still pacing
slowly up and down the long walk. As she looked
at him, he seemed to be older than before. His
hands were still clasped behind his back. There
was no look about him as that of a thriving lover.
Care seemed to be on his face,—nay, even
present, almost visibly, on his very shoulders.
She would go to him and plead for Mrs. Baggett.

But in that case what should become of herself?
She was aware that she could no longer stay
in his house as his adopted daughter. But she
could go forth,—and starve if there was nothing
better for her. But as she thought of starvation,
she stamped with one foot against the other, as
though to punish herself for her own falsehood.
He would not let her starve. He would get
some place for her as a governess. And she was
not in the least afraid of starvation. It would be
sweeter for her to work with any kind of hardship
around her, and to be allowed to think of John
Gordon with her heart free, than to become the

comfortable mistress of his house. She would not admit the plea of starvation even to herself. She wanted to be free of him, and she would tell him so, and would tell him also of the ruin he was about to bring on his old servant.

She watched him as he came back into the house, and then she rose from her chair. 'But I shall never see him again,' she said, as she paused before she left the room.

But what did that matter? Her not seeing him again ought to make, should make, no difference with her. It was not that she might see him, but that she might think of him with unsullied thoughts. That should be her object,—that and the duty that she owed to Mrs. Baggett. Why was not Mrs. Baggett entitled to as much con-sideration as was she herself,—or even he? She turned to the glass, and wiped her eyes with the sponge, and brushed her hair, and then she went across the passage to Mr. Whittlestaff's library.

She knocked at the door,—which she had not been accustomed to do,—and then at his bidding entered the room. 'Oh, Mary,' he said laughing, 'is that the way you begin, by knocking at the door?'

'I think one knocks when one wants a moment of reprieve.'

'You mean to say that you are bashful in assuming your new privileges. Then you had better go back to your old habits, because you always used to come where I was. You must come and go now like my very second self.' Then he came forward from the desk at which he was wont to stand and write, and essayed to put his arm round her waist. She drew back, but still he was not startled. 'It was but a cold kiss I gave you down below. You must kiss me now, you, as a wife kisses her husband.'

'Never.'

'What!' Now he was startled.

'Mr. Whittlestaff, pray—pray do not be angry with me.'

'What is the meaning of it?'

Then she bethought herself,—how she might best explain the meaning. It was hard upon her, this having to explain it, and she told herself, very foolishly, that it would be better for her to begin with the story of Mrs. Baggett. She could more easily speak of Mrs. Baggett than of John Gordon. But it must be remembered, on her behalf, that she had but a second to think how she might best begin her story. 'I have spoken to Mrs. Baggett about your wishes.'

'Well!'

'She has lived with you and your family from before you were born.'

'She is an old fool. Who is going to hurt her? And if it did hurt her, are you and I to be put out of our course because of her? She can remain here as long as she obeys you as her mistress.'

'She says that after so many years she cannot do that.'

'She shall leave the house this very night, if she disturbs your happiness and mine. What! is an old woman like that to tell her master when he may and when he may not marry? I did not think you had been so soft.'

She could not explain it all to him,—all that she thought upon the subject. She could not say that the interference of any domestic between

such a one as John Gordon and his love,—
between him and her if she were happy enough
to be his love,—would be an absurdity too foolish
to be considered. They, that happy two, would
be following the bent of human nature, and
would speak no more than a soft word to the old
woman, if a soft word might avail anything.
Their love, their happy love, would be a thing
too sacred to admit of any question from any
servant, almost from any parent. But why, in this
matter, was not Mrs. Baggett's happiness to be of
as much consequence as Mr. Whittlestaff's;—
especially when her own peace of mind lay in the
same direction as Mrs. Baggett's? 'She says that
you are only laying up trouble for yourself in this,
and I think that it is true.'

Then he rose up in his wrath and spoke his
mind freely, and showed her at once that John
Gordon had not dwelt much on his mind. He
had bade her not to speak of him, and then he
had been contented to look upon him as one
whom he would not be compelled to trouble
himself with any further. 'I think, Mary, that
you are making too little of me, and of yourself,
to talk to me, or even to consider, in such a
matter, what a servant says to you. As you have
given me your affection, you should now allow
nothing that any one can say to you to make
you even think of changing your purpose.' How
grossly must he be mistaken, when he could
imagine that she had given him her heart! Had
she not expressly told him that her love had been
set upon another person? 'To me you are everything. I have been thinking as I walked up and
down the path there, of all that I could do to

make you happy. And I was so happy myself in
feeling that I had your happiness to look after.
How should I not let the wind blow too coldly
on you? How should I be watchful to see that
nothing should ruffle your spirits? What duties,
what pleasures, what society should I provide
for you? How should I change my habits, so as
to make my advanced years fit for your younger
life? And I was teaching myself to hope that
I was not yet too old to make this altogether
impossible. Then you come to me, and tell me
that you must destroy all my dreams, dash all
my hopes to the ground,—because an old woman
has shown her temper and her jealousy!'

This was true,—according to the light in which
he saw her position. Had there been nothing
between them two but a mutual desire to be
married, the reason given by her for changing it
all would be absurd. As he had continued to
speak, slowly adding on one argument to another,
with a certain amount of true eloquence, she
felt that unless she could go back to John Gordon
she must yield. But it was very hard for her to
go back to John Gordon. In the first place, she
must acknowledge, in doing so, that she had only
put forward Mrs. Baggett as a false plea. And
then she must insist on her love for a man who
had never spoken to her of love! It was so hard
that she could not do it openly. 'I had thought
so little of the value I could be to you.'

'Your value to me is infinite. I think, Mary,
that there has come upon you a certain melancholy which is depressing you. Your regard to
me is worth now more than any other possession
or gift that the world can bestow. And I had

taken pride to myself in saying that it had been given.' Yes;—her regard! She could not contradict him as to that. 'And have you thought of your own position? After all that has passed between us, you can hardly go on loving him as you have done.'*

'I know that.'

'Then, what would become of you if you were to break away from me?'

'I thought you would get a place for me as a governess,—or a companion to some lady.'

'Would that satisfy your ambition? I have got a place for you;—but it is here.' As he spoke, he laid his hand upon his heart. 'Not as a companion to a lady are you required to fulfil your duties here on earth. It is a fuller task of work that you must do. I trust,—I trust that it may not be more tedious.' She looked at him again, and he did not now appear so old. There was a power of speech about the man, and a dignity which made her feel that she could in truth have loved him,—had it not been for John Gordon. 'Unfortunately, I am older than you,—very much older. But to you there may be this advantage, that you can listen to what I may say with something of confidence in my knowledge of the world. As my wife, you will fill a position more honourable, and more suitable to your gifts, than could belong to you as a governess or a companion. You will have much more to do, and will be able to go nightly to your rest with a consciousness that you have done more as the mistress of our house than you could have done in that tamer capacity. You will have cares,— and even those will ennoble the world to you,

and you to the world. That other life is a poor
shrunken death,—rather than life. It is a way
of passing her days, which must fall to the lot of
many a female who does not achieve the other;
and it is well that they to whom it falls should
be able to accommodate themselves to it with contentment and self-respect. I think that I may
say of myself that, even as my wife, you will
stand higher than you would do as a companion.'

'I am sure of it.'

'Not on that account should you accept any
man that you cannot love.' Had she not told
him that she did not love him;—even that she
loved another? And yet he spoke to her in this
way! 'You had better tell Mrs. Baggett to come
to me.'

'There is the memory of that other man,' she
murmured very gently.

Then the scowl came back upon his face;—
or not a scowl, but a look rather of cold displeasure. 'If I understand you rightly, the gentleman never addressed you as a lover.'

'Never!'

'I see it all, Mary. Mrs. Baggett has been
violent and selfish, and has made you think
thoughts which should not have been put in your
head to disturb you. You have dreamed a
dream in your early life,—as girls do dream, I
suppose,—and it has now to be forgotten. Is it
not so?'

'I suppose it was a dream.'

'He has passed away, and he has left you to
become the happiness of my life. Send Mrs.
Baggett to me, and I will speak to her.' Then
he came up to her,—for they had been standing

about a yard apart,—and pressed his lips to hers. How was it possible that she should prevent him?

She turned round, and slowly left the room, feeling, as she did so, that she was again engaged to him for ever and ever. She hated herself because she had been so fickle. But how could she have done otherwise? She asked herself, as she went back to her room, at what period during the interview, which was now over, she could have declared to him the real state of her mind. He had, as it were, taken complete possession of her, by right of the deed of gift which she had made of herself that morning. She had endeavoured to resume the gift, but had altogether failed. She declared to herself that she was weak, impotent, purposeless; but she admitted, on the other hand, that he had displayed more of power than she had ever guessed at his possessing. A woman always loves this display of power in a man, and she felt that she could have loved him had it not been for John Gordon.

But there was one comfort for her. None knew of her weakness. Her mind had vacillated like a shuttlecock, but no one had seen the vacillation. She was in his hands, and she must simply do as he bade her. Then she went down to Mrs. Baggett's room, and told the old lady to go upstairs at her master's behest. 'I'm a-going,' said Mrs. Baggett. 'I'm a-going. I hope he'll find every one else as good at doing what he tells 'em. But I ain't a-going to be a-doing for him or for any one much longer.'

CHAPTER VI

John Gordon

MRS. BAGGETT walked into her master's room, loudly knocking at the door, and waiting for a loud answer. He was pacing up and down the library, thinking of the injustice of her interference, and she was full of the injury to which she had been subjected by circumstances. She had been perfectly sincere when she had told Mary Lawrie that Mr. Whittlestaff was entitled to have and to enjoy his own wishes as against both of them. In the first place, he was a man, —and as a man, was to be indulged, at whatever cost to any number of women. And then he was a man whose bread they had both eaten. Mary had eaten his bread, as bestowed upon her from sheer charity. According to Mrs. Baggett's view of the world at large, Mary was bound to deliver herself body and soul to Mr. Whittlestaff, were 'soul sacrifice' demanded from her. As for herself, her first duty in life was to look after him were he to be sick. Unfortunately Mr. Whittlestaff never was sick, but Mrs. Baggett was patiently looking forward to some happy day when he might be brought home with his leg broken. He had no imprudent habits, hunting, shooting, or suchlike; but chance might be good to her. Then the making of all jams and marmalades, for which he did not care a straw, and which he only ate to oblige her, was a comfort to her. She could manage occasionally to be kept out of her bed over some boiling till one

o'clock; and then the making of butter in the
summer would demand that she should be up at
three. Thus she was enabled to consider that
her normal hours of work were twenty-two out
of the twenty-four. She did not begrudge them
in the least, thinking that they were all due to
Mr. Whittlestaff. Now Mr. Whittlestaff wanted
a wife, and, of course, he ought to have her. His
Juggernaut's car must roll on its course over her
body or Mary Lawrie's. But she could not be
expected to remain and behold Mary Lawrie's
triumph and Mary Lawrie's power. That was out
of the question, and as she was thus driven
out of the house, she was entitled to show a little
of her ill humour to the proud bride. She must
go to Portsmouth;—which she knew was tanta-
mount to a living death. She only hated one
person in all the world, and he, as she knew well,
was living at Portsmouth. There were to her only
two places in the world in which anybody could
live,—Croker's Hall and Portsmouth. Croker's
Hall was on the whole the proper region set apart
for the habitation of the blest. Portsmouth was
the other place,—and thither she must go. To
remain, even in heaven, as housekeeper to a young
woman, was not to be thought of. It was written in
the book of Fate that she must go; but not on that
account need she even pretend to keep her temper.

'What's all this that you have been saying to
Miss Lawrie?' began Mr. Whittlestaff, with all
the dignity of anger.

'What have I been saying of to Miss Mary?'

'I am not at all well pleased with you.'

'I haven't said a word again you, sir, nor not
again nothing as you are likely to do.'

'Miss Lawrie is to become my wife.'

'So I hears her say.'

There was something of a check in this—a check to Mr. Whittlestaff's pride in Mary's conduct. Did Mrs. Baggett intend him to understand that Mary had told the whole story to the old woman, and had boasted of her promotion?

'You have taught her to think that she should not do as we have proposed,—because of your wishes.'

'I never said nothing of the kind,—so help me. That I should put myself up again you, sir! Oh no! I knows my place better than that. I wouldn't stand in the way of anything as was for your good,—or even of what you thought was good,—not to be made housekeeper to—— Well, it don't matter where. I couldn't change for the better, nor wages wouldn't tempt me.'

'What was it you said about going away?'

Here Mrs. Baggett shook her head. 'You told Miss Lawrie that you thought it was a shame that you should have to leave because of her.'

'I never said a word of the kind, Mr. Whittlestaff; nor yet, sir, I don't think as Miss Lawrie ever said so. I'm begging your pardon for contradicting you, and well I ought. But anything is better than making ill-blood between lovers.' Mr. Whittlestaff winced at being called a lover, but allowed the word to pass by. 'I never said nothing about shame.'

'What did you say?'

'I said as how I must leave you;—nothing but that. It ain't a matter of the slightest consequence to you, sir.'

'Rubbish!'

'Very well, sir. I mustn't demean me to say*
as anything I had said wasn't rubbish when you
said as it was—— But for all that, I've got to go.'

'Nonsense.'

'Yes, in course.'

'Why have you got to go?'

'Because of my feelings, sir.'

'I never heard such trash.'

'That's true, no doubt, sir. But still, if you'll
think of it, old women does have feelings. Not as
a young one, but still they're there.'

'Who's going to hurt your feelings?'

'In this house, sir, for the last fifteen years I've
been top-sawyer of the female gender.'

'Then I'm not to marry at all.'

'You've gone on and you haven't,—that's all.
I ain't a-finding no fault. But you haven't,—and
I'm the sufferer.' Here Mrs. Baggett began to
sob, and to wipe her eyes with a clean handkerchief, which she must surely have brought into
the room for the purpose. 'If you had taken
some beautiful young lady——'

'I have taken a beautiful young lady,' said
Mr. Whittlestaff, now becoming more angry
than ever.

'You won't listen to me, sir, and then you
boil over like that. No doubt Miss Mary is as
beautiful as the best on 'em. I knew how it would
be when she came among us with her streaky
brown cheeks, ou'd make* an anchor wish to
kiss 'em.' Here Mr. Whittlestaff again became
appeased, and made up his mind at once that
he would tell Mary about the anchor as soon as
things were smooth between them. 'But if it had
been some beautiful young lady out of another

house,—one of them from the Park, for instance,
—who hadn't been here a'most under my own
thumb, I shouldn't 've minded it.'

'The long and the short of it is, Mrs. Baggett,
that I am going to be married.'

'I suppose you are, sir.'

'And, as it happens, the lady I have selected
happens to have been your mistress for the last
two years.'

'She won't be my missus no more,' said Mrs.
Baggett, with an air of fixed determination.

'Of course you can do as you like about that.
I can't compel any one to live in this house
against her will; but I would compel you if I
knew how, for your own benefit.'

'There ain't no compelling.'

'What other place have you got you can go to?
I can't conceive it possible that you should live
in any other family.'

'Not in no family. Wages wouldn't tempt me.
But there's them as supposes that they've a claim
upon me.' Then the woman began to cry in
earnest, and the clean pocket-handkerchief was
used in a manner which would soon rob it of its
splendour.

There was a slight pause before Mr. Whittlestaff rejoined. 'Has he come back again?' he
said, almost solemnly.

'He's at Portsmouth now, sir.' And Mrs.
Baggett shook her head sadly.

'And wants you to go to him?'

'He always wants that when he comes home.
I've got a bit of money, and he thinks there's
some one to earn a morsel of bread for him—or
rayther a glass of gin. I must go this time.'

'I don't see that you need go at all; at any rate, Miss Lawrie's marriage won't make any difference.'

'It do, sir,' she said, sobbing.

'I can't see why.'

'Nor I can't explain. I could stay on here, and wouldn't be afraid of him a bit.'

'Then why don't you stay?'

'It's my feelings. If I was to stay here, I could just send him my wages, and never go nigh him. But when I'm alone about the world and forlorn, I ain't got no excuse but what I must go to him.'

'Then remain where you are, and don't be a fool.'

'But if a person is a fool, what's to be done then? In course I'm a fool. I knows that very well. There's no saying no other. But I can't go on living here, if Miss Mary is to be put over my head in that way. Baggett has sent for me, and I must go. Baggett is at Portsmouth, a-hanging on about the old shop. And he'll be drunk as long as there's gin to be had with or without paying. They do tell me as his nose is got to be awful. There's a man for a poor woman to go and spend her savings on! He's had a'most all on 'em already. Twenty-two pound four and sixpence he had out o' me the last time he was in the country. And he don't do nothing to have him locked up. It would be better for me if he'd get hisself locked up. I do think it's wrong, because a young girl has been once foolish and said a few words before a parson, as she is to be the slave of a drunken red-nosed reprobate for the rest of her life. Ain't there to be no way out of it?'

It was thus that Mrs. Baggett told the tale of

her married bliss,—not, however, without incurring the censure of her master because of her folly in resolving to go. He had just commenced a lecture on the sin of pride, in which he was prepared to show that all the evils which she could receive from the red-nosed veteran at Portsmouth would be due to her own stiff-necked obstinacy, when he was stopped suddenly by the sound of a knock at the front door. It was not only the knock at the door, but the entrance into the hall of some man, for the hall-door had been open into the garden, and the servant-girl had been close at hand. The library was at the top of the low stairs, and Mr. Whittlestaff could not but hear the demand made. The gentleman had asked whether Miss Lawrie was living there.

'Who's that?' said Mr. Whittlestaff to the housekeeper.

'It's not a voice as I know, sir.' The gentleman in the meantime was taken into the drawing-room, and was closeted for the moment with Mary.

We must now go down-stairs and closet ourselves for a few moments with Mary Lawrie before the coming of the strange gentleman. She had left the presence of Mr. Whittlestaff half an hour since, and felt that she had a second time on that day accepted him as her husband. She had accepted him, and now she must do the best she could to suit her life to his requirements. Her first feeling, when she found herself alone, was one of intense disgust at her own weakness. He had spoken to her of her ambition; and he had told her that he had found a place for her, in which that ambition might find a fair scope.

And he had told her also that in reference to John Gordon she had dreamed a dream. It might be so, but to her thinking the continued dreaming of that dream would satisfy her ambition better than the performance of those duties which he had arranged for her. She had her own ideas of what was due from a girl and to a girl, and to her thinking her love for John Gordon was all the world to her. She should not have been made to abandon her thoughts, even though the man had not spoken a word to her. She knew that she loved him; even though a time might come when she should cease to do so, that time had not come yet. She vacillated in her mind between condemnation of the cruelty of Mr. Whittlestaff and of her own weakness. And then, too, there was some feeling of the hardship inflicted upon her by John Gordon. He had certainly said that which had justified her in believing that she possessed his heart. But yet there had been no word on which she could fall back and regard it as a promise.

It might perhaps be better for her that she should marry Mr. Whittlestaff. All her friends would think it to be infinitely better. Could there be anything more moonstruck, more shandy, more wretchedly listless, than for a girl, a penniless girl, to indulge in dreams of an impossible lover, when such a tower of strength presented itself to her as was Mr. Whittlestaff? She had consented to eat his bread, and all her friends had declared how lucky she had been to find a man so willing and so able to maintain her. And now this man did undoubtedly love her very dearly, and there would be, as she was well

aware, no peril in marrying him. Was she to
refuse him because of a soft word once spoken to
her by a young man who had since disappeared
altogether from her knowledge? And she had
already accepted him,—had twice accepted him
on that very day! And there was no longer a
hope for escape, even if escape were desirable.
What a fool must she be to sit there, still dreaming her impossible dream, instead of thinking
of his happiness, and preparing herself for his
wants! He had told her that she might be
allowed to think of John Gordon, though not to
speak of him. She would neither speak of him
nor think of him. She knew herself, she said, too
well to give herself such liberty. He should be
to her as though he had never been. She would
force herself to forget him, if forgetting lies in the
absence of all thought. It was no more than Mr.
Whittlestaff had a right to demand, and no more
than she ought to be able to accomplish. Was
she such a weak simpleton as to be unable to
keep her mind from running back to the words
and to the visage, and to every little personal
trick of one who could never be anything to her?
'He has gone for ever!' she exclaimed, rising up
from her chair. 'He shall be gone; I will not be
a martyr and a slave to my own memory. The
thing came, and has gone, and there is an end
of it.' Then Jane opened the door, with a little
piece of whispered information. 'Please, Miss,
a Mr. Gordon wishes to see you.' The door was
opened a little wider, and John Gordon stood
before her.

There he was, with his short black hair, his
bright pleasant eyes, his masterful mouth, his

dark complexion, and broad, handsome, manly shoulders, such as had dwelt* in her memory every day since he had departed. There was nothing changed, except that his raiment was somewhat brighter, and that there was a look of prosperity about him which he had lacked when he left her. He was the same John Gordon who had seemed to her to be entitled to all that he wanted, and who certainly would have had from her all that he had cared to demand. When he had appeared before her, she had jumped up, ready to rush into his arms; but then she had repressed herself, and had fallen back, and she leant against the table for support.

'So I have found you here,' he said.

'Yes, I am here.'

'I have been after you down to Norwich, and have heard it all. Mary, I am here on purpose to seek you. Your father and Mrs. Lawrie are both gone. He was going when I left you.'

'Yes, Mr. Gordon. They are both gone, and I am alone,——but for the kindness of a most generous friend.'

'I had heard, of course, of Mr. Whittlestaff. I hope I shall not be told now that I am doing no good about the house. At any rate I am not a pauper. I have mended that little fault.' Then he looked at her as though he thought that there was nothing for him but to begin the conversation where it had been so roughly ended at their last meeting.

Did it not occur to him that something might have come across her life during a period of nearly three years, which would stand in his way and in hers? But as she gazed into his face, it

seemed as though no such idea had fallen upon
him. But during those two or three minutes, a
multitude of thoughts crowded on poor Mary's
mind. Was it possible that because of the coming
of John Gordon, Mr. Whittlestaff should withdraw his claim, and allow this happy young hero
to walk off with the reward which he still seemed
to desire? She felt sure that it could not be so. Even
during that short space of time, she resolved that
it could not be so. She knew Mr. Whittlestaff
too well, and was sure that her lover had arrived
too late. It all passed through her brain, and
she was sure that no change could be effected in
her destiny. Had he come yesterday, indeed?
But before she could prepare an answer for John
Gordon, Mr. Whittlestaff entered the room.

She was bound to say something, though she
was little able at the moment to speak at all.
She was aware that some ceremony was necessary. She was but ill able to introduce these two
men to each other, but it had to be done. 'Mr.
Whittlestaff,' she said, 'this is Mr. John Gordon
who used to know us at Norwich.'

'Mr. John Gordon,' said Mr. Whittlestaff,
bowing very stiffly.

'Yes, sir; that is my name. I never had the
pleasure of meeting you at Norwich, though I
often heard of you there. And since I left the
place I have been told how kind a friend you
have been to this young lady. I trust I may live
to thank you for it more warmly though not
more sincerely than I can do at this moment.'

Of John Gordon's fate since he had left Norwich a few words must be told. As Mrs. Lawrie
had then told him, he was little better than a

pauper. He had, however, collected together
what means he had been able to gather, and had
gone to Cape Town in South Africa. Thence he
had made his way up to Kimberley, and had
there been at work among the diamond-fields
for two years. If there be a place on God's earth
in which a man can thoroughly make or mar
himself within that space of time, it is the town
of Kimberley. I know no spot more odious in
every way*to a man who has learned to love the
ordinary modes of English life. It is foul with
dust and flies; it reeks with bad brandy; it is fed
upon potted meats; it has not a tree near it. It
is inhabited in part by tribes of South African
niggers, who have lost all the picturesqueness of
niggerdom in working for the white man's wages.
The white man himself is insolent, ill-dressed,
and ugly. The weather is very hot, and from
morning till night there is no occupation other
than that of looking for diamonds, and the works
attending it. Diamond-grubbers want food and
brandy, and lawyers and policemen. They want
clothes also, and a few horses; and some kind of
education is necessary for their children. But
diamond-searching is the occupation of the
place; and if a man be sharp and clever, and
able to guard what he gets, he will make a fortune there in two years more readily perhaps
than elsewhere. John Gordon had gone out to
Kimberley, and had returned the owner of many
shares in many mines.

CHAPTER VII

John Gordon and Mr. Whittlestaff

MR. GORDON had gone out to South Africa with the settled intention of doing something that might enable him to marry Mary Lawrie, and he had carried his purpose through with a manly resolution. He had not found Kimberley much to his taste, and had not made many dear friends among the settled inhabitants he had found there. But he had worked on, buying and selling shares in mines, owning a quarter of an eighth there, and a half a tenth here, and then advancing till he was the possessor of many complete shares in many various adventures which were quite intelligible to him, though to the ordinary stay-at-home Englishman they seem to be so full of peril as not to be worth possessing. As in other mines, the profit is shared monthly, and the system has the advantage of thus possessing twelve quarter-days in the year. The result is, that time is more spread out, and the man expects to accomplish much more in twelve months than he can at home. In two years a man may have made a fortune and lost it, and be on his way to make it again. John Gordon had suffered no reverses, and with twenty-four quarter-days, at each of which he had received ten or twenty per cent, he had had time to become rich. He had by no means abandoned all his shares in the diamond-mines; but having wealth at command, he had determined to carry out the first purpose for which he had come to

South Africa. Therefore he returned to Norwich, and having there learned Mary's address, now found himself in her presence at Croker's Hall.

Mr. Whittlestaff, when he heard John Gordon's name, was as much astonished as had been Mary herself. Here was Mary's lover,—the very man whom Mary had named to him. It had all occurred on this very morning, so that even the look of her eyes and the tone of her voice, as those few words of hers had been spoken, were fresh in his memory. 'He used to come to our house at Norwich,—and I loved him.' Then she had told him that this lover had been poor, and had gone away. He had, since that, argued it out with himself, and with her too, on the theory, though not expressed, that a lover who had gone away now nearly three years ago, and had not been heard of, and had been poor when he went, was of no use, and should be forgotten. 'Let there be no mention of him between us,' he had intended to say, 'and the memory of him will fade away.' But now on this very day he was back among them, and there was Mary hardly able to open her mouth in his presence.

He had bowed twice very stiffly when Gordon had spoken of all that he had done on Mary's behalf. 'Arrangements have been made,' he said, 'which may, I trust, tend to Miss Lawrie's advantage. Perhaps I ought not to say so myself, but there is no reason why I should trouble a stranger with them.'

'I hope I may never be considered a stranger by Miss Lawrie,' said Gordon, turning round to the young lady.

'No, not a stranger,' said Mary; 'certainly not a stranger.'

But this did not satisfy John Gordon, who felt that there was something in her manner other than he would have it. And yet even to him it seemed to be impossible now, at this first moment, to declare his love before this man, who had usurped the place of her guardian. In fact he could not speak to her at all before Mr. Whittlestaff. He had hurried back from the diamond-fields, in order that he might lay all his suprisingly gotten wealth at Mary's feet, and now he felt himself unable to say a word to Mary of his wealth, unless in this man's presence. He told himself as he had hurried home that there might be difficulties in his way. He might find her married,—or promised in marriage. He had been sure of her love when he started. He had been quite confident that, though no absolute promise had been made from her to him, or from him to her, there had then been no reason for him to doubt. In spite of that, she might have married now, or been promised in marriage. He knew that she must have been poor and left in want when her stepmother had died. She had told him of the intentions for her life, and he had answered that perhaps in the course of events something better might come up for her. Then he had been called a pauper, and had gone away to remedy that evil if it might be possible. He had heard while working among the diamonds that Mr. Whittlestaff had taken her to his own home. He had heard of Mr. Whittlestaff as the friend of her father, and nothing better he thought could have happened. But Mary might have been weak during his absence, and have given herself up to some other man who had asked for her hand. She was still, at heart, Mary Lawrie.* So much had been made known to him. But from the words which had fallen from her own lips, and from the statement which had fallen from Mr. Whittlestaff, he feared that it must be so. Mr. Whittlestaff had said that he need not trouble a stranger with Mary's affairs; and Mary, in answer to his appeal, had declared that he could not be considered as a stranger to her.

He thought a moment how he would act, and then he spoke boldly to both of them. 'I have hurried home from Kimberley, Mr. Whittlestaff, on purpose to find Mary Lawrie.'

Mary, when she heard this, seated herself on the chair that was nearest to her. For any service that it might be to her, his coming was too late. As she thought of this, her voice left her, so that she could not speak to him.

'You have found her,' said Mr. Whittlestaff, very sternly.

'Is there any reason why I should go away again?' He had not at this moment realised the idea that Mr. Whittlestaff himself was the man to whom Mary might be engaged. Mr. Whittlestaff to his thinking had been a paternal providence, a God-sent support in lieu of father, who had come to Mary in her need. He was prepared to shower all kinds of benefits on Mr. Whittlestaff,—diamonds polished, and diamonds in the rough, diamonds pure and white, and diamonds pink-tinted,—if only Mr. Whittlestaff would be less stern to him. But even yet he had no fear of Mr. Whittlestaff himself.

'I should be most happy to welcome you here as an old friend of Mary's,' said Mr. Whittlestaff, 'if you will come to her wedding.' Mr. Whittlestaff also had seen the necessity for open speech; and though he was a man generally reticent as to his own affairs, thought it would be better to let the truth be known at once. Mary, when the word had been spoken as to her wedding, 'blushed black' as her stepmother had said of her. A dark ruby tint covered her cheeks and her forehead; but she turned away her face, and compressed her lips, and clenched her two fists close together.

'Miss Lawrie's wedding!' said John Gordon. 'Is Miss Lawrie to be married?' And he purposely looked at her, as though asking her the question. But she answered never a word.

'Yes. Miss Lawrie is to be married.'

'It is sad tidings for me to hear,' said John Gordon. 'When last I saw her I was rebuked by her step-mother because I was a pauper. It was true. Misfortunes had come in my family, and I was not a fit person to ask Miss Lawrie for her love. But I think she knew that I loved her. I then went off to do the best within my power to remedy that evil. I have come back with such money as might suffice, and now I am told of Miss Lawrie's wedding!' This he said, again turning to her as though for an answer. But from her there came not a word.

'I am sorry you should be disappointed, Mr. Gordon,' said Mr. Whittlestaff; 'but it is so.' Then there came over John Gordon's face a dark frown, as though he intended evil. He was a man whose displeasure, when he was displeased, those around him were apt to fear. But Mr.

Whittlestaff himself was no coward. 'Have you any reason to allege why it should not be so?' John Gordon only answered by looking again at poor Mary. 'I think there has been no promise made by Miss Lawrie. I think that I understand from her that there has been no promise on either side; and indeed no word spoken indicating such a promise.' It was quite clear, at any rate, that this guardian and his ward had fully discussed the question of any possible understanding between her and John Gordon.

'No; there was none: it is true.'

'Well?'

'It is true. I am left without an inch of ground on which to found a complaint. There was no word; no promise. You know the whole story only too well. There was nothing but unlimited love,—at any rate on my part.' Mr. Whittlestaff knew well that there had been love on her part also, and that the love still remained. But she had promised to get over that passion, and there could be no reason why she should not do so, simply because the man had returned. He said he had come from Kimberley. Mr. Whittlestaff had his own ideas about Kimberley. Kimberley was to him a very rowdy place,—the last place in the world from which a discreet young woman might hope to get a well-conducted husband. Under no circumstances could he think well of a husband who presented himself as having come direct from the diamond-fields, though he only looked stern and held his peace. 'If Miss Lawrie will tell me that I may go away,* I will go,' said Gordon, looking again at Mary; but how could Mary answer him?

'I am sure,' said Mr. Whittlestaff, 'that Miss Lawrie will be very sorry that there should be any ground for a quarrel. I am quite well aware that there was some friendship between you two. Then you went, as you say, and though the friendship need not be broken, the intimacy was over. She had no special reason for remembering you, as you yourself admit. She had been left to form any engagement that she may please. Any other expectation on your part must be unreasonable. I have said that, as an old friend of Miss Lawrie's, I should be happy to welcome you here to her wedding. I cannot even name a day as yet; but I trust that it may be fixed soon. You cannot say even to yourself that Miss Lawrie has treated you badly.'

But he could say it to himself. And though he would not say it to Mr. Whittlestaff, had she been there alone, he would have said it to her. There had been no promise,—no word of promise. But he felt that there had been that between them which should have been stronger than any promise. And with every word which came from Mr. Whittlestaff's mouth, he disliked Mr. Whittlestaff more and more. He could judge from Mary's appearance that she was downhearted, that she was unhappy, that she did not glory in her coming marriage. No girl's face ever told her heart's secret more plainly that did Mary's at this moment. But Mr. Whittlestaff seemed to glory in the marriage. To him it seemed that the getting rid of John Gordon was the one thing of importance. So it was, at least, that John Gordon interpreted his manner. But the name of the suitor had not yet been told him, and he did not in the least suspect it. 'May I ask you when it is to be?' he asked.

'That is a question which the lady generally must answer,' said Mr. Whittlestaff, turning on his part also to Mary.

'I do not know,' said Mary.

'And who is the happy man?' said John Gordon. He expected an answer to the question also from Mary, but Mary was still unable to answer him. 'You at any rate will tell me, sir, the name of the gentleman.'

'I am the gentleman,' said Mr. Whittlestaff, holding himself somewhat more erect as he spoke. The position, it must be acknowledged, was difficult. He could see that this strange man, this John Gordon, looked upon him, William Whittlestaff, to be altogether an unfit person to take Mary Lawrie for his wife. By the tone in which he asked the question, and by the look of surprise which he put on when he received the answer, Gordon showed plainly that he had not expected such a reply. 'What! an old man like you to become the husband of such a girl as Mary Lawrie! Is this the purpose for which you have taken her into your house, and given her those good things of which you have boasted?' It was thus that Mr. Whittlestaff had read the look and interpreted the speech conveyed in Gordon's eye. Not that Mr. Whittlestaff had boasted, but it was thus that he read the look. He knew that he had gathered himself up and assumed a special dignity as he made his answer.

'Oh, indeed!' said John Gordon. And now he turned himself altogether round, and gazed with his full frowning eyes fixed upon poor Mary.

'If you knew it all, you would feel that I could not help myself.' It was thus that Mary would have spoken if she could have given vent to the thoughts within her bosom.

'Yes, sir. It is I who think myself so happy as to have gained the affections of the young lady. She is to be my wife, and it is she herself who must name the day when she shall become so. I repeat the invitation which I gave you before. I shall be most happy to see you at my wedding. If, as may be the case, you shall not be in the country when that time comes; and if, now that you are here, you will give Miss Lawrie and myself some token of your renewed friendship, we shall be happy to see you if you will come at once to the house, during such time as it may suit you to remain in the neighbourhood.' Considering the extreme difficulty of the position, Mr. Whittlestaff carried himself quite as well as might have been expected.

'Under such circumstances,' said Gordon, 'I cannot be a guest in your house.' Thereupon Mr. Whittlestaff bowed. 'But I hope that I may be allowed to speak a few words to the young lady not in your presence.'

'Certainly, if the young lady wishes it.'

'I had better not,' said Mary.

'Are you afraid of me?'

'I am afraid of myself. It had better not be so. Mr. Whittlestaff has told you only the truth. I am to be his wife; and in offering me his hand, he has added much to the infinite kindnesses which he has bestowed upon me.'

'Oh, if you think so!'

'I do think so. If you only knew it all, you would think so too.'

'How long has this engagement existed?' asked Gordon. But to this question Mary Lawrie could not bring herself to give an answer.

'If you are not afraid of what he may say to you——?' said Mr. Whittlestaff.

'I am certainly afraid of nothing that Mr Gordon may say.'

'Then I would accede to his wishes. It may be painful, but it will be better to have it over.' Mr. Whittlestaff, in giving this advice, had thought much as to what the world would say of him. He had done nothing of which he was ashamed,—nor had Mary. She had given him her promise, and he was sure that she would not depart from it. It would, he thought, be infinitely better for her, for many reasons, that she should be married to him than to this wild young man, who had just now returned to England from the diamond-mines, and would soon, he imagined, go back there again. But the young man had asked to see the girl whom he was about to marry alone, and it would not suit him to be afraid to allow her so much liberty.

'I shall not hurt you, Mary,' said John Gordon.

'I am sure you would not hurt me.'

'Nor say an unkind word.'

'Oh no! You could do nothing unkind to me, I know. But you might spare me and yourself some pain.'

'I cannot do it,' he said. 'I cannot bring myself to go back at once after this long voyage, instantly, as I should do, without having spoken one word to you. I have come here to England on purpose to see you. Nothing shall induce me to abandon my intention of doing so, but your refusal. I have received a blow,—a great blow, —and it is you who must tell me that there is certainly no cure for the wound.'

'There is certainly none,' said Mary.

'Perhaps I had better leave you together,' said Mr. Whittlestaff, as he got up and left the room.

CHAPTER VIII

John Gordon and Mary Lawrie

THE door was closed, and John Gordon and Mary were alone together. She was still seated, and he, coming forward, stood in front of her. 'Mary,' he said,—and he put out his right hand, as though to take hers. But she sat quite still, making no motion to give him her hand. Nor did she say a word. To her her promise, her reiterated promise, to Mr. Whittlestaff was binding,—not the less binding because it had only been made on this very day. She had already acknowledged to this other man that the promise had been made, and she had asked him to spare her this interview. He had not spared her, and it was for him now to say, while it lasted, what there was to be said. She had settled the matter in her own mind, and had made him understand that it was so settled. There was nothing further that she could tell him. 'Mary, now that we are alone, will you not speak to me?'

'I have nothing to say.'

'Should I not have come to you?'

'You should not have stayed when you found that I had promised myself to another.'

'Is there nothing else that I may wish to say to you?'

'There is nothing else that you should wish to say to the wife of another man.'

'You are not his wife,—not yet.'

'I shall be his wife, Mr. Gordon. You may be sure of that. And I think—think I can say of myself that I shall be a true wife. He has chosen to take me; and as he has so chosen, his wishes must be respected. He has asked you to remain here as a friend, understanding that to be the case. But as you do not choose, you should go.'

'Do you wish me to stay, and to see you become his wife?'

'I say nothing of that. It is not for me to insist on my wishes. I have expressed one wish, and you have refused to grant it. Nothing can pass between you and me which must not, I should say, be painful to both of us.'

'You would have me go then,—so that you should never hear of or see me again?'

'I shall never see you, I suppose. What good would come of seeing you?'

'And you can bear to part with me after this fashion?'

'It has to be borne. The world is full of hard things, which have to be borne. It is not made to run smoothly altogether, either for you or for me. You must bear your cross,—and so must I.'

'And that is the only word I am to receive, after having struggled so hard for you, and having left all my work, and all my cares, and all my property, in order that I might come home, and catch just one glance of your eye. Can you not say a word to me, a word of kindness, that I may carry back with me?'

'Not a word. If you will think of it, you ought not to ask me for a word of kindness. What does a kind word mean—a kind word coming from me to you? There was a time when I wanted a kind word, but I did not ask for it. At the time it did not suit. Nor does it suit now. Put yourself

in Mr. Whittlestaff's case; would you wish the
girl to whom you were engaged to say kind words
behind your back to some other man? If you
heard them, would you not think that she was a
traitor? He has chosen to trust me,—against my
advice, indeed; but he has trusted me, and I
know myself to be trustworthy. There shall be
no kind word spoken.'

'Mary,' said he, 'when did all this happen?'

'It has been happening, I suppose, from the
first day that I came into his house.'

'But when was it settled? When did he ask
you to be his wife? Or when, rather, did you
make him the promise?' John Gordon fancied
that since he had been at Croker's Hall words
had been spoken, or that he had seen signs,
indicating that the engagement had not been
of a long date. And in every word that she had
uttered to him he had heard whispered under
her breath an assurance of her perfect love for
himself. He had been sure of her love when he
had left the house at Norwich, in which he had
been told that he had been lingering there to no
good purpose; but he had never been more certain
than he was at this moment, when she coldly
bade him go and depart back again to his distant
home in the diamond-fields. And now, in her
mock anger and in her indignant words, with the
purpose of her mind written so clearly on her
brow, she was to him more lovable and more
beautiful than ever. Could it be fair to him as
a man that he should lose the prize which was
to him of such inestimable value, merely for a
word of cold assent given to this old man, and
given, as he thought, quite lately? His devotion

to her was certainly assured. Nothing could be more fixed, less capable of a doubt, than his love. And he, too, was somewhat proud of himself in that he had endeavoured to entangle her by no promise till he had secured for himself and for her the means of maintaining her. He had gone out and he had come back with silent hopes, with hopes which he had felt must be subject to disappointment, because he knew himself to be a reticent, self-restrained man; and because he had been aware that 'the world,' as she had said, 'is full of hard things which have to be borne.'

But now if, as he believed, the engagement was but of recent date, there would be a hardship in it, which even he could not bear patiently,—a hardship, the endurance of which must be intolerable to her. If it were so, the man could hardly be so close-fisted, so hard-hearted, so cruel-minded, as to hold the girl to her purpose! 'When did you promise to be his wife?' he said, repeating his question. Now there came over Mary's face a look of weakness, the opposite to the strength which she had displayed when she had bade him not ask her for a word of kindness. To her the promise was the same, was as strong, even though it had been made but that morning, as though weeks and months had intervened. But she felt that to him there would be an apparent weakness in the promise of her engagement, if she told him that it was made only on that morning. 'When was it, Mary?'

'It matters nothing,' she said.

'But it does matter—to me.'

Then a sense of what was fitting told her that it was incumbent on her to tell him the truth.

Sooner or later he would assuredly know, and it was well that he should know the entire truth from her lips. She could not put up with the feeling that he should go away deceived in any degree by herself.

'It was this morning,' she said.

'This very morning?'

'It was on this morning that I gave my word to Mr. Whittlestaff, and promised to become his wife.'

'And had I been here yesterday I should not have been too late?'

Here she looked up imploringly into his face. She could not answer that question, nor ought he to press for an answer. And the words were no sooner out of his mouth than he felt that it was so. It was not to her that he must address any such remonstrance as that. 'This morning!' he repeated—'only this morning!'

But he did not know, nor could she tell him, that she had pleaded her love for him when Mr. Whittlestaff had asked her. She could not tell him of that second meeting, at which she had asked Mr. Whittlestaff that even yet he should let her go. It had seemed to her, as she had thought of it, that Mr. Whittlestaff had behaved well to her, had intended to do a good thing to her, and had ignored the other man, who had vanished, as it were, from the scene of their joint lives, because he had become one who ought not to be allowed to interest her any further. She had endeavoured to think of it with stern justice, accusing herself of absurd romance, and giving Mr. Whittlestaff credit for all goodness. This had been before John Gordon had appeared among them; and now she struggled hard not to be less just to Mr. Whittlestaff than before, because of this accident. She knew him well enough to be aware that he could not easily be brought to abandon the thing on which he had set his mind.* It all passed through her mind as she prepared her answer for John Gordon. 'It can make no difference,' she said. 'A promise is a promise, though it be but an hour old.'

'That is to be my answer?'

'Yes, that is to be your answer. Ask yourself, and you will know that there is no other answer that I can honestly make you.'

'How is your own heart in the affair?'

There she was weak, and knew as she spoke that she was weak. 'It matters not at all,' she said.

'It matters not at all?' he repeated after her. 'I can understand that my happiness should be nothing. If you and he were satisfied, of course it would be nothing. If you were satisfied, there would be an end to it; because if your pleasure and his work together, I must necessarily be left out in the cold. But it is not so. I take upon myself to say that you are not satisfied.'

'You will not allow me to answer for myself?'

'No, not in this matter. Will you dare to tell me that you do not love me?' She remained silent before him, and then he went on to reason with her. 'You do not deny it. I hear it in your voice and see it in your face. When we parted in Norwich, did you not love me then?'

'I shall answer no such question. A young woman has often to change her mind as to whom she loves, before she can settle down as one man's wife or another's.'

'You do not dare to be true. If I am rough with you, it is for your sake as well as my own. We are young, and, as was natural, we learnt to love each other. Then you came here and were alone in the world, and I was gone. Though there had been no word of marriage between us, I had hoped that I might be remembered in my absence. Perhaps you did remember me. I cannot think that I was ever absent from your heart; but I was away, and you could not know how loyal I was to my thoughts of you. I am not blaming you, Mary. I can well understand that you were eating his bread and drinking his cup, and that it appeared to you that everything was due to him. You could not have gone on eating his bread unless you had surrendered yourself to his wishes. You must have gone from this, and have had no home to which to go. It is all true. But the pity of it, Mary; the pity of it!'*

'He has done the best he could by me.'

'Perhaps so; but if done from that reason, the surrender will be the easier.'

'No, no, no; I know more of him than you do. No such surrender will come easy to him. He has set his heart upon this thing, and as far as I am concerned he shall have it.'

'You will go to him with a lie in your mouth?'

'I do not know. I cannot say what the words may be. If there be a lie, I will tell it.'

'Then you do love me still?'

'You may cheat me out of my thoughts, but it will be to no good. Whether I lie or tell the truth, I will do my duty by him. There will be no lying. To the best of my ability I will love him, and him only. All my care shall be for him. I have resolved, and I will force myself to love him. All his qualities are good. There is not a thought in his mind of which he need be ashamed.'

'Not when he will use his power to take you out of my arms.'

'No, sir; for I am not your property. You speak of dealing with me, as though I must necessarily belong to you if I did not belong to him. It is not so.'

'Oh, Mary!'

'It is not so. What might be the case I will not take upon myself to say,—or what might have been. I was yesterday a free woman, and my thoughts were altogether my own. To-day I am bound to him, and whether it be for joy or for sorrow, I will be true to him. Now, Mr. Gordon, I will leave you.'

'Half a moment,' he said, standing between her and the door. 'It cannot be that this should be the end of all between us. I shall go to him, and tell him what I believe to be the truth.'

'I cannot hinder you; but I shall tell him that what you say is false.'

'You know it to be true.'

'I shall tell him that it is false.'

'Can you bring yourself to utter a lie such as that?'

'I can bring myself to say whatever may be best for him, and most conducive to his wishes.' But as she said this, she was herself aware that she had told Mr. Whittlestaff only on this morning that she had given her heart to John Gordon, and that she would be unable to keep her thoughts from running to him. She had implored him to leave her to herself, so that the memory of her love might be spared. Then, when this young man had been still absent, when there was no dream of his appearing again before her, when the consequence would be that she must go forth into the world, and earn her own bitter bread alone,—at that moment she knew that she had been true to the memory of the man. What had occurred since, to alter her purpose so violently? Was it the presence of the man she did love, and the maidenly instincts which forbade her to declare her passion in his presence? Or was it simply the conviction that her promise to Mr. Whittlestaff had been twice repeated, and could not now admit of being withdrawn? But in spite of her asseverations, there must have been present to her mind some feeling that if Mr. Whittlestaff would yield to the prayer of John Gordon, all the gulf would be bridged over which yawned between herself and perfect happiness. Kimberley? Yes, indeed; or anywhere else in the wide world. As he left the room, she did now tell herself that in spite of all that she had said she could accompany him anywhere over the world with perfect bliss. How well had he spoken for himself, and for his love! How like a man he had looked, when he had asked her that question, 'Will you dare to tell me that you do not love me?' She had not dared; even though at the moment she had longed to leave upon him the impression that it was so. She had told him that she would lie to Mr. Whittlestaff,—lie on Mr. Whittlestaff's own behalf. But such a lie as this she could not tell to John Gordon. He had heard it in her voice and seen it in her face. She knew it well, and was aware that it must be so.

'The pity of it,' she too said to herself; 'the pity of it!' If he had but come a week sooner,— but a day sooner, before Mr. Whittlestaff had spoken out his mind,—no love-tale would ever have run smoother. In that case she would have accepted John Gordon without a moment's consideration. When he should have told her of his distant home, of the roughness of his life, of the changes and chances to which his career must be subject, she would have assured him, with her heart full of joy, that she would accept it all and think her lot so happy as to admit of no complaint. Mr. Whittlestaff would then have known the condition of her heart, before he had himself spoken a word. And as the trouble would always have been in his own bosom, there would, so to say, have been no trouble at all. A man's sorrows of that kind do not commence, or at any rate are not acutely felt, while the knowledge of the matter from which they grow is confined altogether to his own bosom.

But she resolved, sitting there after John Gordon had left her, that in the circumstances as they existed, it was her duty to bear what sorrow there was to be borne. Poor John Gordon! He must bear some sorrow too, if there should be cause to him for grief. There would be loss of money, and loss of time, which would of themselves cause him grief. Poor John Gordon! She did not blame him in that he had gone away, and not said one word to draw from her some assurance of her love. It was the nature of the man, which in itself was good and noble. But in this case it had surely been unfortunate. With such a passion at his heart, it was rash in him to have gone across the world to the diamond-fields without speaking a word by which they two might have held themselves as bound together. The pity of it!

But as circumstances had gone, honour and even honesty demanded that Mr. Whittlestaff should not be allowed to suffer. He at least had been straightforward in his purpose, and had spoken as soon as he had been assured of his own mind. Mr. Whittlestaff should at any rate have his reward.

CHAPTER IX

The Rev. Montagu Blake

JOHN GORDON, when he left the room, went out to look for Mr. Whittlestaff, but was told that he had gone into the town. Mr. Whittlestaff had had his own troubles in thinking of the unlucky coincidence of John Gordon's return, and had wandered forth, determined to leave those two together, so that they might speak to each other as they pleased. And during his walk he did come to a certain resolution. Should a request of any kind be made to him by John Gordon, it should receive not the slightest attention. He was a man to whom he owed nothing, and for whose welfare he was not in the least solicitous. 'Why should I be punished and he be made happy?' It was thus he spoke to himself. Should he encounter the degradation of disappointment, in order that John Gordon should win the object on which he had set his heart? Certainly not. His own heart was much dearer to him than that of John Gordon.

But if a request should be made to him by Mary Lawrie? Alas! if it were so, then there must be sharp misery in store for him. In the first place, were she to make the request, were she to tell him to his face, she who had promised to be his wife, that this man was dear to her, how was it possible that he should go to the altar with the girl, and there accept from her her troth? She had spoken already of a fancy which had crossed her mind respecting a man who could have been no more than a dream to her, of whose whereabouts and condition—nay, of his very existence—she was unaware. And she had told him that no promise, no word of love, had passed between them. 'Yes, you may think of him,' he had said, meaning not to debar her from the use of thought, which should be open to all the world, 'but let him not be spoken of.' Then she had promised; and when she had come again to withdraw her promise, she had done so with some cock-and-bull story about the old woman, which had had no weight with him. Then he had her presence during the interview between the three on which to form his judgment. As far as he could remember, as he wandered through the fields thinking of it, she had not spoken hardly above a word during that interview. She had sat silent, apparently unhappy, but not explaining the cause of her unhappiness. It might well be that she should be unhappy in the presence of her affianced husband and her old lover. But now if she would tell him that she wished to be relieved from him, and to give herself to this stranger, she should be allowed to go. But he told himself also that he would carry his generosity no further. He was not called upon to offer to surrender himself. The man's coming had been a misfortune; but let him go, and in process of time he would be forgotten. It was thus that Mr. Whittlestaff resolved as he walked across the country, while he left the two lovers to themselves in his own parlour.

It was now nearly five o'clock, and Mr. Whittlestaff, as Gordon was told, dined at six. He felt that he would not find the man before dinner unless he remained at the house,—and for doing so he had no excuse. He must return in the evening, or sleep at the inn and come back the next morning. He must manage to catch the man alone, because he was assuredly minded to use upon him all the power of eloquence which he had at his command. And as he thought it improbable so to find him in the evening, he determined to postpone his task. But in doing so he felt that he should be at a loss. The eager words were hot now within his memory, having been sharpened against the anvil of his thoughts by his colloquy with Mary Lawrie. To-morrow they might have cooled. His purpose might be as strong; but a man when he wishes to use burning words should use them while the words are on fire.

John Gordon had a friend at Alresford, or rather an acquaintance, on whom he had determined to call, unless circumstances, as they should occur at Croker's Hall, should make him too ecstatic in his wish* for any such operation. The ecstasy certainly had not come as yet, and he went forth therefore to call on the Reverend Mr. Blake. Of Mr. Blake he only knew that he was a curate of a neighbouring parish, and that they two had been at Oxford together. So he walked down to the inn to order his dinner, not feeling his intimacy with Mr. Blake sufficient to justify him in looking for his dinner with him. A man always dines, let his sorrow be what it may. A woman contents herself with tea, and mitigates her sorrow, we must suppose, by an extra cup. John Gordon ordered a roast fowl,—the safest dinner at an English

country inn,—and asked his way to the
curate's house.

The Rev. Montagu Blake was curate of Little
Alresford, a parish, though hardly to be called
a village, lying about three miles from the town.
The vicar was a feeble old gentleman who had
gone away to die in the Riviera, and Mr. Blake
had the care of souls to himself. He was a man
to whom his lines had fallen in pleasant places.
There were about 250 men, women, and children,
in his parish, and not a Dissenter among them.
For looking after these folk he had £120 per
annum, and as pretty a little parsonage as could
be found in England. There was a squire with
whom he was growing in grace and friendship,
who, being the patron of the living, might probably bestow it upon him. It was worth only
£250, and was not, therefore, too valuable to be
expected. He had a modest fortune of his own,
£300 a-year perhaps, and,—for the best of his
luck shall be mentioned last,—he was engaged to
the daughter of one of the prebendaries of Winchester,* a pretty bright little girl, with a further
sum of £5000 belonging to herself. He was
thirty years of age, in the possession of perfect
health, and not so strict in matters of religion as
to make it necessary for him to abandon any of
the innocent pleasures of this world. He could
dine out, and play cricket, and read a novel. And
should he chance, when riding his cob about the
parish, or visiting some neighbouring parish, to
come across the hounds, he would not scruple
to see them over a field or two. So that the Rev.
Montagu Blake was upon the whole a happy
fellow.

He and John Gordon had been thrown together at Oxford for a short time during the last months of their residence, and though they were men quite unlike each other in their pursuits, circumstances had made them intimate. It was well that Gordon should take a stroll for a couple of hours before dinner, and therefore he started off for Little Alresford. Going into the parsonage gate he was overtaken by Blake, and of course introduced himself. 'Don't you remember Gordon at Exeter?'

'John Gordon! Gracious me! Of course I do. What a good fellow you are to come and look a fellow up! Where have you come from, and where are you going to, and what brings you to Alresford, beyond the charitable intention of dining with me? Oh, nonsense! not dine; but you will, and I can give you a bed too, and breakfast, and shall be delighted to do it for a week. Ordered your dinner? Then we'll unorder it. I'll send the boy in and put that all right. Shall I make him bring your bag back?' Gordon, however, though he assented to the proposition as regarded dinner, made his friend understand that it was imperative that he should be at the inn that night.

'Yes,' said Blake, when they had settled down to wait for their dinner, 'I am parson here,—a sort of a one at least. I am not only curate, but live in expectation of higher things. Our squire here, who owns the living, talks of giving it to me. There isn't a better fellow living than Mr. Furnival,* or his wife, or his four daughters.'

'Will he be as generous with one of them as with the living?'

'There is no necessity, as far as I am concerned. I came here already provided in that respect. If you'll remain here till September, you'll see me a married man. One Kattie Forrester intends to condescend to become Mrs. Montagu Blake. Though I say it as shouldn't, a sweeter human being doesn't live on the earth. I met her soon after I had taken orders. But I had to wait till I had some sort of a house to put her into. Her father is a clergyman like myself, so we are all in a boat together. She's got a little bit of money, and I've got a little bit of money, so that we shan't absolutely starve. Now you know all about me; and what have you been doing yourself?'

John Gordon thought that this friend of his had been most communicative. He had been told everything concerning his friend's life. Had Mr. Blake written a biography of himself down to the present period, he could not have been more full or accurate in his details. But Gordon felt that as regarded himself he must be more reticent. 'I intended to have joined my father's bank, but that came to grief.'

'Yes; I did hear of some trouble in that respect.'

'And then I went out to the diamond-fields.'

'Dear me! that was a long way.'

'Yes, it is a long way,—and rather rough towards the end.'

'Did you do any good at the diamond-fields? I don't fancy that men often bring much money home with them.'

'I brought some.'

'Enough to do a fellow any good in his after life?'

'Well, yes; enough to content me, only that a man is not easily contented who has been among diamonds.'

'Crescit amor diamonds!'*said the parson. 'I can easily understand that. And then, when a fellow goes back again, he is so apt to lose it all. Don't you expect to see your diamonds turn into slate-stones?'*

'Not except in the ordinary way of expenditure. I don't think the gnomes or the spirits will interfere with them,—though the thieves may, if they can get a hand upon them. But my diamonds have, for the most part, been turned into ready money, and at the present moment take the comfortable shape of a balance at my banker's.'

'I'd leave it there,—or buy land, or railway shares. If I had realized in that venture enough to look at, I'd never go out to the diamond-fields again.'

'It's hard to bring an occupation of that kind to an end all at once,' said John Gordon

'Crescit amor diamonds!' repeated the Reverend Montagu Blake, shaking his head. 'If you gave me three, I could easily imagine that I should toss up with another fellow who had three also, double or quits, till I lost them all. But we'll make sure of dinner, at any rate, without any such hazardous proceeding.' Then they went into the dining-room, and enjoyed themselves, without any reference having been made as yet to the business which had brought John Gordon into the neighbourhood of Alresford.

'You'll find that port wine rather good. I can't afford claret, because it takes such a lot to go far enough. To tell the truth, when I'm alone I confine myself to whisky and water. Blake is a very good name for whisky.'*

'Why do you make a ceremony with me?'

'Because it's so pleasant to have an excuse for such a ceremony. It wasn't you only I was thinking of when I came out just now, and uncorked the bottle. Think what it is to have a prudent mind. I had to get it myself out of the cellar, because girls can't understand that wine shouldn't be treated in the same way as physic. By-the-by, what brought you into this part of the world at all?'

'I came to see one Mr. Whittlestaff.'

'What! old William Whittlestaff? Then, let me tell you, you have come to see as honest a fellow, and as good-hearted a Christian, as any that I know.'

'You do know him?'

'Oh yes, I know him. I'd like to see the man whose bond is better than old Whittlestaff's. Did you hear what he did about that young lady who is living with him? She was the daughter of a friend,—simply of a friend who died in pecuniary distress. Old Whittlestaff just brought her into his house, and made her his own daughter. It isn't every one who will do that, you know.'

'Why do you call him old?' said John Gordon.

'Well; I don't know. He is old.'

'Just turned fifty.'

'Fifty is old. I don't mean that he is a cripple or bedridden. Perhaps if he had been a married man, he'd have looked younger. He has got a very nice girl there with him; and if he isn't too old to think of such things, he may marry her. Do you know Miss Lawrie?'

'Yes; I know her.'

'Don't you think she's nice? Only my goose is cooked, I'd go in for her sooner than any one I see about.'

'Sooner than your own squire's four daughters?'

'Well,—yes. They're nice girls too. But I don't quite fancy one out of four. And they'd look higher than the curate.'

'A prebendary is as high as a squire,' said Gordon.

'There are prebendaries and there are squires. Our squire isn't a swell, though he's an uncommonly good fellow. If I get a wife from one and a living from the other, I shall think myself very lucky. Miss Lawrie is a handsome girl, and everything that she ought to be; but if you were to see Kattie Forrester, I think you would say that she was A 1. I sometimes wonder whether old Whittlestaff will think of marrying.'

Gordon sat silent, turning over one or two matters in his mind. How supremely happy was this young parson with his Kattie Forrester and his promised living,—in earning the proceeds of which there need be no risk, and very little labour,—and with his bottle of port wine and comfortable house! All the world seemed to have smiled with Montagu Blake. But with him, though there had been much success, there had been none of the world's smiles. He was aware at this moment, or thought he was aware, that the world would never smile on him,—unless he should succeed in persuading Mr. Whittlestaff to give up the wife whom he had chosen. Then he felt tempted to tell his own story to this young parson. They were alone together, and it seemed as though Providence had provided him with a friend. And the subject of Mary Lawrie's intended marriage had been brought forward in a peculiar manner. But he was by nature altogether different from Mr. Blake, and could not blurt out his love-story with easy indifference. 'Do you know Mr. Whittlestaff well?' he asked.

'Pretty well. I've been here four years; and he's a near neighbour. I think I do know him well.'

'Is he a sort of man likely to fall in love with such a girl as Miss Lawrie, seeing that she is an inmate of his house?'

'Well,' said the parson, after some consideration, 'if you ask me, I don't think he is. He seems to have settled himself down to a certain manner of life, and will not, I should say, be stirred from it very quickly. If you have any views in that direction, I don't think he'll be your rival.'

'Is he a man to care much for a girl's love?'

'I should say not.'

'But if he had once brought himself to ask her?' said Gordon.

'And if she had accepted him?' suggested the other.

'That's what I mean.'

'I don't think he'd let her go very easily. He's a sort of dog whom you cannot easily persuade to give up a bone. If he has set his heart upon matrimony, he will not be turned from it. Do you know anything of his intentions?'

'I fancy that he is thinking of it.'

'And you mean that you were thinking of it, too, with the same lady.'

'No, I didn't mean that.' Then he added, after a pause, 'That is just what I did not mean to say. I did not mean to talk about myself. But since you ask me the question, I will answer it truly,—I have thought of the same lady. And my thoughts were earlier in the field than his. I must say good-night now,' he said, rising somewhat brusquely from his chair. 'I have to walk back to Alresford, and must see Mr. Whittlestaff early in the morning. According to your view of the case I shan't do much with him. And if it be so, I shall be off to the diamond-fields again by the first mail.'*

'You don't say so!'

'That is to be my lot in life. I am very glad to have come across you once again, and am delighted to find you so happy in your prospects. You have told me everything, and I have done pretty much the same to you. I shall disappear from Alresford, and never more be heard of. You needn't talk much about me and my love; for though I shall be out of the way at Kimberley, many thousand miles from here, a man does not care to have his name in every one's mouth.'

'Oh no,' said Blake. 'I won't say a word about Miss Lawrie;—unless indeed you should be successful.'

'There is not the remotest possibility of that,' said Gordon, as he took his leave.

'I wonder whether she is fond of him,' said the curate to himself, when he resolved to go to bed instead of beginning his sermon that night. 'I shouldn't wonder if she is, for he is just the sort of man to make a girl fond of him.'

CHAPTER X

John Gordon again goes to Croker's Hall

ON the next morning, when John Gordon reached the corner of the road at which stood Croker's Hall, he met, outside on the roadway, close to the house, a most disreputable old man with a wooden leg and a red nose. This was Mr. Baggett, or Sergeant Baggett as he was generally called, and was now known about all Alresford to be the husband of Mr. Whittlestaff's housekeeper. For news had got abroad, and tidings were told that Mr. Baggett was about to arrive in the neighbourhood to claim his wife. Everybody knew it before the inhabitants of Croker's Hall. And now, since yesterday afternoon, all Croker's Hall knew it, as well as the rest of the world. He was standing there close to the house, which stood a little back from the road, between nine and ten in the morning, as drunk as a lord. But I think his manner of drunkenness was perhaps in some respects different from that customary with lords. Though he had only one leg of the flesh, and one of wood, he did not tumble down, though he brandished in the air the stick with which he was accustomed to disport himself. A lord would, I think, have got himself taken to bed. But the Sergeant did not appear to have any such intention. He had come out on to the road from the yard into which the back-door of the house opened, and seemed to John Gordon as though, having been so far expelled, he was determined to be driven no further,—and he was accompanied, at a distance, by his wife. 'Now, Timothy Baggett,' began the unfortunate woman, 'you may just take yourself away out of that, as fast as your legs can carry you, before the police comes to fetch you.'

'My legs! Whoever heared a fellow told of his legs when there was one of them wooden. And as for the perlice, I shall want the perlice to fetch my wife along with me. I ain't a-going to stir out of this place without Mrs. B. I'm a hold man, and wants a woman to look arter me. Come along, Mrs. B.' Then he made a motion as though to run after her, still brandishing the stick in his hand. But she retreated, and he came down, seated on the pathway by the roadside, as though he had only accomplished an intended manœuvre. 'Get me a drop o' summat, Mrs. B., and I don't mind if I stay here half an hour longer.' Then he laughed loudly, nodding his head merrily at the bystanders,—as no lord under such circumstances certainly would have done.

All this happened just as John Gordon came up to the corner of the road, from whence, by a pathway, turned the main entrance into Mr. Whittlestaff's garden. He could not but see the drunken red-nosed man, and the old woman, whom he recognised as Mr. Whittlestaff's servant, and a crowd of persons around, idlers out of Alresford, who had followed Sergeant Baggett up to the scene of his present exploits. Croker's Hall was not above a mile from the town, just where the town was beginning to become country, and where the houses all had gardens belonging to them, and the larger houses a field or two. 'Yes, sir, master is at home. If you'll please to ring the bell, one of the girls will come out.' This was said by Mrs. Baggett, advancing almost over the body of her prostrate husband. 'Drunken brute!' she said, by way of a salute, as she passed him. He only laughed aloud, and looked around upon the bystanders with triumph.

At this moment Mr. Whittlestaff came down through the gate into the road. 'Oh, Mr. Gordon! good morning, sir. You find us rather in a disturbed condition this morning. I am sorry I did not think of asking you to come to breakfast. But perhaps, under all the circumstances, it was better not. That dreadful man has put us sadly about. He is the unfortunate husband of my hardly less unfortunate housekeeper.'

'Yes, sir, he is my husband,—that's true,' said Mrs. Baggett.

'I'm wery much attached to my wife, if you knew all about it, sir; and I wants her to come home with me. Service ain't no inheritance; nor yet ain't wages, when they never amounts to more than twenty pounds a-year.'

'It's thirty, you false ungrateful beast!' said Mrs. Baggett. But in the meantime Mr. Whittlestaff had led the way into the garden, and John Gordon had followed him. Before they reached the hall-door, Mary Lawrie had met them.

'Oh, Mr. Whittlestaff!' she said, 'is it not annoying? that dreadful man with the wooden leg is here, and collecting a crowd round the place. Good morning, Mr. Gordon. It is the poor woman's ne'er-do-well husband. She is herself so decent and respectable, that she will be greatly harassed. What can we do, Mr. Whittlestaff?

Can't we get a policeman?' In this way the conversation was led away to the affairs of Sergeant
and Mrs. Baggett, to the ineffable distress of
John Gordon. When we remember the kind of
speeches which Gordon intended to utter, the
sort of eloquence which he desired to use, it must
be admitted that the interruption was provoking.
Even if Mary would leave them together, it
would be difficult to fall back upon the subject
which Gordon had at heart.

It is matter of consideration whether, when
important subjects are to be brought upon the
tapis, the ultimate result will or will not depend
much on the manner in which they are introduced. It ought not to be the case that they shall
be so prejudiced. 'By-the-by, my dear fellow,
now I think of it, can you lend me a couple of
thousand pounds for twelve months?' Would
that generally be as efficacious as though the
would-be borrower had introduced his request
with the general paraphernalia of distressing
solemnities? The borrower, at any rate, feels
that it would not, and postpones the moment till
the fitting solemnities can be produced. But
John Gordon could not postpone his moment.
He could not go on residing indefinitely at the
Claimant's Arms till he could find a proper
opportunity for assuring Mr. Whittlestaff that it
could not be his duty to marry Mary Lawrie. He
must rush at his subject, let the result be what it
might. Indeed he had no hopes as to a favour-
able result. He had slept upon it, as people say
when they intend to signify that they have lain
awake, and had convinced himself that all eloquence would be vain. Was it natural that a man

should give up his intended wife, simply because he was asked? Gordon's present feeling was an anxious desire to be once more on board the ship that should take him again to the diamond-fields, so that he might be at peace, knowing then, as he would know, that he had left Mary Lawrie behind for ever. At this moment he almost repented that he had not left Alresford without any farther attempt. But there he was on Mr. Whittlestaff's ground, and the attempt must be made, if only with the object of justifying his coming.

'Miss Lawrie,' he began, 'if you would not mind leaving me and Mr. Whittlestaff alone together for a few minutes, I will be obliged to you.' This he said with quite sufficient solemnity, so that Mr. Whittlestaff drew himself up, and looked hard and stiff, as though he were deter-mined to forget Sergeant Baggett and all his peccadilloes for the moment.

'Oh, yes; certainly; but——' Mr. Whittlestaff looked sternly at her, as though to bid her go at once. 'You must believe nothing as coming from me unless it comes out of my own mouth.' Then she put her hand upon his arm, as though half embracing him.

'You had better leave us, perhaps,' said Mr. Whittlestaff. And then she went.

Now the moment had come, and John Gordon felt the difficulty. It had not been lessened by the assurance given by Mary herself that nothing was to be taken as having come from her unless it was known and heard to have so come. And yet he was thoroughly convinced that he was altogether loved by her, and that had he appeared on the scene but a day sooner, she would have accepted him with all her heart. 'Mr. Whittlestaff,' he said, 'I want to tell you what passed yesterday between me and Miss Lawrie.'

'Is it necessary?' he asked.

'I think it is.'

'As far as I am concerned, I doubt the necessity. Miss Lawrie has said a word to me,—as much, I presume, as she feels to be necessary.'

'I do not think that her feeling in the matter should be a guide for you or for me. What we have both of us to do is to think what may be best for her, and to effect that as far as may be within our power.'

'Certainly,' said Mr. Whittlestaff. 'But it may so probably be the case that you and I shall differ materially as to thinking what may be best for her. As far as I understand the matter, you wish that she should be your wife. I wish that she should be mine. I think that as my wife she would live a happier life than she could do as yours; and as she thinks also——' Here Mr. Whittlestaff paused.

'But does she think so?'

'You heard what she said just now.'

'I heard nothing as to her thoughts of living,' said John Gordon 'Nor in the interview which I had with her yesterday did I hear a word fall from her as to herself. We have got to form our ideas as to that from circumstances which shall certainly not be made to appear by her own speech. When you speak against me——'

'I have not said a word against you, sir.'

'Perhaps you imply,' said Gordon, not stopping to notice Mr. Whittlestaff's last angry tone,

—'perhaps you imply that my life may be that of a rover, and as such would not conduce to Miss Lawrie's happiness.'

'I have implied nothing.'

'To suit her wishes I would remain altogether in England. I was very lucky, and am not a man greedy of great wealth. She can remain here, and I will satisfy you that there shall be enough for our joint maintenance.'

'What do I care for your maintenance, or what does she? Do you know, sir, that you are talking to me about a lady whom I intend to make my wife,—who is engaged to marry me? Goodness gracious me!'

'I own, sir, that it is singular.'

'Very singular,—very singular indeed. I never heard of such a thing. It seems that you knew her at Norwich.'

'I did know her well.'

'And then you went away and deserted her.'

'I went away, Mr. Whittlestaff, because I was poor. I was told by her step-mother that I was not wanted about the house, because I had no means. That was true, and as I loved her dearly, I started at once, almost in despair, but still with something of hope,—with a shade of hope,—that I might put myself in the way of enabling her to become my wife. I did not desert her.'

'Very well. Then you came back and found her engaged to be my wife. You had it from her own mouth. When a gentleman hears that, what has he to do but to go away?'

'There are circumstances here.'

'What does she say herself? There are no circumstances to justify you. If you would come here as a friend, I offered to receive you. As you had been known to her, I did not turn my back upon you. But now your conduct is so peculiar that I cannot ask you to remain here any longer.' They were walking up and down the long walk, and now Mr. Whittlestaff stood still, as though to declare his intention that the interview should be considered as over.

'I know that you wish me to go away,' said Gordon.

'Well, yes; unless you withdraw all idea of a claim to the young lady's hand.'

'But I think you should first hear what I have to say. You will not surely have done your duty by her unless you hear me.'

'You can speak if you wish to speak,' said Mr. Whittlestaff.

'It was not till yesterday that you made your proposition to Miss Lawrie.'

'What has that to do with it?'

'Had I come on the previous day, and had I been able then to tell her all that I can tell her now, would it have made no difference?'

'Did she say so?' asked the fortunate lover, but in a very angry tone.

'No; she did not say so. It was with difficulty that I forced from her an avowal that her engagement was so recent. But she did confess that it was so. And she confessed, not in words, but in her manner, that she had found it impossible to refuse to you the request that you had asked.'

'I never heard a man assert so impudently that he was the sole owner of a lady's favours. Upon my word, I think that you are the vainest man whom I ever met.'

'Let it be so. I do not dare to defend myself, but only her. Whether I am vain or not, is it not true that which I say? I put it to you, as man to man, whether you do not know that it is true? If you marry this girl, will you not marry one whose heart belongs to me? Will you not marry one of whom you knew two days since that her heart was mine? Will you not marry one who, if she was free this moment, would give herself to me without a pang of remorse?'

'I never heard anything like the man's vanity!'

'But is it true? Whatever may be my vanity, or self-seeking, or unmanliness if you will, is not what I say God's truth? It is not about my weaknesses, or your weaknesses, that we should speak, but about her happiness.'

'Just so; I don't think she would be happy with you.'

'Then it is to save her from me that you are marrying her,—so that she may not sink into the abyss of my unworthiness.'

'Partly that.'

'But if I had come two days since, when she would have received me with open arms——'

'You have no right to make such a statement.'

'I ask yourself whether it is not true? She would have received me with open arms, and would you then have dared, as her guardian, to bid her refuse the offer made to her, when you had learned, as you would have done, that she loved me; that I had loved her with all my heart before I left England; that I had left it with the view of enabling myself to marry her; that I had been wonderfully successful; that I had come back with no other hope in the world than that of giving it all to her; that I had been able to show you my whole life, so that no girl need be afraid to become my wife——'

'What do I know about your life? You may have another wife living at this moment.'

'No doubt; I may be guilty of any amount of villainy, but then, as her friend, you should make inquiry. You would not break a girl's heart because the man to whom she is attached may possibly be a rogue. In this case you have no ground for the suspicion.'

'I never heard of a man who spoke of himself so grandiloquently!'

'But there is ample reason why you should make inquiry. In truth, as I said before, it is her happiness and not mine nor your own that you should look to. If she has taken your offer because you had been good to her in her desolation, —because she had found herself unable to refuse aught to one who had treated her so well; if she had done all this, believing that I had disappeared from her knowledge, and doubting altogether my return; if it be so—and you know that it is so—then you should hesitate before you lead her to her doom.'

'You heard her say that I was not to believe any of these things unless I got them from her own mouth?'

'I did; and her word should go for nothing either with you or with me. She has promised, and is willing to sacrifice herself to her promise. She will sacrifice me too because of your goodness,—and because she is utterly unable to put a fair value upon herself. To me she is all the world. From the first hour in which I saw her to the present, the idea of gaining her has been everything. Put aside the words which she just spoke, what is your belief of the state of her wishes?'

'I can tell you my belief of the state of her welfare.'

'There your own prejudice creeps in, and I might retaliate by charging you with vanity as you have done me,—only that I think such vanity very natural. But it is her you should consult on such a matter. She is not to be treated like a child. Of whom does she wish to become the wife? I boldly say that I have won her love, and that if it be so, you should not desire to take her to yourself. You have not answered me, nor can I expect you to answer me; but look into your-self and answer it there. Think how it will be with you, when the girl who lies upon your shoulder shall be thinking ever of some other man from whom you have robbed her. Good-bye, Mr. Whittlestaff. I do not doubt but that you will turn it all over in your thoughts.' Then he escaped by a wicket-gate into the road at the far end of the long walk, and was no more heard of at Croker's Hall on that day.

CHAPTER XI

Mrs. Baggett trusts only in the Funds

Mr. WHITTLESTAFF, when he was left alone
in the long walk, was disturbed by many
troublesome thoughts. The knowledge that his
housekeeper was out on the road, and that her
drunken disreputable husband was playing the
fool for the benefit of all the idlers that had
sauntered out from Alresford to see him, added
something to his grief. Why should not the stupid
woman remain indoors, and allow him, her
master, to send for the police? She had declared
that she would go with her husband, and he
could not violently prevent her. This was not
much when added to the weight of his care as to
Mary Lawrie, but it seemed to be the last ounce
destined to break the horse's back, as is the
proverbial fate of all last ounces.

Just as he was about to collect his thoughts,
so as to resolve what it might be his duty to do
in regard to Mary, Mrs. Baggett appeared before
him on the walk with her bonnet on her head.
'What are you going to do, you stupid woman?'

'I am a-going with he,' she said, in the midst
of a torrent of sobs and tears. 'It's a dooty.
They says if you does your dooty all will come
right in the end. It may be, but I don't see it no
further than taking him back to Portsmouth.'

'What on earth are you going to Portsmouth
for now? And why? why now? He's not more
drunk than he has been before, nor yet less
abominable. Let the police lock him up for the

night, and send him back to Portsmouth in the morning. Why should you want to go with him now?'

'Because you're going to take a missus,' said Mrs. Baggett, still sobbing.

'It's more than I know; or you know; or anyone knows,' and Mr. Whittlestaff spoke as though he had nearly reduced himself to his housekeeper's position.

'Not marry her!' she exclaimed.

'I cannot say. If you will let me alone to manage my own affairs, it will be best.'

'That man has been here interfering. You don't mean to say that you're going to be put upon by such a savage as that, as has just come home from South Africa. Diamonds, indeed! I'd diamond him! I don't believe, not in a single diamond. They're all rubbish and paste. If you're going to give her up to that fellow, you're not the gentleman I take you for.'

'But if I don't marry you won't have to go,' he said, unable to refrain from so self-evident an argument.

'Me going! What's me going? What's me or that drunken old reprobate out there to the likes of you? I'd stay, only if it was to see that Mr. John Gordon isn't let to put his foot here in this house; and then I'd go. John Gordon, indeed! To come up between you and her, when you had settled your mind and she had settled hern! If she favours John Gordon, I'll tear her best frock off her back.'

'How dare you speak in that way of the lady who is to be your mistress?'

'She ain't to be my mistress. I won't have no

mistress. When her time is come, I shall be in the poorhouse at Portsmouth, because I shan't be able to earn a penny to buy gin for him.' As she said this, Mrs. Baggett sobbed bitterly.

'You're enough to drive a man mad. I don't know what it is you want, or you don't want.'

'I wishes to see Miss Lawrie do her dooty, and become your wife, as a lady should do. You wishes it, and she ought to wish it too. Drat her! If she is going back from her word——'

'She is not going back from her word. Nothing is more excellent, nothing more true, nothing more trustworthy than Miss Lawrie. You should not allow yourself to speak of her in such language.'

'Is it you, then, as is going back?'

'I do not know. To tell the truth, Mrs. Baggett, I do not know.'

'Then let me tell you, sir. I'm an old woman whom you've known all your life pretty nigh, and you can trust me. Don't give up to none of 'em. You've got her word, and keep her to it. What's the good o' your fine feelings if you're to break your heart. You means well by her, and will make her happy. Can you say as much for him? When them diamonds is gone, what's to come next? I ain't no trust in diamonds, not to live out of, but only in the funds,* which is reg'lar. I wouldn't let her see John Gordon again,— never, till she was Mrs. Whittlestaff. After that she'll never go astray; nor yet won't her thoughts.'

'God bless you! Mrs. Baggett,' he said.

'She's one of them when she's your own she'll remain your own all out. She'll stand the washing. I'm an old woman, and I knows 'em.'

'And yet you cannot live with such a lady as her?'

'No! if she was one of them namby-pambys as'd let an old woman keep her old place, it might do.'

'She shall love you always for what you said just now.'

'Love me! I don't doubt her loving me. She'll love me because she is loving—not that I am lovable. She'll want to do a'most everything about the house, and I shall want the same; and her wants are to stand uppermost,—that is, if she is to be Mrs. Whittlestaff.'

'I do not know; I have to think about it.'

'Don't think about it no more; but just go in and do it. Don't have no more words with him nor yet with her,—nor yet with yourself. Let it come on just as though it were fixed by fate. It's in your own hands now, sir, and don't you be thinking of being too good-natured; there ain't no good comes from it. A man may maunder away his mind in softnesses till he ain't worth nothing, and don't do no good to no one. You can give her bread to eat, and clothes to wear, and can make her respectable before all men and women. What has he to say? Only that he is twenty years younger than you. Love! Rot it! I suppose you'll come in just now, sir, and see my boxes when they're ready to start.' So saying, she turned round sharply on the path and left him.

In spite of the excellent advice which Mr. Whittlestaff had received from his housekeeper, bidding him not have any more words even with himself on the matter, he could not but think of all the arguments which John Gordon had used to him. According to Mrs. Baggett, he ought to content himself with knowing that he could find food and raiment and shelter for his intended wife, and also in feeling that he had her promise, and her assurance that that promise should be respected. There was to him a very rock in all this, upon which he could build his house with absolute safety. And he did not believe of her that, were he so to act, she would turn round upon him with future tears or neglect her duty, because she was ever thinking of John Gordon. He knew that she would be too steadfast for all that, and that even though there might be some sorrow at her heart, it would be well kept down, out of his sight, out of the sight of the world at large, and would gradually sink out of her own sight too. But if it be given to a man 'to maunder away his mind in softnesses,' he cannot live otherwise than as nature has made him. Such a man must maunder. Mrs. Baggett had understood accurately the nature of his character; but had not understood that, as was his character, so must he act. He could not alter his own self. He could not turn round upon himself, and bid himself be other than he was. It is necessary to be stern and cruel and determined, a man shall say to himself. In this particular emergency of my life I will be stern and cruel. General good will come out of such a line of conduct. But unless he be stern and cruel in other matters also,— unless he has been born stern and cruel, or has so trained himself,—he cannot be stern and cruel for that occasion only. All this Mr. Whittlestaff knew of himself. As sure as he was there thinking over John Gordon and Mary Lawrie, would he maunder away his mind in softnesses. He feared it of himself, was sure of it of himself, and hated himself because it was so.

He did acknowledge to himself the truth of the position as asserted by John Gordon. Had the man come but a day earlier, he would have been in time to say the first word; and then, as Mr. Whittlestaff said to himself, there would not for him have been a chance. And in such case there would have been no reason, as far as Mr. Whittlestaff could see, why John Gordon should be treated other than as a happy lover. It was the one day in advance which had given him the strength of his position. But it was the one day also which had made him weak. He had thought much about Mary for some time past. He had told himself that by her means might be procured some cure to the wound in his heart which had made his life miserable for so many years. But had John Gordon come in time, the past misery would only have been prolonged, and none would have been the wiser. Even Mrs. Baggett would have held her peace, and not thrown it in his teeth that he had attempted to marry the girl and had failed. As it was, all the world of Alresford would know how it had been with him, and all the world of Alresford as they looked at him would tell themselves that this was the man who had attempted to marry Mary Lawrie, and had failed.

It was all true,—all that John Gordon alleged on his own behalf. But then he was able to salve his own conscience by telling himself that when John Gordon had run through his diamonds, there would be nothing but poverty and distress. There was no reason for supposing that the diamonds would be especially short-lived, or that John Gordon would probably be a spendthrift. But diamonds as a source of income are volatile, —not trustworthy, as were the funds to Mrs. Baggett. And then the nature of the source of income offered, enabled him to say so much as a plea to himself. Could he give the girl to a man who had nothing but diamonds with which to pay his weekly bills? He did tell himself again and again, that Mary Lawrie should not be encouraged to put her faith in diamonds. But he felt that it was only an excuse. In arguing the matter backwards and forwards, he could not but tell himself that he did believe in John Gordon.

And then an idea, a grand idea, but one very painful in its beauty, crept into his mind. Even though these diamonds should melt away, and become as nothing, there was his own income, fixed and sure as the polar star, in the consolidated British three per cents. If he really loved this girl, could he not protect her from poverty, even were she married to a John Gordon, broken down in the article of his diamonds? If he loved her, was he not bound, by some rule of chivalry which he could not define even to himself, to do the best he could for her happiness? He loved her so well that he thought that, for her sake, he could abolish himself. Let her have his money, his house, and his horses. Let her even have John Gordon. He could with a certain feeling of delight imagine it all. But then he could not abolish himself. There he would be, subject to the

remarks of men. 'There is he,' men would say of
him, 'who has maundered away his mind in softnesses;—who in his life has loved two girls, and
has, at last, been thrown over by both of them
because he has been no better than a soft maundering idiot.' It would be thus that his neighbours would speak of him in his vain effort to
abolish himself.

It was not yet too late. He had not yielded an
inch to this man. He could still be stern and unbending. He felt proud of himself in that he had
been stern and unbending, as far as the man was
concerned. And as regarded Mary, he did feel
sure of her. If there was to be weakness displayed,
it would be in himself. Mary would be true to her
promise;—true to her faith, true to the arrangement made for her own life. She would not
provoke him with arguments as to her love for
John Gordon; and, as Mrs. Baggett has assured
him, even in her thoughts she would not go
astray. If it were but for that word, Mrs. Baggett
should not be allowed to leave his house.

But what as to Mary's love? Any such question was maunderingly soft. It was not for him
to ask it. He did believe in her altogether, and
was perfectly secure that his name and his honour
were safe in her hands. And she certainly would
learn to love him. 'She'll stand the washing,'
he said to himself, repeating another morsel of
Mrs. Baggett's wisdom. And thus he made up
his mind that he would, on this occasion, if only
on this occasion, be stern and cruel. Surely a
man could bring himself to sternness and cruelty
for once in his life, when so much depended on it.

Having so resolved, he walked back into the

house, intending to see Mary Lawrie, and so to
speak to her as to give her no idea of the conversation which had taken place between him
and John Gordon. It would not be necessary,
he thought, that he should mention to her John
Gordon's name any more. Let his marriage go
on, as though there were no such person as John
Gordon. It would be easier to be stern and cruel
when he could enact the character simply by
silence. He would hurry on his wedding as
quickly as she would allow him, and then the
good thing—the good that was to come out of
sternness and cruelty—would be achieved.

He went through from the library to knock at
Mary's door, and in doing so, had to pass the
room in which Mrs. Baggett had slept tranquilly
for fifteen years. There, in the doorway, was a
big trunk, and in the lock of the door was a key.
A brilliant idea at once occurred to Mr. Whittlestaff. He shoved the big box in with his foot,
locked the door, and put the key in his pocket.
At that moment the heads of the gardener and
the groom appeared up the back staircase, and
after them Mrs. Baggett.

'Why, Mrs. Baggett, the door is locked!' said
the gardener.

'It is, to be sure,' said the groom. 'Why, Mrs.
Baggett, you must have the key in your own
pocket!'

'I ain't got no such thing. Do you bring the
box down with you.'

'I have got the key in my pocket,' said Mr.
Whittlestaff, in a voice of much authority. 'You
may both go down. Mrs. Baggett's box is not to
be taken out of that room to-day.'

'Not taken out! Oh, Mr. Whittlestaff! Why, the porter is here with his barrow to take it down to the station.'

'Then the porter must have a shilling and go back again empty.' And so he stalked on, to bid Miss Lawrie come to him in the library.

'I never heard of such a go in all my life;— and he means it, too,' said Thornybush, the gardener.

'I never quite know what he means,' said Hayonotes, the groom; 'but he's always in earnest, whatever it is. I never see one like the master for being in earnest. But he's too deep for me in his meaning. I suppose we is only got to go back.' So they retreated down the stairs, leaving Mrs. Baggett weeping in the passage.

'You should let a poor old woman have her box,' she said, whining to her master, whom she followed to the library.

'No; I won't! You shan't have your box. You're an old fool!'

'I know I'm an old fool;—but I ought to have my box.'

'You won't have it. You may just go down and get your dinner. When you want to go to bed, you shall have the key.'

'I ought to have my box, Miss Mary. It's my own box. What am I to do with Baggett? They have given him more gin out there, and he's as drunk as a beast. I think I ought to have my own box. Shall I tell Thornybush as he may come back? The train'll be gone, and then what am I to do with Baggett? He'll get hisself that drunk, you won't be able to stir him. And it is my own box, Mr. Whittlestaff?'

To all which Mr. Whittlestaff turned a deaf ear. She should find that there was no maundering softness with him now. He felt within his own bosom that it behoved him to learn to become stern and cruel. He knew that the key was in his pocket, and found that there was a certain satisfaction in being stern and cruel. Mrs. Baggett might sob her heart out after her box, and he would decline to be moved.

'What'll I do about Baggett, sir?' said the poor woman, coming back. 'He's a lying there at the gate, and the perlice doesn't like to touch him because of you, sir. He says as how if you could take him into the stables, he'd sleep it off among the straw. But then he'd be just as bad after this first go, to-morrow.'

To this, however, Mr. Whittlestaff at once acceded. He saw a way out of the immediate difficulty. He therefore called Hayonotes to him, and succeeded in explaining his immediate meaning. Hayonotes and the policeman between them lifted Baggett, and deposited the man in an empty stall, where he was accommodated with ample straw. And an order was given that as soon as he had come to himself, he should be provided with something to eat.

'Summat to eat!' said Mrs. Baggett, in extreme disgust. 'Provide him with a lock-up and plenty of cold water!'

CHAPTER XII

Mr. Blake's Good News

IN the afternoon, after lunch had been eaten, there came a ring at the back-door, and Mr. Montagu Blake was announced. There had been a little *contretemps* or misadventure. It was Mr. Blake's habit when he called at Croker's Hall to ride his horse into the yard, there to give him up to Hayonotes, and make his way in by the back entrance. On this occasion Hayonotes had been considerably disturbed in his work, and was discussing the sad condition of Mr. Baggett with Thornybush over the gate of the kitchen-garden. Consequently, Mr. Blake had taken his own horse into the stable, and as he was about to lead the beast up to the stall, had been stopped and confused by Sergeant Baggett's protruding wooden leg.

''Alloa! what's up now?' said a voice addressing Mr. Blake from under the straw. 'Do you go down, old chap, and get us three-penn'orth of cream o' the valley from the Cock.'

Then Mr. Blake had been aware that this prior visitor was not in a condition to be of much use to him, and tied up his own horse in another stall. But on entering the house, Mr. Blake announced the fact of there being a stranger in the stables, and suggested that the one-legged gentleman had been looking at somebody taking a glass of gin.* Then Mrs. Baggett burst out into a loud screech of agony. 'The nasty drunken beast! he ought to be locked up into the darkest hole they've got in all Alresford.'

'But who is the gentleman?' said Mr. Blake.

'My husband, sir; I won't deny him. He is the cross as I have to carry, and precious heavy he is. You must have heard of Sergeant Baggett;— the most drunkenest, beastliest, idlest scoundrel as ever the Queen had in the army, and the most difficultest for a woman to put up with in the way of a husband! Let a woman be ever so decent, he'd drink her gowns and her petticoats, down to her very underclothing. How would you like, sir, to have to take up with such a beast as that, after living all your life as comfortable as any lady in the land? Wouldn't that be a come-down, Mr. Blake? And then to have your box locked up, and be told that the key of your bedroom door is in the master's pocket.' Thus Mrs. Baggett continued to bewail her destiny.

Mr. Blake having got rid of the old woman, and bethinking himself of the disagreeable incidents to which a gentleman with a larger establishment than his own might be liable, made his way into the sitting-room, where he found Mary Lawrie alone; and having apologised for the manner of his intrusion, and having said something intended to be jocose as to the legs of the warrior in the stable, at once asked a question as to John Gordon.

'Mr. Gordon!' said Mary. 'He was here this morning with Mr. Whittlestaff, but I know nothing of him since.'

'He hasn't gone back to London?'

'I don't know where he has gone. He slept in

Alresford last night, but I know nothing of him since.'

'He sent his bag by the boy at the inn down to the railway station when he came up here. I found his bag there, but heard nothing of him. They told me at the inn that he was to come up here, and I thought I should either find him here or meet him on the road.'

'Do you want to find him especially?'

'Well, yes.'

'Do you know Mr. Gordon?'

'Well, yes; I do. That is to say, he dined with me last night. We were at Oxford together, and yesterday evening we got talking about our adventures since.'

'He told you that he had been at the diamond-fields?'

'Oh, yes; I know all about the diamond-fields. But Mr. Hall particularly wants to see him up at the Park.' (Mr. Hall was the squire with four daughters who lived at Little Alresford.) 'Mr. Hall says that he knew his father many years ago, and sent me out to look for him. I shall be wretched if he goes away without coming to Little Alresford House. He can't go back to London before four o'clock, because there is no train. You know nothing about his movements?'

'Nothing at all. For some years past Mr. Gordon has been altogether a stranger to me.' Mr. Blake looked into her face, and was aware that there was something to distress her. He at once gathered from her countenance that Mr. Whittlestaff had been like the dog that stuck to his bone, and that John Gordon was like the other dog—the disappointed one—and had been

turned out from the neighbourhood of the kennel.
'I should imagine that Mr. Gordon has gone
away, if not to London, then in some other direction.' It was clear that the young lady intended
him to understand that she could say nothing
and knew nothing as to Mr. Gordon's movements.

'I suppose I must go down to the station and
leave word for him there,' said Mr. Blake. Miss
Lawrie only shook her head. 'Mr. Hall will be
very sorry to miss him. And then I have some
special good news to tell him.'

'Special good news!' Could it be that something had happened which would induce Mr.
Whittlestaff to change his mind. That was the
one subject which to her, at the present moment,
was capable of meaning specially good tidings.

'Yes, indeed, Miss Lawrie; double good news,
I may say. Old Mr. Harbottle has gone at last
at San Remo.' Mary did know who Mr. Harbottle
was,—or had been. Mr. Harbottle had been
the vicar at Little Alresford, for whose death Mr.
Blake was waiting, in order that he might enter
in together upon the good things of matrimony
and the living. He was a man so contented, and
talked so frequently of the good things which
Fortune was to do for him, that the tidings of his
luck had reached even the ears of Mary Lawrie.
'That's an odd way of putting it, of course,' continued Mr. Blake; 'but then he was quite old and
very asthmatic, and couldn't ever come back
again. Of course I'm very sorry for him,—in one
way; but then I'm very glad in another. It is
a good thing to have the house in my own hands,
so as to begin to paint at once, ready for her

coming. Her father wouldn't let her be married till I had got the living, and I think he was right, because I shouldn't have liked to spend money in painting and such like on an uncertainty. As the old gentleman had to die, why shouldn't I tell the truth? Of course I am glad, though it does sound so terrible.'

'But what are the double good news?'

'Oh, I didn't tell you. Miss Forrester is to come to the Park. She is not coming because Mr. Harbottle is dead. That's only a coincidence. We are not going to be married quite at once,—straight off the reel,* you know. I shall have to go to Winchester for that. But now that old Harbottle has gone, I'll get the day fixed; you see if I don't. But I must really be off, Miss Lawrie. Mr. Hall will be terribly vexed if I don't find Gordon, and there's no knowing where he may go whilst I'm talking here.' Then he made his adieux, but returned before he had shut the door after him. 'You couldn't send somebody with me, Miss Lawrie? I shall be afraid of that wooden-legged man in the stables, for fear he should get up and abuse me. He asked me to get him some gin,—which was quite unreasonable.' But on being assured that he would find the groom about the place, he went out, and the trot of his horse was soon heard upon the road.

He did succeed in finding John Gordon, who was listlessly waiting at the Claimant's Arms for the coming of the four o'clock train which was to take him back to London, on his way, as he told himself, to the diamond-fields. He had thrown all his heart, all the energy of which he was the master, into the manner in which he had

pleaded for himself and for Mary with Mr.
Whittlestaff. But he felt the weakness of his
position in that he could not remain present upon
the ground and see the working of his words.
Having said what he had to say, he could only
go; and it was not to be expected that the eloquence of an absent man, of one who had declared that he was about to start for South Africa,
should be regarded. He knew that what he had
said was true, and that, being true, it ought to
prevail; but, having declared it, there was nothing
for him to do but to go away. He could not see
Mary herself again, nor, if he did so, would she
be so likely to yield to him as was Mr. Whittlestaff. He could have no further excuse for addressing himself to the girl who was about to
become the wife of another man. Therefore he
sat restless, idle, and miserable in the little parlour at the Claimant's Arms, thinking that the
long journey which he had made had been taken
all in vain, and that there was nothing left for
him in the world but to return to Kimberley, and
add more diamonds to his stock-in-trade.

'Oh, Gordon!' said Blake, bursting into the
room, 'you're the very man I want to find. You
can't go back to London to-day.'

'Can't I?'

'Quite out of the question. Mr. Hall knew
your father intimately when you were only a
little chap.'

'Will that prevent my going back to London?'

'Certainly it will. He wants to renew the
acquaintance. He is a most hospitable, kind-
hearted man; and who knows, one of the four
daughters might do yet.'

'Who is Mr. Hall?' No doubt he had heard the name on the previous evening; but Hall is common, and had been forgotten.

'Who is Mr. Hall? Why, he is the squire of Little Alresford, and my patron. I forget you haven't heard that Mr. Harbottle is dead at last. Of course I am very sorry for the old gentleman in one sense; but it is such a blessing in another. I'm only just thirty, and it's a grand thing my tumbling into the living in this way.'

'I needn't go back because Mr. Harbottle is dead.'

'But Kattie Forrester is coming to the Park. I told you last night, but I daresay you've forgotten it; and I couldn't tell then that Mr. Hall was acquainted with you, or that he would be so anxious to be hospitable. He says that I'm to tell you to take your bag up to the house at once. There never was anything more civil than that. Of course I let him know that we had been at Oxford together. That does go for something.'

'The university and your society together,' suggested Gordon.

'Don't chaff, because I'm in earnest. Kattie Forrester will be in by the very train that was to take you on to London, and I'm to wait and put her into Mr. Hall's carriage. One of the daughters, I don't doubt, will be there, and you can wait and see her if you like it. If you'll get your bag ready, the coachman will take it with Kattie's luggage. There's the Park carriage coming down the street now. I'll go out and stop old Steady-pace the coachman; only don't you keep him long, because I shouldn't like Kattie to find that there was no one to look after her at the station.'

There seemed to be an opening in all this for John Gordon to remain at any rate a day longer in the neighbourhood of Mary Lawrie, and he determined that he would avail himself of the opportunity. He therefore, together with his friend Blake, saw the coachman, and gave instructions as to finding the bag at the station, and prepared himself to walk out to the Park. 'You can go down to the station,' he said to Blake, 'and can ride back with the carriage.'

'Of course I shall see you up at the house,' said Blake. 'Indeed I've been asked to stay there whilst Kattie is with them. Nothing can be more hospitable than Mr. Hall and his four daughters. I'd give you some advice, only I really don't know which you'd like the best. There is a sort of similarity about them; but that wears off when you come to know them. I have heard people say that the two eldest are very much alike. If that be so, perhaps you'll like the third the best. The third is the nicest, as her hair may be a shade darker than the others. I really must be off now, as I wouldn't for worlds that the train should come in before I'm on the platform.' With that he went into the yard, and at once trotted off on his cob.

Gordon paid his bill, and started on his walk to Little Alresford Park. Looking back into his early memories, he could just remember to have heard his father speak of Mr. Hall. But that was all. His father was now dead, and, certainly, he thought, had not mentioned the name for many years. But the invitation was civil, and as he was to remain in the neighbourhood, it might be that he should again have the opportunity of seeing

Mary Lawrie or Mr. Whittlestaff. He found that Little Alresford Park lay between the town and Mr. Blake's church, so that he was at the gate sooner than he expected. He went in, and having time on his hands, deviated from the road and went up a hill, which was indeed one of the downs, though between the park paling. Here he saw deer feeding, and he came after a while to a beech grove. He had now gone down the hill on the other side, and found himself close to as pretty a labourer's cottage as he remembered ever to have seen. It was still June, and it was hot, and he had been on his legs nearly the whole morning. Then he began to talk, or rather to think to himself. 'What a happy fellow is that man Montagu Blake! He has every thing,—not that he wants, but that he thinks that he wants. The work of his life is merely play. He is going to marry a wife,—not who is, but whom he thinks to be perfection. He looks as though he were never ill a day in his life. How would he do if he were grubbing for diamonds amidst the mud and dust of Kimberley? Instead of that, he can throw himself down on such a spot as this, and meditate his sermon among the beech-trees.' Then he began to think whether the sermon could be made to have some flavour of the beech-trees, and how much better in that case it would be, and as he so thought he fell asleep.

He had not been asleep very long, perhaps not five minutes, when he became aware in his slumbers that an old man was standing over him. One does thus become conscious of things before the moment of waking has arrived, so positively as to give to the sleeper a false sense of the reality of existence. 'I wonder whether you can be Mr. Gordon,' said the old man.

'But I am,' said Gordon. 'I wonder how you know me.'

'Because I expect you.' There was something very mysterious in this,—which, however, lost all mystery as soon as he was sufficiently awake to think of things. 'You are Mr. Blake's friend.'

'Yes; I am Mr. Blake's friend.'

'And I am Mr. Hall. I didn't expect to find you sleeping here in Gar Wood. But when I find a strange gentleman asleep in Gar Wood, I put two and two together, and conclude that you must be Mr. Gordon.'

'It's the prettiest place in all the world, I think.'

'Yes; we are rather proud of Gar Wood,—especially when the deer are browsing on the hill-side to the left, as they are now. If you don't want to go to sleep again, we'll walk up to the house. There's the carriage. I can hear the wheels. The girls have gone down to fetch your friend's bride. Mr. Blake is very fond of his bride,—as I dare say you have found out.'

Then, as the two walked together to the house, Mr. Hall explained that there had been some little difference in years gone by between old Mr. Gordon and himself as to money. 'I was very sorry, but I had to look after myself. You knew nothing about it, I dare say.'

'I have heard your name—that's all.'

'I need not say anything more about it,' said Mr. Hall; 'only when I heard that you were in the country, I was very glad to have the opportunity of seeing you. Blake tells me that you know my friend Whittlestaff.'

'I did not know him till yesterday morning.'

'Then you know the young lady there; a charming young lady she is. My girls are extremely fond of Mary Lawrie. I hope we may get them to come over while you are staying here.'

'I can only remain one night,—or at the most two, Mr. Hall.'

'Pooh, pooh! We have other places in the neighbourhood to show you quite as pretty as Gar Wood. Though that's a bounce: I don't think there is any morsel quite so choice as Gar Wood when the deer are there. What an eye you must have, Mr. Gordon, to have made it out by yourself at once; but then, after all, it only put you to sleep. I wonder whether the Rookery will put you to sleep. We go in this way, so as to escape the formality of the front door, and I'll introduce you to my daughters and Miss Forrester.'

CHAPTER XIII

At Little Alresford

Mr. HALL was a pleasant English gentleman, now verging upon seventy years of age, who had 'never had a headache in his life,' as he was wont to boast, but who lived very carefully, as one who did not intend to have many headaches. He certainly did not intend to make his head ache by the cares of the work of the world. He was very well off;—that is to say, that with so many thousands a year, he managed to live upon half. This he had done for very many years, because the estate was entailed on a distant relative, and because he had not chosen to leave his children paupers. When the girls came he immediately resolved that he would never go up to London, —and kept his resolve. Not above once in three or four years was it supposed to be necessary that he showed his head to a London hairdresser. He was quite content to have a practitioner out from Alresford, and to pay him one shilling, including the journey. His tenants in these bad times* had always paid their rents, but they had done so because their rents had not been raised since the squire had come to the throne. Mr. Hall knew well that if he was anxious to save himself from headaches in that line, he had better let his lands on easy terms. He was very hospitable, but he never gave turtle from London, or fish from Southampton, or strawberries or peas on the first of April. He could give a dinner without champagne, and thought forty shillings a dozen price

enough for port or sherry, or even claret. He
kept a carriage for his four daughters, and did
not tell all the world that the horses spent a fair
proportion of their time at the plough. The four
daughters had two saddle-horses between them,
and the father had another for his own use.
He did not hunt,—and living in that part of
Hampshire, I think he was right. He did shoot
after the manner of our forefathers;—would go
out, for instance, with Mr. Blake, and perhaps
Mr. Whittlestaff, and would bring home three
pheasants, four partridges, a hare, and any
quantity of rabbits that the cook might have
ordered. He was a man determined on no account to live beyond his means; and was not very
anxious to seem to be rich. He was a man of no
strong affections, or peculiarly generous feelings.
Those who knew him, and did not like him, said
that he was selfish. They who were partial to
him declared that he never owed a shilling that
he could not pay, and that his daughters were
very happy in having such a father. He was a
good-looking man, with well-formed features,
but one whom you had to see often before you
could remember him. And as I have said before,
he 'never had a headache in his life.' 'When your
father wasn't doing quite so well with the bank
as his friends wished, he asked me to do something for him. Well; I didn't see my way.'

'I was a boy then, and I heard nothing of my
father's business.'

'I dare say not; but I cannot help telling you.
He thought I was unkind. I thought that he
would go on from one trouble to another;—and
he did. He quarrelled with me, and for years we

never spoke. Indeed I never saw him again. But for the sake of old friendship, I am very glad to meet you.' This he said, as he was walking across the hall to the drawing-room.

There Gordon met the young ladies with the clergyman, and had to undergo the necessary introductions. He thought that he could perceive at once that his story, as it regarded Mary Lawrie, had been told to all of them. Gordon was quick, and could learn from the manners of his companions what had been said about him, and could perceive that they were aware of something of his story. Blake had no such quickness, and could attribute none of it to another. 'I am very proud to have the pleasure of making you acquainted with these five young ladies.' As he said this he had just paused in his narrative of Mr. Whittlestaff's love, and was certain that he had changed the conversation with great effect. But the young ladies were unable not to look as young ladies would have looked when hearing the story of an unfortunate gentleman's love. And Mr. Blake would certainly have been unable to keep such a secret.

'This is Miss Hall, and this is Miss Augusta Hall,' said the father. 'People do think that they are alike.'

'Oh, papa, what nonsense! You needn't tell Mr. Gordon that.'

'No doubt he would find it out without telling,' continued the father.

'I can't see it, for the life of me,' said Mr. Blake. He evidently thought that civility demanded such an assertion. Mr. Gordon, looking at the two young ladies, felt that he would never know them apart though he might live in the house for a year.

'Evelina is the third,' continued Mr. Hall, pointing out the one whom Mr. Blake had specially recommended to his friend's notice. ' Evelina is not quite so like, but she's like too.'

'Papa, what nonsense you do talk!' said Evelina.

'And this is Mary. Mary considers herself to be quite the hope of the family; *spem gregis*. Ha, ha!'

'What does *spem gregis* mean?* I'm sure I don't know,' said Mary. The four young ladies were about thirty, varying up from thirty to thirty-five. They were fair-haired, healthy young women, with good common-sense, not beautiful, though very like their father.

'And now I must introduce you to Miss Forrester,—Kattie Forrester,' said Mr. Blake, who was beginning to think that his own young lady was being left out in the cold.

'Yes, indeed,' said Mr. Hall. 'As I had begun with my own, I was obliged to go on to the end. Miss Forrester—Mr. Gordon. Miss Forrester is a young lady whose promotion has been fixed in the world.'

'Mr. Hall, how can you do me so much injury as to say that? You take away from me the chance of changing my mind.'

'Yes,' said the oldest Miss Hall; 'and Mr. Gordon the possibility of changing his.* Mr. Gordon, what a sad thing it is that Mr. Harbottle should never have had an opportunity of seeing his old parish once again.'

'I never knew him,' said Gordon.

'But he had been here nearly fifty years. And then to leave the parish without seeing it any more. It's very sad when you look at it in that light.'

'He has never resided here permanently for a quarter of a century,' said Mr. Blake.

'Off and on in the summer time,' said Augusta. 'Of course he could not take much of the duty, because he had a clergyman's throat.* I think it a great pity that he should have gone off so suddenly.'

'Miss Forrester won't wish to have his *resurgam* sung,* I warrant you,' said Mr. Hall.

'I don't know much about *resurgams*,' said the young lady, 'but I don't see why the parish shall not be just as well in Mr. Blake's hands.' Then the young bride was taken away by the four elder ladies to dress, and the gentlemen followed them half an hour afterwards.

They were all very kind to him, and sitting after dinner, Mr. Hall suggested that Mr. Whittlestaff and Miss Lawrie should be asked over to dine on the next day. John Gordon had already promised to stay until the third, and had made known his intention of going back to South Africa as soon as he could arrange matters. 'I've got nothing to keep me here,' he said, 'and as there is a good deal of money at stake, I should be glad to be there as soon as possible.'

'Oh, come! I don't know about your having nothing to keep you here,' said Blake. But as to Mr. Hall's proposition regarding the inhabitants of Croker's Lodge, Gordon said nothing. He could not object to the guests whom a gentleman might ask to his own house; but he thought it improbable that either Mr. Whittlestaff or Mary should come. If he chose to appear and to bring her with him, it must be his own look-out. At any rate he, Gordon, could say and could do nothing on such an occasion. He had been betrayed into telling his secret to this garrulous young parson. There was no help for spilt milk; but it was not probable that Mr. Blake would go any further, and he at any rate must be content to bear the man's society for one other evening. 'I don't see why you shouldn't manage to make things pleasant even yet,' said the parson. But to this John Gordon made no reply.

In the evening some of the sisters played a few pieces at the piano, and Miss Forrester sang a few songs. Mr. Hall in the meantime went fast asleep. John Gordon couldn't but tell himself that his evenings at Kimberley were, as a rule, quite as exciting. But then Kattie Forrester did not belong to him, and he had not found himself able as yet to make a choice between the young ladies. It was, however, interesting to see the manner in which the new vicar hung about the lady of his love, and the evident but innocent pride with which she accepted the attentions of her admirer.

'Don't you think she's a beautiful girl?' said Blake, coming to Gordon's room after they had all retired to bed; 'such genuine wit, and so bright, and her singing, you know, is quite perfect,—absolutely just what it ought to be. I do know something about singing myself, because I've had all the parish voices under my own charge for the last three years. A practice like that goes a long way, you know.' To this Mr.

Gordon could only give that assent which silence is intended to imply. 'She'll have £5000 at once, you know, which does make her in a manner equal to either of the Miss Halls. I don't quite know what they'll have, but not more than that, I should think. The property is entailed, and he's a saving man. But if he can have put by £20,000 he has done very well; don't you think so?'

'Very well indeed.'

'I suppose I might have had one of them; I don't mind telling you in strictest confidence. But, goodness gracious, after I had once seen Kattie Forrester, there was no longer a doubt. I wish you'd tell me what you think about her.'

'About Miss Forrester?'

'You needn't mind speaking quite openly to me. I'm that sort of fellow that I shouldn't mind what any fellow said. I've formed my own ideas, and am not likely to change them. But I should like to hear, you know, how she strikes a fellow who has been at the diamond-fields. I cannot imagine but that you must have a different idea about women to what we have.' Then Mr. Blake sat himself down in an arm-chair at the foot of the bed, and prepared himself to discuss the opinion which he did not doubt that his friend was about to deliver.

'A very nice young woman indeed,' said John Gordon, who was anxious to go to bed.

'Ah, you know,—that's a kind of thing that anybody can say. There is no real friendship in that. I want to know the true candid opinion of a man who has travelled about the world, and has been at the diamond-fields. It isn't

everybody who has been at the diamond-fields,'
continued he, thinking that he might thereby
flatter his friend.

'No, not everybody. I suppose a young woman
is the same there as here, if she have the same
natural gifts. Miss Forrester would be pretty
anywhere.'

'That's a matter of course. Any fellow can see
that with half an eye. Absolutely beautiful, I
should say, rather than pretty.'

'Just so. It's only a variation in terms, you
know.'

'But then her manner, her music, her language, her wit, and the colour of her hair! When
I remember it all, I think I'm the luckiest fellow
in the world. I shall be a deal happier with her
than with Augusta Hall. Don't you think so?
Augusta was the one intended for me; but, bless
you, I couldn't look at her after I had seen Kattie
Forrester. I don't think you've given me your
true unbiassed opinion yet.'

'Indeed I have,' said John Gordon.

'Well; I should be more free-spoken than that,
if you were to ask me about Mary Lawrie. But
then, of course, Mary Lawrie is not your engaged
one. It does make a difference. If it does turn
out that she marries Mr. Whittlestaff, I shan't
think much of her, I can tell you that. As it is,
as far as looks are concerned, you can't compare
her to my Kattie.'

'Comparisons are odious,' said Gordon.

'Well, yes; when you are sure to get the worst
of them. You wouldn't think comparisons odious
if you were going to marry Kattie, and it was my
lot to have Mary Lawrie. Well, yes; I don't mind

going to bed now, as you have owned so much as that.'

'Of all the fools,' said Gordon to himself, as he went to his own chamber,—'of all the fools who were ever turned out in the world to earn their own bread, he is the most utterly foolish. Yet he will earn his bread, and will come to no especial grief in the work. If he were to go out to Kimberley, no one would pay him a guinea a-week. But he will perform the high work of a clergyman of the Church of England indifferently well.'

On the next morning a messenger was sent over to Croker's Hall, and came back after due lapse of time with an answer to the effect that Mr. Whittlestaff and Miss Lawrie would have pleasure in dining that day at Little Alresford Park. 'That's right,' said Mr. Blake to the lady of his love. 'We shall now, perhaps, be able to put the thing into a proper groove. I'm always very lucky in managing such matters. Not that I think that Gordon cares very much about the young lady, judging from what he says of her.'

'Then I don't see why you should interest yourself.'

'For the young lady's sake. A lady always prefers a young gentleman to an old one. Only think what you'd feel if you were married to Mr. Whittlestaff.'

'Oh, Montagu! how can you talk such nonsense?'

'I don't suppose you ever would, because you are not one of those sort of young ladies. I don't suppose that Mary Lawrie likes it herself; and therefore I'd break the match off in a moment if I could. That's what I call good-natured.'

After lunch they all went off to the Rookery, which was at the other side of the park from Gar Wood. It was a beautiful spot, lying at the end of the valley, through which they had to get out from their carriage, and to walk for half a mile. Only for the sake of doing honour to Miss Forrester, they would have gone on foot. But as it was, they had all the six horses among them. Mr. Gordon was put up on one of the young ladies' steeds, the squire and the parson each had his own, and Miss Evelina was also mounted, as Mr. Blake had suggested, perhaps with the view to the capture of Mr. Gordon. 'As it's your first day,' whispered Mr. Blake to Kattie, 'it is so nice, I think, that the carriage and horses should all come out. Of course there is nothing in the distance, but there should be a respect shown on such an occasion. Mr. Hall does do everything of this kind just as it should be.'

'I suppose you know the young lady who is coming here to-night,' said Evelina to Mr. Gordon.

'Oh, yes; I knew her before I went abroad.'

'But not Mr. Whittlestaff?'

'I had never met Mr. Whittlestaff, though I had heard much of his goodness.'

'And now they are to be married. Does it not seem to you to be very hard?'

'Not in the least. The young lady seems to have been left by her father and step-mother without any engagement, and, indeed, without any provision. She was brought here, in the first place, from sheer charity, and I can certainly understand that when she was here Mr. Whittlestaff should have admired her.'

'That's a matter of course,' said Evelina.

'Mr. Whittlestaff is not at all too old to fall in love with any young lady. This is a pretty place,—a very lovely spot. I think I like it almost better than Gar Wood.' Then there was no more said about Mary Lawrie till they all rode back to dinner.

CHAPTER XIV

Mr. Whittlestaff is going out to Dinner

'THERE's an invitation come, asking us to dine at Little Alresford to-day.' This was said, soon after breakfast, by Mr. Whittlestaff to Mary Lawrie, on the day after Mr. Gordon's coming. 'I think we'll go.'

'Could you not leave me behind?'

'By no means. I want you to become intimate with the girls, who are good girls.'

'But Mr. Gordon is there.'

'Exactly. That is just what I want. It will be better that you and he should meet each other, without the necessity of making a scene.' From this it may be understood that Mr. Whittlestaff had explained to Mary as much as he had thought necessary of what had occurred between him and John Gordon, and that Mary's answers had been satisfactory to his feelings. Mary had told him that she was contented with her lot in life, as Mr. Whittlestaff had proposed it for her. She had not been enthusiastic; but then he had not expected it. She had not assured him that she would forget John Gordon. He had not asked her. She had simply said that if he were satisfied, —so was she. 'I think that with me, dearest, at any rate, you will be safe.' 'I am quite sure that I shall be safe,' she had answered. And that had been sufficient.

But the reader will also understand from this that he had sought for no answer to those burning questions which John Gordon had put to him. Had she loved John Gordon the longest? Did she love him the best? There was no doubt a certain cautious selfishness in the way in which he had gone to work. And yet of general selfishness it was impossible to accuse him. He was willing to give her everything,—to do all for her. And he had first asked her to be his wife, with every observance. And then he could always protect himself on the plea that he was doing the best he could for her. His property was assured, —in the three per cents, as Mrs. Baggett had suggested; whereas John Gordon's was all in diamonds. How frequently do diamonds melt and come to nothing? They are things which a man can carry in his pocket, and lose or give away. They cannot,—so thought Mr. Whittlestaff,—be settled in the hands of trustees, or left to the charge of an executor. They cannot be substantiated. Who can say that, when looking to a lady's interest, this bit of glass may not come up instead of that precious stone? 'John Gordon might be a very steady fellow; but we have only his own word for that,'—as Mr. Whittlestaff observed to himself. There could not be a doubt but that Mr. Whittlestaff himself was the safer staff of the two on which a young lady might lean. He did make all these excuses for himself, and determined that they were of such a nature that he might rely upon them with safety. But still there was a pang in his bosom—a silent secret—which kept on whispering to him that he was not the best beloved. He had, however, resolved steadfastly that he would not put that question to Mary. If she did not wish to declare her love, neither did he. It was a pity, a thousand

pities, that it should be so. A change in her heart
might, however, take place. It would come to
pass that she would learn that he was the superior
staff on which to lean. John Gordon might disappear among the diamond-fields, and no more
be heard of. He, at any rate, would do his best
for her, so that she should not repent her bargain.
But he was determined that the bargain, as it
had been struck, should be carried out. Therefore, in communicating to Mary the invitation
which he had received from Little Alresford, he
did not find it necessary to make any special
speech in answer to her inquiry about John
Gordon.

She understood it all, and could not in her
very heart pronounce a judgment against him.
She knew that he was doing that which he
believed would be the best for her welfare. She,
overwhelmed by the debt of her gratitude, had
acceded to his request, and had been unable
afterwards to depart from her word. She had
said that it should be so, and she could not then
turn upon him and declare that when she had
given him her hand, she had been unaware of the
presence of her other lover. There was an injustice, an unkindness, an ingratitude, a selfishness in this, which forbade her to think of it as
being done by herself. It was better for her that
she should suffer, though the suffering should be
through her whole life, than that he should be
disappointed. No doubt the man would suffer
too,—her hero, her lover,—he with whom she
would so willingly have risked everything, either
with or without the diamonds. She could not,
however, bear to think that Mr. Whittlestaff

should be so very prudent and so very wise solely
on her behalf. She would go to him, but for
other reasons than that. As she walked about the
place half the day, up and down the long walk,
she told herself that it was useless to contend
with her love. She did love John Gordon; she
knew that she loved him with her whole heart;
she knew that she must be true to him;—but
still she would marry Mr. Whittlestaff, and do
her duty in that state of life to which it had
pleased God to call her. There would be a sacrifice—a sacrifice of two—but still it was justice.

Had she not consented to take everything
from Mr. Whittlestaff; her bread, her meat, her
raiment, the shelter under which she lived, and
the position in the world which she now enjoyed?
Had the man come but a day earlier, it would all
have been well. She would have told her love
before Mr. Whittlestaff had spoken of his wants.
Circumstances had been arranged differently,
and she must bear it. But she knew that it would
be better for her that she should see John Gordon
no more. Had he started at once to London and
gone thence to the diamond-fields without seeing
her again there would be a feeling that she had
become the creature of stern necessity; there
would have been no hope for her,—as also no
fear. Had he started a second time for South
Africa, she would have looked upon his further
return with any reference to her own wants as a
thing impossible. But now how would it be with
her? Mr. Whittlestaff had told her with a stern
indifference that she must again meet this man,
sit at the table with him as an old friend, and be
again subject to his influence. 'It will be better

that you and he should meet,' he had said, 'without the necessity of making a scene.' How could she assure him that there would be no scene?

Then she thought that she would have recourse to that ordinary feminine excuse, a headache; but were she to do so she would own the whole truth to her master; she would have declared that she so loved the man that she could not endure to be in his presence. She must now let the matter pass as he had intended. She must go to Mr. Hall's house, and there encounter him she loved with what show of coldness she might be able to assume.

But the worst of it all lay in this,—that she could not but think that he had been induced to remain in the neighbourhood in order that he might again try to gain his point. She had told herself again and again that it was impossible, that she must decide as she had decided, and that Mr. Whittlestaff had decided so also. He had used what eloquence was within his reach, and it had been all in vain. He could now appeal only to herself, and to such appeal there could be but one answer. And how was such appeal to be made in Mr. Hall's drawing-room? Surely John Gordon had been foolish in remaining in the neighbourhood. Nothing but trouble could come of it.

'So you are going to see this young man again!' This came from Mrs. Baggett, who had been in great perturbation all the morning. The Sergeant had slept in the stables through the night, and had had his breakfast brought to him, warm, by his own wife; but he had sat up among the straw, and had winked at her, and had asked her to give him threepence of gin with the cat-lap. To this she had acceded, thinking probably that she could not altogether deprive him of the food to which he was accustomed without injury. Then, under the influence of the gin and the promise of a ticket to Portsmouth, which she undertook to get for him at the station, he was induced to go down with her, and was absolutely despatched. Her own box was still locked up, and she had slept with one of the two maids. All this had not happened without great disturbance in the household. She herself was very angry with her master because of the box; she was very angry with Mary, because Mary was, she thought, averse to her old lover; she was very angry with Mr. Gordon, because she well understood that Mr. Gordon was anxious to disturb the arrangement which had been made for the family. She was very angry with her husband, not because he was generally a drunken old reprobate, but because he had especially disgraced her on the present occasion by the noise which he had made in the road. No doubt she had been treated unfairly in the matter of the box, and could have succeeded in getting the law of her master. But she could not turn against her master in that way. She could give him a bit of her own mind, and that she did very freely; but she could not bring herself to break the lock of his door. And then, as things went now, she did think it well that she should remain a few days longer at Croker's Hall. The occasion of her master's marriage was to be the cause of her going away. She could not endure not to be foremost among all the women at Croker's Hall. But it was intolerable to her feelings that any one should interfere with her master; and she thought that, if need were, she could assist him by her tongue. Therefore she was disposed to remain yet a few days in her old place, and had come, after she had got the ticket for her husband,—which had been done before Mr. Whittlestaff's breakfast,— to inform her master of her determination. 'Don't be a fool,' Mr. Whittlestaff had said.

'I'm always a fool, whether I go or stay, so that don't much matter.' This had been her answer, and then she had gone in to scold the maids.

As soon as she had heard of the intended dinner-party, she attacked Mary Lawrie. 'So you're going to see this young man again?'

'Mr. Whittlestaff is going to dine at Little Alresford, and intends to take me with him.'

'Oh yes; that's all very well. He'd have left you behind if he'd been of my way of thinking. Mr. Gordon here, and Mr. Gordon there! I wonder what's Mr. Gordon! He ain't no better than an ordinary miner. Coals and diamonds is all one to me;—I'd rather have the coals for choice.' But Mary was not in a humour to contest the matter with Mrs. Baggett, and left the old woman the mistress of the field.

When the time arrived for going to the dinner, Mr. Whittlestaff took Mary in the pony carriage with him. 'There is always a groom about there,' he said, 'so we need not take the boy.' His object was, as Mary in part understood, that he should be able to speak what last words he might have to utter without having other ears than hers to listen to them.

Mary would have been surprised had she known how much painful thought Mr. Whittlestaff gave to the matter. To her it seemed as though he had made up his mind without any effort, and was determined to abide by it. He had thought it well to marry her; and having asked her, and having obtained her consent, he intended to take advantage of her promise. That was her idea of Mr. Whittlestaff, as to which she did not at all blame him. But he was, in truth, changing his purpose every quarter of an hour;—or not changing it, but thinking again and again throughout the entire day whether he would not abandon himself and all his happiness to the romantic idea of making this girl supremely happy. Were he to do so, he must give up everything. The world would have nothing left for him as to which he could feel the slightest interest. There came upon him at such moments insane ideas as to the amount of sacrifice which would be demanded of him. She should have everything—his house, his fortune; and he, John Gordon, as being a part of her, should have them also. He, Whittlestaff, would abolish himself as far as such abolition might be possible. The idea of suicide was abominable to him—was wicked, cowardly, and inhuman. But if this were to take place he could wish to cease to live. Then he would comfort himself by assuring himself again and again that of the two he would certainly make the better husband. He was older. Yes; it was a pity that he should be so much the elder. And he knew that he was old of his age,—such a one as a girl like Mary Lawrie could hardly be brought to love passionately. He brought up against himself all the hard facts as sternly as could any younger rival. He looked at himself in the glass over and over again, and always gave the verdict against his own appearance. There was nothing to recommend him. So he told himself,—judging of himself most unfairly. He set against himself as evils little points by which Mary's mind and Mary's judgment would never be affected. But in truth throughout it all he thought only of her welfare. But there came upon him constantly an idea that he hardly knew how to be as good to her as he would have been had it not been for Catherine Bailey. To have attempted twice, and twice to have failed so disastrously! He was a man to whom to have failed once in such a matter was almost death. How should he bear it twice and still live? Nevertheless he did endeavour to think only of her welfare. 'You won't find it cold, my dear?' he said.

'Cold! Why, Mr. Whittlestaff, it's quite hot.'

'I meant hot. I did mean to say hot.'

'I've got my parasol.'

'Oh!—ah!—yes; so I perceive. Go on, Tommy. That foolish old woman will settle down at last, I think.' To this Mary could make no answer, because, according to her ideas, Mrs. Baggett's settling down must depend on her master's marriage. 'I think it very civil of Mr. Hall asking us in this way.'

'I suppose it is.'

'Because you may be sure he had heard of your former acquaintance with him.'

'Do you think so?'

'Not a doubt about it. He said as much to me in his note. That young clergyman of his will have told him everything. "Percontatorem fugito nam garrulus idem est."* I've taught you Latin enough to understand that. But, Mary, if you wish to change your mind, this will be your last opportunity.' His heart at that moment had been very tender towards her, and she had resolved that hers should be very firm to him.

CHAPTER XV

Mr. Whittlestaff goes out to Dinner

THIS would be her last opportunity. So Mary told herself as she got out of the carriage at Mr. Hall's front door. It was made manifest to her by such a speech that he did not expect that she should do so, but looked upon her doing so as within the verge of possibility. She could still do it, and yet not encounter his disgust or his horror. How terrible was the importance to herself, and, as she believed, to the other man also. Was she not justified in so thinking? Mr. Gordon had come home, travelling a great distance, at much risk to his property, at great loss of time, through infinite trouble and danger, merely to ask her to be his wife. Had a letter reached her from him but a week ago bidding her to come, would she not have gone through all the danger and all the trouble? How willingly would she have gone! It was the one thing that she desired; and, as far as she could understand the signs which he had given, it was the one, one thing which he desired. He had made his appeal to that other man, and, as far as she could understand the signs which had reached her, had been referred with confidence to her decision. Now she was told that the chance of changing her mind was still in her power.

The matter was one of terrible importance; but was its importance to Mr. Whittlestaff as great as to John Gordon? She put herself altogether out of the question. She acknowledged to herself, with a false humility, that she was nobody;—she was a poor woman living on charity, and was not to be thought of when the position of these two men was taken into consideration. It chanced that they both wanted her. Which wanted the most? Which of the two would want her for the longest? To which would her services be of the greater avail in assisting him to his happiness. Could there be a doubt? Was it not in human nature that she should bind herself to the younger man, and with him go through the world, whether safely or in danger?

But though she had had time to allow these questions to pass through her mind between the utterance of Mr. Whittlestaff's words and her entrance into Mr. Hall's drawing-room, she did not in truth doubt. She knew that she had made up her mind on the matter. Mr. Gordon would in all probability have no opportunity of saying another word to her. But let him say what word he might, it should be in vain. Nothing that he could say, nothing that she could say, would avail anything. If this other man would release her,—then indeed she would be released. But there was no chance of such release coming. In truth, Mary did not know how near the chance was to her;—or rather, how near the chance had been. He had now positively made up his mind, and would say not a word further unless she asked him. If Mary said nothing to John Gordon on this evening, he would take an opportunity before they left the house to inform Mr. Hall of his intended marriage. When once the word should have passed his mouth, he could not live under the stigma of a second Catherine Bailey.

'Miss Lawrie, pray let me make you known to my intended.' This came from Mr. Montagu Blake, who felt himself to be justified by his peculiar circumstances in so far taking upon himself the work of introducing the guests in Mr. Hall's house. 'Of course, you've heard all about it. I am the happiest young man in Hampshire, —and she is the next.'

'Speak for yourself, Montagu. I am not a young man at all.'

'You're a young man's darling, which is the next thing to it.'

'How are you, Whittlestaff?' said Mr. Hall. 'Wonderful weather, isn't it? I'm told that you've been in trouble about that drunken husband which plagues the life out of that respectable housekeeper of yours.'

'He is a trouble; but if he is bad to me, how much worse must he be to her?'

'That's true. He must be very bad, I should think. Miss Mary, why don't you come over this fine weather, and have tea with my girls and Kattie Forrester in the woods? You should take your chance while you have a young man willing to wait upon you.'

'I shall be quite delighted,' said Blake, 'and so will John Gordon.'

'Only that I shall be in London this time to-morrow,' said Gordon.

'That's nonsense. You are not going to Kimberley all at once. The young ladies expect you to bring out a lot of diamonds and show them before you start. Have you seen diamonds, Miss Lawrie?'*

'Indeed no,' said Mary.

'I think I should have asked just to see them,' said Evelina Hall. Why should they join her name with his in this uncivil manner, or suppose that she had any special power to induce him to show his treasures.

'When you first find a diamond,' said Mr. Hall, 'what do you do with it? Do you ring a bell and call together your friends, and begin to rejoice.'

'No, indeed. The diamond is generally washed out of the mud by some nigger, and we have to look very sharp after him to see that he doesn't hide it under his toe-nails. It's not a very romantic kind of business from first to last.'

'Only profitable,' said the curate.

'That's as may be. It is subject to greater losses than the preaching of sermons.'

'I should like to go out and see it all,' said Miss Hall, looking into Miss Lawrie's face. This also appeared to Mary to be ill-natured.

Then the butler announced the dinner, and they all followed Mr. Hall and the curate's bride out of one room into the other. 'This young lady,' said he, 'is supposed to be in the ascendant just at the present moment. She can't be married above two or three times at the most. I say this to excuse myself to Miss Lawrie, who ought perhaps to have the post of honour.' To this some joking reply was made, and they all sat down to their dinner. Miss Lawrie was at Mr. Hall's left hand, and at her left hand John Gordon was seated. Mary could perceive that everything was arranged so as to throw herself and John Gordon together,—as though they had some special interest in each other. Of all this

Mr. Whittlestaff saw nothing. But John Gordon did perceive something, and told himself that that ass Blake had been at work. But his perceptions in the matter were not half as sharp as those of Mary Lawrie.

'I used to be very fond of your father, Gordon,' said Mr. Hall, when the dinner was half over. 'It's all done and gone now. Dear, dear, dear!'

'He was an unfortunate man, and perhaps expected too much from his friends.'

'I am very glad to see his son here, at any rate. I wish you were not going to settle down so far away from us.'

'Kimberley is a long way off.'

'Yes, indeed; and when a fellow gets out there he is apt to stay, I suppose.'

'I shall do so, probably. I have nobody near enough to me here at home to make it likely that I shall come back.'

'You have uncles and aunts?' said Mr. Hall.

'One uncle and two aunts. I shall suit their views and my cousins' better by sending home some diamonds than by coming myself.'

'How long will that take?' asked Mr. Hall. The conversation was kept up solely between Mr. Hall and John Gordon. Mr. Whittlestaff took no share in it unless when he was asked a question, and the four girls kept up a whisper with Miss Forrester and Montagu Blake.

'I have a share in rather a good thing,' said Gordon; 'and if I could get out of it so as to realise my property, I think that six months might suffice.'

'Oh, dear! Then we may have you back again before the year's out?' Mr. Whittlestaff looked up at this, as though apprised that the danger was not yet over. But he reflected that before twelve months were gone he would certainly have made Mary Lawrie his wife.

'Kimberley is not a very alluring place,' said John Gordon. 'I don't know any spot on God's earth that I should be less likely to choose for my abiding resting-place.'

'Except for the diamonds.'

'Except for the diamonds, as you remark. And therefore when a man has got his fill of diamonds, he is likely to leave.'

'His fill of diamonds!' said Augusta Hall.

'Shouldn't you like to try your fill of diamonds?' asked Blake.

'Not at all,' said Evelina. 'I'd rather have strawberries and cream.'

'I think I should like diamonds best,' said Mary. Whereupon Evelina suggested that her younger sister was a greedy little creature.

'As soon as you've got your fill of diamonds, which won't take more than six months longer,' suggested Mr. Hall, 'you'll come back again?'

'Not exactly. I have an idea of going up the country across the Zambesi. I've a notion that I should like to make my way out somewhere in the Mediterranean,—Egypt, for instance, or Algiers.'

'What!—across the equator? You'd never do that alive?'

'Things of that kind have been done. Stanley crossed the continent.'*

'But not from south to north. I don't believe in that. You had better remain at Kimberley and get more diamonds.'

'He'd be with diamonds like the boy with the bacon,' said the clergyman; 'when prepared for another wish,* he'd have more than he could eat.'

'To tell the truth,' said John Gordon, 'I don't quite know what I should do. It would depend perhaps on what somebody else would join me in doing. My life was very lonely at Kimberley, and I do not love being alone.'

'Then, why don't you take a wife?' said Montagu Blake, very loudly, as though he had hit the target right in the bull's-eye. He so spoke as to bring the conversation to an abrupt end. Mr. Whittlestaff immediately looked conscious. He was a man who, on such an occasion, could not look otherwise than conscious. And the five girls, with all of whom the question of the loves of John Gordon and Mary Lawrie had been fully discussed, looked conscious. Mary Lawrie was painfully conscious; but endeavoured to hide it, not unsuccessfully. But in her endeavour she had to look unnaturally stern,—and was conscious, too, that she did that. Mr. Hall, whose feelings of romance were not perhaps of the highest order, looked round on Mr. Whittlestaff and Mary Lawrie. Montagu Blake felt that he had achieved a triumph. 'Yes,' said he, 'if those are your feelings, why don't you take a wife?'

'One man may not be so happy as another,' said Gordon, laughing. 'You have suited yourself admirably, and seem to think it quite easy for a man to make a selection.'

'Not quite such a selection as mine, perhaps,' said Blake.

'Then think of the difficulty. Do you suppose

that any second Miss Forrester would dream of going to the diamond-fields with me?'

'Perhaps not,' said Blake. 'Not a second Miss Forrester—but somebody else.'

'Something inferior?'

'Well—yes; inferior to my Miss Forrester, certainly.'

'You are the most conceited young man that I ever came across,' said the young lady herself.

'And I am not inclined to put up with anything that is very inferior,' said John Gordon. He could not help his eye from glancing for a moment round upon Mary Lawrie. She was aware of it, though no one else noticed it in the room. She was aware of it, though any one watching her would have said that she had never looked at him.

'A man may always find a woman to suit him, if he looks well about him,' said Mr. Hall, sententiously. 'Don't you think so, Whittlestaff?'

'I dare say he may,' said Mr. Whittlestaff, very flatly. And as he said so he made up his mind that he would, for that day, postpone the task of telling Mr. Hall of his intended marriage.

The evening passed by, and the time came for Mr. Whittlestaff to drive Miss Lawrie back to Croker's Hall. She had certainly spent a most uneventful period, as far as action or even words of her own was concerned. But the afternoon was one which she would never forget. She had been quite, quite sure, when she came into the house; but she was more than sure now. At every word that had been spoken she had thought of herself and of him. Would he not have known how to have chosen a fit companion,—only for this great misfortune? And would she have been so much inferior to Miss Forrester? Would he have thought her inferior to any one? Would he not have preferred her to any other female whom the world had at the present moment produced? Oh, the pity of it; the pity of it!

Then came the bidding of adieu. Gordon was to sleep at Little Alresford that night, and to take his departure by early train on the next morning. Of the adieux spoken the next morning we need take no notice, but only of the word or two uttered that night. 'Good-bye, Mr. Gordon,' said Mr. Whittlestaff, having taken courage for the occasion, and having thought even of the necessary syllables to be spoken.

'Good-bye, Mr. Whittlestaff,' and he gave his rival his hand in apparently friendly grasp. To those burning questions he had asked he had received no word of reply; but they were questions which he would not repeat again.

'Good-bye, Mr. Gordon,' said Mary. She had thought of the moment much, but had determined at last that she would trust herself to nothing further. He took her hand, but did not say a word. He took it and pressed it for a moment, and then turned his face away, and went in from the hall back to the door leading to the drawing-room. Mr. Whittlestaff was at the moment putting on his great-coat, and Mary stood with her bonnet and cloak on at the open front door, listening to a word or two from Kattie Forrester and Evelina Hall. 'Oh, I wish, I wish it might have been!' said Kattie Forrester.

'And so do I,' said Evelina. 'Can't it be?'

'Good-night,' said Mary, boldly, stepping out

rapidly into the moonlight, and mounting without assistance to her plaçe in the open carriage.

'I beg your pardon,' said Mr. Hall, following
her; but there came not a word from her.

Mr. Whittlestaff had gone back after John
Gordon. 'By-the-by,' he said, 'what will be your
address in London?'

'The "Oxford and Cambridge" in Pall Mall,'*
said he.

'Oh, yes; the club there. It might be that I
should have a word to send to you. But I don't
suppose I shall,' he added, as he turned round
to go away. Then he shook hands with the party
in the hall, and mounting up into the carriage,
drove Mary and himself away homewards towards Croker's Hall.

Not a word was spoken between them for the
first mile, nor did a sound of a sob or an audible
suspicion of a tear come from Mary. Why did
those girls know the secret of her heart in that
way? Why had they dared to express a hope as
to an event, or an idea as to a disappointment,
all knowledge of which ought to be buried in her
own bosom? Had she spoken of her love for
John Gordon? She was sure that no word had
escaped her. And were it surmised, was it not
customary that such surmises should be kept in
the dark? But here these young ladies had dared
to pity her for her vain love, as though, like some
village maiden, she had gone about in tears be-
wailing herself that some groom or gardener had
been faithless. But sitting thus for the first mile,
she choked herself to keep down her sobs.

'Mary,' at last he whispered to her.

'Well, Mr. Whittlestaff?'

'Mary, we are both of us unhappy.'

'I am not unhappy,' she said, plucking up herself suddenly. 'Why do you say that I am unhappy?'

'You seem so. I at any rate am unhappy.'

'What makes you so?'

'I did wrong to take you to dine in company with that man.'

'It was not for me to refuse to go.'

'No; there is no blame to you in it;—nor is there blame to me. But it would have been better for us both had we remained away.' Then he drove on in silence, and did not speak another word till they reached home.

'Well!' said Mrs. Baggett, following them into the dining-room.

'What do you mean by "well"?'

'What did the folks say to you at Mr. Hall's? I can see by your face that some of them have been saying summat.'

'Nobody has been saying anything that I know of,' said Mr. Whittlestaff. 'Do you go to bed.' Then when Mrs. Baggett was gone, and Mary had listlessly seated herself on a chair, her lover again addressed her. 'I wish I knew what there is in your heart.' Yet she would not tell him; but turned away her face and sat silent. 'Have you nothing to say to me?'

'What should I have to say to you? I have nothing to say of that of which you are thinking.'

'He has gone now, Mary.'

'Yes; he has gone.'

'And you are contented?' It did seem hard upon her that she should be called upon to tell a lie,—to say that which he must know to be a lie,—and to do so in order that he might be encouraged to persevere in achieving his own object. But she did not quite understand him. 'Are you contented?' he repeated again.

Then she thought that she would tell the lie. If it was well that she should make the sacrifice for his sake, why should it not be completed? If she had to give herself to him, why should not the gift be as satisfactory as it might be made to his feelings? 'Yes; I am contented.'

'And you do not wish to see him again?'

'Certainly not, as your wife.'

'You do not wish it at all,' he rejoined, 'whether you be my wife or otherwise?'

'I think you press me too hard.' Then she remembered herself, and the perfect sacrifice which she was minded to make. 'No; I do not wish again to see Mr. Gordon at all. Now, if you will allow me, I will go to bed. I am thoroughly tired out, and I hardly know what I am saying.'

'Yes; you can go to bed,' he said. Then she gave him her hand in silence, and went off to her own room.

She had no sooner reached her bed, than she threw herself on it and burst into tears. All this which she had to endure,—all that she would have to bear,—would be, she thought, too much for her. And there came upon her a feeling of contempt for his cruelty. Had he sternly resolved to keep her to her promised word, and to forbid her all happiness for the future,—to make her his wife, let her heart be as it might;—had he said: 'you have come to my house, and have eaten my bread and have drunk of my cup, and have then promised to become my wife, and now you shall not depart from it because this interloper has come between us;'—then, though she might have felt him to be cruel, still she would have respected him. He would have done, as she believed, as other men do. But he wished to gain his object, and yet not appear to be cruel. It was so that she thought of him. 'And it shall be as he would have it,' she said to herself. But though she saw far into his character, she did not quite read it aright.

He remained there alone in his library into the late hours of the night. But he did not even take up a book with the idea of solacing his hours. He too had his idea of self-sacrifice, which went quite as far as hers. But yet he was not as sure as was she that the self-sacrifice would be a duty. He did not believe, as did she, in the character of John Gordon. What if he should give her up to one who did not deserve her,—to one whose future would not be stable enough to secure the happiness and welfare of such a woman as was Mary Lawrie! He had no knowledge to guide him, nor had she;—nor, for the matter of that, had John Gordon himself any knowledge of what his own future might be. Of his own future Mr. Whittlestaff could speak and think with the greatest confidence. It would be safe, happy, and bright, should Mary Lawrie become his wife. Should she not do so, it must be altogether ruined and confounded.

He could not conceive it to be possible that he should be required by duty to make such a sacrifice; but he knew of himself that if her happiness, her true and permanent happiness, would require it, then the sacrifice should be made.

CHAPTER XVI

Mrs. Baggett's Philosophy

THE next day was Saturday, and Mr. Whittle-staff came out of his room early, intending to speak to Mrs. Baggett. He had declared to himself that it was his purpose to give her some sound advice respecting her own affairs,—as far as her affairs and his were connected together. But low down in his mind, below the stratum in which his declared resolution was apparent to himself, there was a hope that he might get from her some comfort and strength as to his present purpose. Not but that he would ultimately do as he himself had determined; but, to tell the truth, he had not quite determined, and thought that a word from Mrs. Baggett might assist him.

As he came out from his room, he encountered Mary, intent upon her household duties. It was something before her usual time, and he was surprised. She had looked ill overnight and worn, and he had expected that she would keep her bed. 'What makes you so early, Mary?' He spoke to her with his softest and most affectionate tone.

'I couldn't sleep, and I thought I might as well be up.' She had followed him into the library, and when there he put his arm round her waist and kissed her forehead. It was a strange thing for him to do. She felt that it was so—very, very strange; but it never occurred to her that it behoved her to be angry at his caress. He had kissed her once before, and only once, and it had seemed to her that he had intended that their love-making should go on without kisses. But was she not his property, to do as he pleased with her? And there could be no ground for displeasure on her part.

'Dear Mary,' he said, 'if you could only know how constant my thoughts are to you.' She did not doubt that it was so; but just so constant were her thoughts to John Gordon. But from her to him there could be no show of affection—nothing but the absolute coldness of perfect silence. She had passed the whole evening with him last night, and had not been allowed to speak a single word to him beyond the ordinary greetings of society. She had felt that she had not been allowed to speak a single word to any one, because he had been present. Mr. Whittlestaff had thrown over her the deadly mantle of his ownership, and she had consequently felt herself to be debarred from all right over her own words and actions. She had become his slave; she felt herself in very truth to be a poor creature whose only duty it was in the world to obey his volition. She had told herself during the night that, with all her motives for loving him, she was learning to regard him with absolute hatred. And she hated herself because it was so. Oh, what a tedious affair was this of living! How tedious, how sad and miserable, must her future days be, as long as days should be left to her! Could it be made possible to her that she should ever be able to do her duty by this husband of hers,—for her, in whose heart of hearts would be seated continually the image of this other man?

'By-the-by,' said he, 'I want to see Mrs. Baggett. I suppose she is about somewhere.'

'Oh dear, yes. Since the trouble of her husband has become nearer, she is earlier and earlier every day. Shall I send her?' Then she departed, and in a few minutes Mrs. Baggett entered the room.

'Come in, Mrs. Baggett.'

'Yes, sir.'

'I have just a few words which I want to say to you. Your husband has gone back to Portsmouth?'

'Yes sir; he have.' This she said in a very decided tone, as though her master need trouble himself no further about her husband.

'I am very glad that it should be so. It's the best place for him,—unless he could be sent to Australia.'

'He ain't a-done nothing to fit himself for Botany Bay,* Mr. Whittlestaff,' said the old woman, bobbing her head at him.

'I don't care what place he has fitted himself for, so long as he doesn't come here. He is a disreputable old man.'

'You needn't be so hard upon him, Mr. Whittlestaff. He ain't a-done nothing much to you, barring sleeping in the stable one night when he had had a drop o' drink too much.' And the old woman pulled out a great handkerchief, and began to wipe her eyes piteously.

'What a fool you are, Mrs. Baggett.'

'Yes; I am a fool. I knows that.'

'Here's this disreputable old man eating and drinking your hard-earned wages.'

'But they are my wages. And who's a right to them, only he?'

'I don't say anything about that, only he comes here and disturbs you.'

'Well, yes; he is disturbing; if it's only because of his wooden leg and red nose. I don't mean to say as he's the sort of a man as does a credit to a gentleman's house to see about the place. But he was my lot in matrimony, and I've got to put up with him. I ain't a-going to refuse to bear the burden which came to be my lot. I don't suppose he's earned a single shilling since he left the regiment, and that is hard upon a poor woman who's got nothing but her wages.'

'Now, look here, Mrs. Baggett.'

'Yes, sir.'

'Send him your wages.'

'And have to go in rags myself,—in your service.'

'You won't go in rags. Don't be a fool.'

'I am a fool, Mr. Whittlestaff; you can't tell me that too often.'

'You won't go in rags. You ought to know us well enough——'

'Who is us, Mr. Whittlestaff? They ain't no us;—just yet.'

'Well;—me.'

'Yes, I know you, Mr. Whittlestaff.'

'Send him your wages. You may be quite sure that you'll find yourself provided with shoes and stockings, and the rest of it.'

'And be a woluntary burden beyond what I earns! Never;—not as long as Miss Mary is coming to live here as missus of your house. I should do summat as I should have to repent of. But, Mr. Whittlestaff, I've got to look the world in the face, and bear my own crosses. I never can do it no younger.'

'You're an old woman now, and you talk of

throwing yourself upon the world without the means of earning a shilling.'

'I think I'd earn some, at something, old as I am, till I fell down flat dead,' she said. 'I have that sperit in me, that I'd still be doing something. But it don't signify; I'm not going to remain here when Miss Mary is to be put over me. That's the long and the short of it all.'

Now had come the moment in which, if ever, Mr. Whittlestaff must get the strength which he required. He was quite sure of the old woman, —that her opinion would not be in the least influenced by any desire on her own part to retain her position as his housekeeper. 'I don't know about putting Miss Mary over you,' he said.

'Don't know about it!' she shouted.

'My mind is not absolutely fixed.'

''As she said anything?'

'Not a word.'

'Or he? Has he been and dared to speak up about Miss Mary. And he,—who, as far as I can understand, has never done a ha'porth for her since the beginning. What's Mr. Gordon? I should like to know. Diamonds! What's diamonds in the way of a steady income? They're all a flash in the pan, and moonshine and dirtiness. I hates to hear of diamonds. There's all the ill in the world comes from them; and you'd give her up to be taken off by such a one as he among the diamonds! I make bold to tell you, Mr. Whittlestaff, that you ought to have more strength of mind than what that comes to. You're telling me every day as I'm an old fool.'

'So you are.'

'I didn't never contradict you; nor I don't

mean, if you tells me so as often again. And I don't mean to be that impident as to tell my master as I ain't the only fool about the place. It wouldn't be no wise becoming.'

'But you think it would be true.'

'I says nothing about that. That's not the sort of language anybody has heard to come out of my mouth, either before your face or behind your back. But I do say as a man ought to behave like a man. What! Give up to a chap as spends his time in digging for diamonds! Never!'

'What does it matter what he digs for; you know nothing about his business.'

'But I know something about yours, Mr. Whittlestaff. I know where you have set your wishes. And I know that when a man has made up his mind in such an affair as this, he shouldn't give way to any young diamond dealer of them all.'

'Not to him.'

'And what's she? Are you to give up everything because she's love-sick for a day or two? Is everything to be knocked to pieces here at Croker's Hall, because he has come and made eyes at her? She was glad enough to take what you offered before he had come this way.'

'She was not glad enough. That is it. She was not glad enough.'

'She took you, at any rate, and I'd never make myself mean enough to make way for such a fellow as that.'

'It isn't for him, Mrs. Baggett.'

'It is for him. Who else? To walk away and just leave the game open because he has come down to Hampshire! There ain't no spirit of standing up and fighting about it.'

'With whom am I to fight?'

'With both of 'em;—till you have your own way. A foolish, stupid, weak girl like that!'

'I won't have her abused.'

'She's very well. I ain't a-saying nothing against her. If she'll do what you bid her, she'll turn out right enough. You asked her, and she said she'd do it. Is not that so? There's nothing I hate so much as them romantic ways. And everything is to be made to give way because a young chap is six foot high! I hates romance and manly beauty, as they call it, and all the rest of it. Where is she to get her bread and meat? That's what I want to know.'

'There'll be bread and meat for her.'

'I dare say. But you'll have to pay for it, while she's philandering about with him! And that's what you call fine feelings. I call it all rubbish. If you've a mind to make her Mrs. Whittlestaff, make her Mrs. Whittlestaff. Drat them fine feelings. I never knew no good come of what people call fine feelings. If a young woman does her work as it should be, she's got no time to think of 'em. And if a man is master, he should be master. How's a man to give way to a girl like that, and then stand up and face the world around him? A man has to be master; and when he's come to be a little old-like, he has to see that he will be master. I never knew no good come of one of them soft-going fellows who is minded to give up whenever a woman wants anything. What's a woman? It ain't natural that she should have her way; and she don't like a man a bit better in the long-run because he lets her. There's Miss Mary; if you're stiff with her now, she'll come out right enough in a month or two. She's lived without Mr. Gordon well enough since she's been here. Now he's come, and we hear a deal about these fine feelings. You take my word, and say nothing to nobody about the young man. He's gone by this time, or he's a-going. Let him go, say I; and if Miss Mary takes on to whimper a bit, don't you see it.'

Mrs. Baggett took her departure, and Mr. Whittlestaff felt that he had received the comfort, or at any rate the strength, of which he had been in quest. In all that the woman had said to him, there had been a re-echo of his own thoughts,—of one side, at any rate, of his own thoughts. He knew that true affection, and the substantial comforts of the world, would hold their own against all romance. And he did not believe,—in his theory of ethics he did not believe,—that by yielding to what Mrs. Baggett called fine feelings, he would in the long-run do good to those with whom he was concerned in the world. Were he to marry Mary Lawrie now, Mary Whittlestaff would, he thought, in ten years' time, be a happier woman than were he to leave her. That was the solid conviction of his mind, and in that he had been strengthened by Mrs. Baggett's arguments. He had desired to be so strengthened, and therefore his interview had been successful.

But as the minutes passed by, as every quarter of an hour added itself to the quarters that were gone, and as the hours grew on, and the weakness of evening fell upon him, all his softness came back again. They had dined at six o'clock, and at seven he declared his purpose of strolling out by himself. On these summer evenings he would often take Mary with him; but he now told her, with a sort of apology, that he would rather go alone. 'Do,' she said, smiling up into his face; 'don't let me ever be in your way. Of course, a man does not always want to have to find conversation for a young lady.'

'If you are the young lady, I should always want it—only that I have things to think of.'

'Go and think of your things. I will sit in the garden and do my stitching.'

About a mile distant, where the downs began to rise, there was a walk supposed to be common to all who chose to frequent it, but which was entered through a gate which gave the place within the appearance of privacy. There was a little lake inside crowded with water-lilies, when the time for the water-lilies had come; and above the lake a path ran up through the woods, very steep, and as it rose higher and higher, altogether sheltered. It was about a mile in length till another gate was reached; but during the mile the wanderer could go off on either side, and lose himself on the grass among the beech-trees. It was a favourite haunt with Mr. Whittlestaff. Here he was wont to sit and read his Horace, and think of the affairs of the world as Horace depicted them. Many a morsel of wisdom he had here made his own, and had then endeavoured to think whether the wisdom had in truth been taken home by the poet to his own bosom, or had only been a glitter of the intellect, never appropriated for any useful purpose. '"Gemmas, marmor, ebur,"' he had said. '"Sunt qui non habeant; est qui non curat habere."* I suppose he did care for jewels, marble, and ivory, as much as any one. "Me lentus Glycerae torret amor meæ."* I don't suppose he ever loved her really, or any other girl.' Thus he would think over his Horace, always having the volume in his pocket.

Now he went there. But when he had sat himself down in a spot to which he was accustomed, he had no need to take out his Horace. His own thoughts came to him free enough without any need of his looking for them to poetry. After all, was not Mrs. Baggett's teaching a damnable philosophy? Let the man be the master, and let him get everything he can for himself, and enjoy to the best of his ability all that he can get. That was the lesson as taught by her. But as he sat alone there beneath the trees, he told himself that no teaching was more damnable. Of course it was the teaching by which the world was kept going in its present course; but when divested of its plumage was it not absolutely the philosophy of selfishness? Because he was a man, and as a man had power and money and capacity to do the things after which his heart lusted, he was to do them for his own gratification, let the consequences be what they might to one whom he told himself that he loved! Did the lessons of Mrs. Baggett run smoothly with those of Jesus Christ?*

Then within his own mind he again took Mrs. Baggett's side of the question. How mean a creature must he not become, if he were now to surrender this girl whom he was anxious to make his wife! He knew of himself that in such a matter he was more sensitive than others. He could not let her go, and then walk forth as though little or nothing were the matter with him. Now for the second time in his life he had essayed to marry. And now for the second time all the world would know that he had been accepted and then rejected. It was, he thought, more than he could endure,—and live.

Then after he had sat there for an hour he got up and walked home; and as he went he tried to resolve that he would reject the philosophy of Mrs. Baggett and accept the other. 'If I only knew!' he said as he entered his own gate. 'If one could only see clearly!' Then he found Mary still seated in the garden. 'Nothing is to be got,' he said, 'by asking you for an answer.'

'In what have I failed?'

'Never mind. Let us go in and have a cup of tea.' But she knew well in what he accused her of failing, and her heart turned towards him again.

CHAPTER XVII

*Mr. Whittlestaff meditates a Journey**

THE next day was Sunday, and was passed in
absolute tranquillity. Nothing was said either
by Mr. Whittlestaff or by Mary Lawrie; nor, to
the eyes of those among whom they lived, was
there anything to show that their minds were
disturbed. They went to church in the morning,
as was usual with them, and Mary went also to
the evening service. It was quite pleasant to see
Mrs. Baggett start for her slow Sabbath morning
walk, and to observe how her appearance altogether belied that idea of rags and tatters which
she had given as to her own wardrobe. A nicer
dressed old lady, or a more becoming black silk
gown, you shall not see on a Sunday morning
making her way to any country church in England. While she was looking so pleasant and
demure,—one may say almost so handsome, in
her old-fashioned and apparently new bonnet,
—what could have been her thoughts respecting the red-nosed, one-legged warrior, and her
intended life, to be passed in fetching two-
penn'orths of gin for him, and her endeavours
to get for him a morsel of wholesome food? She
had had her breakfast out of her own china tea-
cup, which she used to boast was her own
property, as it had been given to her by Mr.
Whittlestaff's mother, and had had her little drop
of cream, and, to tell the truth, her boiled egg,
which she always had on a Sunday morning, to
enable her to listen to the long sermon of the

Rev. Mr. Lowlad.* She would talk of her hopes and her burdens, and undoubtedly she was in earnest. But she certainly did seem to make her hay very comfortably while the sun shone.

Everything on this Sunday morning was pleasant, or apparently pleasant, at Croker's Hall. In the evening, when Mary and the maid-servants went to church, leaving Mrs. Baggett at home to look after the house and go to sleep, Mr. Whittlestaff walked off to the wooded path with his Horace. He did not read it very long. The bits which he did usually read never amounted to much at a time. He would take a few lines and then digest them thoroughly, wailing over them or rejoicing, as the case might be. He was not at the present moment much given to joy. 'Intermissa, Venus, diu rursus bella moves? Parce, precor, precor.'* This was the passage to which he turned at the present moment; and very little was the consolation which he found in it. What was so crafty, he said to himself, or so vain as that an old man should hark back to the pleasures of a time of life which was past and gone! 'Non sum qualis eram,'*he said, and then thought with shame of the time when he had been jilted by Catherine Bailey,—the time in which he had certainly been young enough to love and be loved, had he been as lovable as he had been prone to love. Then he put the book in his pocket. His latter effort had been to recover something of the sweetness of life, and not, as had been the poet's, to drain those dregs to the bottom. But when he got home he bade Mary tell him what Mr. Lowlad had said in his sermon, and was quite cheery in his manner of picking Mr. Lowlad's theology to pieces;—for Mr. Whittlestaff did not altogether agree with Mr. Lowlad as to the uses to be made of the Sabbath.

On the next morning he began to bustle about a little, as was usual with him before he made a journey; and it did escape him, while he was talking to Mrs. Baggett about a pair of trousers which it turned out that he had given away last summer, that he meditated a journey to London on the next day.

'You ain't a-going?' said Mrs. Baggett.

'I think I shall.'

'Then don't. Take my word for it, sir,—don't.' But Mr. Whittlestaff only snubbed her, and nothing more was said about the journey at the moment.

In the course of the afternoon visitors came. Miss Evelina Hall with Miss Forrester had been driven into Alresford, and now called in company with Mr. Blake. Mr. Blake was full of his own good tidings, but not so full but that he could remember, before he took his departure, to say a half whispered word on behalf of John Gordon. 'What do you think, Mr. Whittlestaff? Since you were at Little Alresford we've settled the day.'

'You needn't be telling it to everybody about the county,' said Kattie Forrester.

'Why shouldn't I tell it to my particular friends? I am sure Miss Lawrie will be delighted to hear it.'

'Indeed I am,' said Mary.

'And Mr. Whittlestaff also. Are you not, Mr. Whittlestaff?'

'I am very happy to hear that a couple whom I like so well are soon to be made happy. But you have not yet told us the day.'

'The 1st of August,' said Evelina Hall.

'The 1st of August,' said Mr. Blake, 'is an auspicious day. I am sure there is some reason for regarding it as auspicious, though I cannot exactly remember what. It is something about Augustus, I think.'*

'I never heard of such an idea to come from a clergyman of the Church of England,' said the bride. 'I declare Montagu never seems to think that he's a clergyman at all.'

'It will be better for him,' said Mr. Whittlestaff, 'and for all those about him, that he should ever remember the fact and never seem to do so.'

'All the same,' said Blake, 'although the 1st of August is auspicious, I was very anxious to be married in July, only the painters said they couldn't be done with the house in time. One is obliged to go by what these sort of people say and do. We're to have a month's honeymoon,—only just a month, because Mr. Lowlad won't make himself as agreeable as he ought to do about the services; and Newface, the plumber and glazier, says he can't have the house done as Kattie would like to live in it before the end of August. Where do you think we're going to, Miss Lawrie? You would never guess.'

'Perhaps to Rome,' said Mary at a shot.

'Not quite so far. We're going to the Isle of Wight. It's rather remarkable that I never spent but one week in the Isle of Wight since I was born. We haven't quite made up our mind whether it's to be Black Gang Chine or Ventnor.* It's a matter of dresses, you see.'

'Don't be a fool, Montagu,' said Miss Forrester.

'Well, it is. If we decide upon Ventnor, she must have frocks and things to come out with.'

'I suppose so,' said Mr. Whittlestaff.

'But she'll want nothing of the kind at Black Gang.'

'Do hold your tongue, and not make an ass of yourself. What do you know what dresses I shall want? As it is, I don't think I shall go either to the one place or the other. The Smiths are at Ryde, and the girls are my great friends. I think we'll go to Ryde, after all.'

'I'm so sorry, Mr. Whittlestaff, that we can't expect the pleasure of seeing you at our wedding. It is, of course, imperative that Kattie should be married in the cathedral. Her father is one of the dignitaries, and could not bear not to put his best foot foremost on such an occasion. The Dean will be there, of course. I'm afraid the Bishop cannot come up from Farnham, because he will have friends with him. I am afraid John Gordon will have gone by that time, or else we certainly would have had him down. I should like John Gordon to be present, because he would see how the kind of thing is done.' The name of John Gordon at once silenced all the matrimonial chit-chat which was going on among them. It was manifest both to Mr. Whittlestaff and to Mary that it had been lugged in without a cause, to enable Mr. Blake to talk about the absent man. 'It would have been pleasant; eh, Kattie?'

'We should have been very glad to see Mr.

Gordon, if it would have suited him to come,'
said Miss Forrester.

'It would have been just the thing for him;
and we at Oxford together, and everything.
Don't you think he would have liked to be there?
It would have put him in mind of other things,
you know.'

To this appeal there was no answer made. It
was impossible that Mary should bring herself
to talk about John Gordon in mixed company.
And the allusion to him stirred Mr. Whittlestaff's
wrath. Of course it was understood as having
been spoken in Mary's favour. And Mr. Whittlestaff had been made to perceive by what had
passed at Little Alresford that the Little Alresford people all took the side of John Gordon, and
were supposed to be taking the side of Mary at
the same time. There was not one of them, he
said to himself, that had half the sense of Mrs.
Baggett. And there was a vulgarity about their
interference of which Mrs. Baggett was not
guilty.

'He is half way on his road to the diamond-
fields,' said Evelina.

'And went away from here on Saturday morning!' said Montagu Blake. 'He has not started
yet,—not dreamed of it. I heard him whisper to
Mr. Whittlestaff about his address. He's to be
in London at his club. I didn't hear him say for
how long, but when a man gives his address at
his club he doesn't mean to go away at once. I
have a plan in my head. Some of those boats go
to the diamond-fields from Southampton. All the
steamers go everywhere from Southampton. Winchester is on the way to Southampton. Nothing

will be easier for him than to drop in for our
marriage on his way out. That is, if he must
go at last.' Then he looked hard at Mary
Lawrie.

'And bring some of his diamonds with him,'
said Evelina Hall. 'That would be very nice.'
But not a word more was said then about John
Gordon by the inhabitants of Croker's Hall.
After that the visitors went, and Montagu Blake
chaperoned the girls out of the house, without
an idea that he had made himself disagreeable.

'That young man is a most egregious ass,' said
Mr. Whittlestaff.

'He is good-natured and simple, but I doubt
whether he sees things very plainly.'

'He has not an idea of what a man may talk
about and when he should hold his tongue. And
he is such a fool as to think that his idle chatter
can influence others. I don't suppose a bishop
can refuse to ordain a gentleman because he is a
general idiot. Otherwise I think the bishop is
responsible for letting in such an ass as this.'
Mary said to herself, as she heard this, that it was
the most ill-natured remark which she had ever
known to fall from the mouth of Mr Whittlestaff.

'I think I am going away for a few days,' Mr.
Whittlestaff said to Mary, when the visitors were
gone.

'Where are you going?'

'Well, I suppose I shall be in London. When
one goes anywhere, it is generally to London;
though I haven't been there for more than two
months.'*

'Not since I came to live with you,' she said.
'You are the most stay-at-home person by way

of a gentleman that I ever heard of.' Then there was a pause for a few minutes, and he said nothing further. 'Might a person ask what you are going for?' This she asked in the playful manner which she knew he would take in good part.

'Well; I don't quite know that a person can. I am going to see a man upon business, and if I began to tell you part of it, I must tell it all,— which would not be convenient.'

'May I not ask how long you will be away? There can't be any dreadful secret in that. And I shall want to know what to get for your dinner when you come back.' She was standing now at his elbow, and he was holding her by the arm. It was to him almost as though she were already his wife, and the feeling to him was very pleasant. Only if she were his wife, or if it were positively decided among them that she would become so, he would certainly tell her the reason for which he might undertake any journey. Indeed there was no reason connected with any business of his which might not be told, other than that special reason which was about to take him to London. He only answered her now by pressing her hand and smiling into her face. 'Will it be for a month?'

'Oh dear, no! what should I do away from home for a month?'

'How can I tell? The mysterious business may require you to be absent for a whole year. Fancy my being left at home all that time. You don't think of it; but you have never left me for a single night since you first brought me to live here.'

'And you have never been away.'

'Oh, no! why should I go away? What

business can a woman have to move from home, especially such a woman as I am.'

'You are just like Mrs. Baggett. She always talks of women with supreme contempt. And yet she is just as proud of herself as the queen when you come to contradict her.'

'You never contradict me.'

'Perhaps the day may come when I shall.' Then he recollected himself, and added, 'Or perhaps the day may never come. Never mind. Put up my things for one week. At any rate I shall not be above a week gone.' Then she left him, and went away to his room to do what was necessary.

She knew the business on which he was about to travel to London, as well as though he had discussed with her the whole affair. In the course of the last two or three days there had been moments in which she had declared to herself that he was cruel. There had been moments in which she had fainted almost with sorrow when she thought of the life which fate had in store for her. There must be endless misery, while there might have been joy, so ecstatic in its nature as to make it seem to her to be perennial. Then she had almost fallen, and had declared him to be preternaturally cruel. But these moments had been short, and had endured only while she had allowed herself to dream of the ecstatic joy, which she confessed to herself to be an unfit condition of life for her. And then she had told herself that Mr. Whittlestaff was not cruel, and that she herself was no better than a weak, poor, flighty creature unable to look in its face life and all its realities. And then she would be lost in amazement as she thought of herself and all her vacillations.

She now was resolved to take his part, and to fight his battle to the end. When he had told her that he was going up to London, and going up on business as to which he could tell her nothing, she knew that it behoved her to prevent him from taking the journey. John Gordon should be allowed to go in quest of his diamonds, and Mr. Whittlestaff should be persuaded not to interfere with him. It was for her sake, and not for John Gordon's, that he was about to make the journey. He had asked her whether she were willing to marry him, and she had told him that he was pressing her too hard. She would tell him now,—now before it was too late,—that this was not so. His journey to London must at any rate be prevented.*

CHAPTER XVIII

Mr. and Mrs. Tookey

ON the day arranged, early on the morning after the dinner at Little Alresford Park, John Gordon went up to London. He had not been much moved by the intimation made to him by Mr. Whittlestaff that some letter should be written to him at his London address. He had made his appeal to Mr. Whittlestaff, and had received no answer whatever. And he had, after a fashion, made his appeal also to the girl. He felt sure that his plea must reach her. His very presence then in this house had been an appeal to her. He knew that she so far believed in him as to be conscious that she could at once become his wife—if she were willing to throw over his rival. He knew also that she loved him,—or had certainly loved him. He did not know the nature of her regard; nor was it possible that he should ever know that,—unless she were his wife. She had given a promise to that other man, and—it was thus he read her character—she could be true to her promise without any great heartbreak. At any rate, she intended to be true to it. He did not for a moment suspect that Mr. Whittlestaff was false. Mary had declared that she would not withdraw her word,—that only from her own mouth was to be taken her intention of such withdrawal, and that such intention she certainly would never utter. Of her character he understood much,—but not quite all. He was not aware of the depth of her feeling. But

Mr. Whittlestaff he did not understand at all. Of all those vacillating softnesses he knew nothing,—or of those moments spent with the poet, in which he was wont to fight against the poet's pretences, and of those other moments spent with Mrs. Baggett, in which he would listen to, and always finally reject, those invitations to manly strength which she would always pour into his ears. That Mr. Whittlestaff should spend hour after hour, and now day after day, in teaching himself to regard nothing but what might best suit the girl's happiness,—of that he was altogether in the dark. To his thinking, Mr. Whittlestaff was a hard man, who, having gained his object, intended to hold fast by what he had gained. He, John Gordon, knew, or thought that he knew, that Mary, as his wife, would lead a happier life than with Mr. Whittlestaff. But things had turned out unfortunately, and there was nothing for him but to return to the diamond-fields.

Therefore he had gone back to London with the purpose of preparing for his journey. A man does not start for South Africa to-morrow, or, if not to-morrow, then the next day. He was aware that there must be some delay; but any place would be better in which to stay than the neighbourhood of Croker's Hall. There were things which must be done, and people with whom he must do it; but of all that, he need say nothing down at Alresford. Therefore, when he got back to London, he meant to make all his arrangements—and did so far settle his affairs as to take a berth on board one of the mail steamers.

He had come over in company with a certain

lawyer, who had gone out to Kimberley with a view to his profession, and had then, as is the case with all the world that goes to Kimberley, gone into diamonds. Diamonds had become more to him than either briefs or pleadings. He had been there for fifteen years, and had ruined himself and made himself half-a-dozen times. He had found diamonds to be more pleasant than law, and to be more compatible with champagne, tinned lobsters, and young ladies. He had married a wife, and had parted with her, and taken another man's wife, and paid for her with diamonds. He had then possessed nothing, and had afterwards come forth a third-part owner of the important Stick-in-the-Mud claim, which at one time was paying 12 per cent per month. It must be understood that the Stick-in-the-Mud claim was an almost infinitesimal portion of soil in the Great Kimberley mine. It was but the sixteenth part of an original sub-division. But from the centre of the great basin,* or rather bowl, which forms the mine, there ran up two wires to the high mound erected on the circumference, on which continually two iron cages were travelling up and down, coming back empty, but going up laden with gemmiferous dirt. Here travelled the diamonds of the Stick-in-the-Mud claim, the owner of one-third of which, Mr. Fitzwalker Tookey, had come home with John Gordon.

Taking a first general glance at affairs in the diamond-fields, I doubt whether we should have been inclined to suspect that John Gordon and Fitzwalker Tookey would have been likely to come together as partners in a diamond speculation. But John Gordon had in the course of things become owner of the other two shares, and when Fitzwalker Tookey determined to come home, he had done so with the object of buying his partner's interest. This he might have done at once,—only that he suffered under the privation of an insufficiency of means. He was a man of great intelligence, and knew well that no readier mode to wealth had ever presented itself to him than the purchase of his partner's shares. Much was said to persuade John Gordon; but he would not part with his documents without seeing security for his money. Therefore Messrs. Gordon and Tookey put the old Stick-in-the-Mud into the hands of competent lawyers, and came home together.

'I am not at all sure that I shall sell,' John Gordon had said.

'But I thought that you offered it.'

'Yes; for money down. For the sum named I will sell now. But if I start from here without completing the bargain, I shall keep the option in my own hands. The fact is, I do not know whether I shall remain in England or return. If I do come back I am not likely to find anything better than the old Stick-in-the-Mud.' To this Mr. Tookey assented, but still he resolved that he would go home. Hence it came to pass that Mr. Fitzwalker Tookey was now in London, and that John Gordon had to see him frequently. Here Tookey had found another would-be partner, who had the needed money, and it was fervently desired by Mr. Tookey that John Gordon might not go back to South Africa.

The two men were not at all like in their

proclivities; but they had been thrown together, and each had learned much of the inside life of the other. The sort of acquaintance with whom a steady man becomes intimate in such a locality often surprises the steady man himself. Fitzwalker Tookey had the antecedents and education of a gentleman. Champagne and lobster suppers— the lobster coming out of tin cases,—diamonds and strange ladies, even with bloated cheeks and strong language, had not altogether destroyed the vestiges of the Temple. He at any rate was fond of a companion with whom he could discuss his English regrets, and John Gordon was not inclined to shut himself up altogether among his precious stones, and to refuse the conversation of a man who could talk. Tookey had told him of his great distress in reference to his wife. 'By G——! you know, the cruellest thing you ever heard in the world. I was a little tight one night, and the next morning she was off with Atkinson, who got away with his pocket full of diamonds. Poor girl! she went down to the Portuguese settlement, and he was nabbed. He's doing penal service now down at Cape Town. That's a kind of thing that does upset a fellow.' And poor Fitzwalker began to cry.

Among such confidences Gordon allowed it to escape from him that were he to become married in England, he did not think it probable that he should return. Thus it was known, at least to his partner, that he was going to look for a wife, and the desire in Mr. Tookey's breast that the wife might be forthcoming was intense. 'Well!' he said, immediately on Gordon's return to London.

'What does "well" mean?'

'Of course you went down there to look after the lady.'

'I have never told you so.'

'But you did—did you not?'

'I have told you nothing about any lady, though you are constantly asking questions. As a fact, I think I shall go back next month.'

'To Kimberley?'

'I think so. The stake I have there is of too great importance to be abandoned.'

'I have the money ready to pay over;—absolute cash on the nail. You don't call that abandoning it?'

'The claim has gone up in value 25 per cent, as you have already heard.'

'Yes; it has gone up a little, but not so much as that. It will come down as much by the next mail. With diamonds you never can stick to anything.'

'That's true. But you can only go by the prices as you see them quoted. They may be up 25 per cent again by next mail. At any rate, I am going back.'

'The devil you are!'

'That's my present idea. As I like to be on the square with you altogether, I don't mind saying that I have booked a berth by the Kentucky Castle.'

'The deuce you have! And you won't take a wife with you?'

'I am not aware that I shall have such an impediment.'

Then Fitzwalker Tooker assumed a very long face. It is difficult to trace the workings of such a man's mind, or to calculate the meagre chances on which he is too often driven to base his hopes of success. He feared that he could not show his face in Kimberley, unless as the representative of the whole old Stick-in-the-Mud. And with that object he had declared himself in London to have the actual power of disposing of Gordon's shares. Gordon had gone down to Hampshire, and would no doubt be successful with the young lady. At any rate,—as he described it to himself, —he had 'gone in for that.' He could see his way in that direction, but in no other. 'Upon my word, this, you know, is—what I call—rather throwing a fellow over.'

'I am as good as my word.'

'I don't know about that, Gordon.'

'But I do, and I won't hear any assertion to the contrary. I offered you the shares for a certain price, and you rejected them.'

'I did not do that.'

'You did do that,—exactly. Then there came up in my mind a feeling that I might probably wish to change my purpose.'

'And I am to suffer for that.'

'Not in the least. I then told you that you should still have the shares for the price named. But I did not offer them to any one else. So I came home,—and you chose to come with me. But before I started, and again after, I told you that the offer did not hold good, and that I should not make up my mind as to selling till after I got to England.'

'We understood that you meant to be married.'

'I never said so. I never said a word about marriage. I am now going back, and mean to manage the mine myself.'

'Without asking me?'

'Yes; I shall ask you. But I have two-thirds. I will give you for your share 10 per cent more than the price you offered me for each of my shares. If you do not like that, you need not accept the offer; but I don't mean to have any more words about it.'

Mr. Fitzwalker Tookey's face became longer and longer, and he did in truth feel himself to be much aggrieved within his very soul. There were still two lines of conduct open to him. He might move the stern man by a recapitulation of the sorrow of his circumstances, or he might burst out into passionate wrath, and lay all his ruin to his partner's doing. He might still hope that in this latter way he could rouse all Kimberley against Gordon, and thus creep back into some vestige of property under the shadow of Gordon's iniquities. He would try both. He would first endeavour to move the stern man to pity. 'I don't think you can imagine the condition in which you are about to place me.'

'I can't admit that I am placing you any-where.'

'I'll just explain. Of course I know that I can tell you everything in strictest confidence.'

'I don't know it at all.'

'Oh yes; I can. You remember the story of my poor wife?'

'Yes; I remember.'

'She's in London now.'

'What! She got back from the Portuguese settlement?'

'Yes. She did not stay there long. I don't suppose that the Portuguese are very nice people.'

'Perhaps not.'

'At any rate they don't have much money among them.'

'Not after the lavish expenditure of the diamond-fields,' suggested Gordon.

'Just so. Poor Matilda had been accustomed to all that money could buy for her. I never used to be close-fisted with her, though sometimes I would be tight.'

'As far as I could understand, you never used to agree at all.'

'I don't think we did hit it off. Perhaps it was my fault.'

'You used to be a little free in your way of living.'

'I was. I confess that I was so. I was young then, but I am older now. I haven't touched a B. and S.* before eleven o'clock since I have been in London above two or three times. I do mean to do the best I can for my young family.' It was the fact that Mr. Tookey had three little children boarding out in Kimberley.

'And what is the lady doing in London?'

'To tell the truth, she's at my lodgings.'

'Oh—h!'

'I do admit it. She is.'

'She is indifferent to the gentleman in the Cape Town penal settlement?'

'Altogether, I don't think she ever really cared for him. To tell the truth, she only wanted some one to take her away from—me.'

'And now she trusts you again?'

'Oh dear, yes;—completely. She is my wife, you know, still.'

'I suppose so.'

'That sacred tie has never been severed. You must always remember that. I don't know what your feelings are on such a subject, but according to my views it should not be severed roughly. When there are children, that should always be borne in mind. Don't you think so?'

'The children should be borne in mind.'

'Just so. That's what I mean. Who can look after a family of young children so well as their young mother? Men have various ways of looking at the matter.' To this John Gordon gave his ready consent, and was anxious to hear in what way his assistance was to be asked in again putting Mr. and Mrs. Tookey, with their young children, respectably on their feet. 'There are men, you know, stand-off sort of fellows, who think that a woman should never be forgiven.'

'It must depend on how far the husband has been in fault.'

'Exactly. Now these stand-off sort of fellows will never admit that they have been in fault at all. That's not my case.'

'You drank a little.'

'For the matter of that, so did she. When a woman drinks she gets herself to bed somehow. A man gets out upon a spree. That's what I used to do, and then I would hit about me rather recklessly. I have no doubt Matilda did get it sometimes. When there has been that kind of thing, forgive and forget is the best thing you can do.'

'I suppose so.'

'And then at the Fields there isn't the same sort of prudish life which one is accustomed to in England. Here in London a man is nowhere if he takes his wife back. Nobody knows her, because there are plenty to know of another sort. But there things are not quite so strict. Of course she oughtn't to have gone off with Atkinson;— a vulgar low fellow, too.'

'And you oughtn't to have licked her.'

'That's just it. It was tit for tat, I think. That's the way I look at it. At any rate we are living together now, and no one can say we're not man and wife.'

'There'll be a deal of trouble saved in that way.'

'A great deal. We are man and wife, and can begin again as though nothing had happened. No one can say that black's the white of our eye. She'll take to those darling children as though nothing had happened. You can't conceive how anxious she is to get back to them. And there's no other impediment. That's a comfort.'

'Another impediment would have upset you rather?'

'I couldn't have put up with that.' Mr. Fitzwalker Tookey looked very grave and high-minded as he made the assertion. 'But there's nothing of that kind. It's all open sailing. Now, —what are we to live upon, just for a beginning?'

'You have means out there.'

'Not as things are at present,—I am sorry to say. To tell the truth, my third share of the old Stick-in-the-Mud is gone. I had to raise money when it was desirable that I should come with you.'

'Not on my account.'

'And then I did owe something. At any rate, it's all gone now. I should find myself stranded at Kimberley without a red cent.'*

'What can I do?'

'Well,—I will explain. Poker & Hodge* will buy your shares for the sum named. Joshua Poker, who is out there, has got my third share. Poker & Hodge have the money down, and when I have arranged the sale, will undertake to give me the agency at one per cent on the whole take for three years certain. That'll be £1000 a-year, and it's odd if I can't float myself again in that time.' Gordon stood silent, scratching his head. 'Or if you'd give me the agency on the same terms, it would be the same thing. I don't care a straw for Poker & Hodge.'

'I daresay not.'

'But you'd find me as true as steel.'

'What little good I did at the Fields I did by looking after my own business.'

'Then what do you propose? Let Poker & Hodge have them, and I shall bless you for ever.' To this mild appeal Mr. Tookey had been brought by the manner in which John Gordon had scratched his head. 'I think you are bound to do it, you know.' To this he was brought by the subsequent look which appeared in John Gordon's eyes.

'I think not.'

'Men will say so.'

'I don't care a straw what men say, or women.'

'And you to come back in the same ship with me and my wife! You couldn't do it. The Fields wouldn't receive you.' Gordon bethought himself whether this imagined rejection might not arise rather from the character of his travelling companions. 'To bring back the mother of three little sainted babes, and then to walk in upon

every shilling of property which had belonged
to their father! You never could hold up your
head in Kimberley again.'

'I should have to stand abashed before your
virtue?'

'Yes, you would. I should be known to have
come back with my poor repentant wife,—the
mother of three dear babes. And she would be
known to have returned with her misguided
husband. The humanity of the Fields would not
utter a word of reproval to either of us. But,
upon my word, I should not like to stand in your
shoes. And how you could sit opposite to her
and look her in the face on the journey out, I
don't know.'

'It would be unpleasant.'

'Deuced unpleasant, I should say. You remember the old Roman saying, "Never be conscious
of anything within your own bosom."* Only
think how you would feel when you were swell-
ing it about in Kimberley, while that poor lady
won't be able to buy a pair of boots for herself
or her children. I say nothing about myself. I
didn't think you were the man to do it;—
I didn't indeed.'

Gordon did find himself moved by the diver-
sity of lights through which he was made to look
at the circumstances in question. In the first
place, there was the journey back with Mr.
Tookey and his wife, companions he had not
anticipated. The lady would probably begin by
soliciting his intimacy, which on board ship he
could hardly refuse. With a fellow-passenger,
whose husband has been your partner, you must
quarrel bitterly or be warm friends. Upon the

whole, he thought that he could not travel to South Africa with Mr. and Mrs. Fitzwalker Tookey. And then he understood what the man's tongue would do if he were there for a month in advance. The whole picture of life, too, at the Fields was not made attractive by Mr. Tookey's description. He was not afraid of the reception which might be accorded to Mrs. Tookey, but saw that Tookey found himself able to threaten him with violent evils, simply because he would claim his own. Then there shot across his brain some reminiscence of Mary Lawrie, and a comparison between her and her life and the sort of life which a man must lead under the auspices of Mrs. Tookey. Mary Lawrie was altogether beyond his reach; but it would be better to have her to think of than the other to know. His idea of the diamond-fields was disturbed by the promised return of his late partner and his wife.

'And you mean to reduce me to this misery?' asked Mr. Tookey.

'I don't care a straw for your misery.'

'What!'

'Not for your picture of your misery. I do not doubt but that when you have been there for a month you will be drunk as often as ever, and just as free with your fists when a woman comes in your way.'

'Never!'

'And I do not see that I am at all bound to provide for you and for your wife and children. You have seen many ups and downs, and will be doomed to see many more, as long as you can get hold of a bottle of wine.'

'I mean to take the pledge,—I do indeed. I

must do it gradually, because of my constitution, —but I shall do it.'

'I don't in the least believe in it;—nor do I believe in any man who thinks to redeem himself after such a fashion. It may still be possible that I shall not go back.'

'Thank God!'

'I may kill beasts in Buenos Ayres, or take a tea-farm in Thibet, or join the colonists in Tennessee.* In that case I will let you know what arrangement I may propose to make about the Kimberley claim. At any rate, I may say this,— I shall not go back in the same vessel with you.'

'I thought it would have been so comfortable.'

'You and Mrs. Tookey would find yourself more at your ease without me.'

'Not in the least. Don't let that thought disturb you. Whatever misery fate may have in store for me, you will always find that, for the hour, I will endeavour to be a good companion. "Sufficient for the day is the evil thereof." That is the first of my mottoes.'

'At any rate, I shall not go back in the Kentucky Castle if you do.'

'I'm afraid our money is paid.'

'So is mine; but that does not signify. You have a week yet, and I will let you know by eleven o'clock on Thursday what steps I shall finally take. If in any way I can serve you, I will do so; but I can admit no claim.'

'A thousand thanks! And I am so glad you approve of what I have done about Matilda. I'm sure that a steady-going fellow like you would have done the same.' To this John Gordon could make no answer, but left his friend,

and went away about his own business. He had
to decide between Tennessee, Thibet, and Buenos
Ayres, and wanted his time for his own purposes.

When he got to dinner at his club, he found
a letter from Mr. Whittlestaff, which had come
by the day-mail. It was a letter which, for the
time, drove Thibet and Buenos Ayres, and Tennessee also, clean out of his mind. It was as
follows:—

'CROKER'S HALL, — *June* 188–.

'DEAR MR. JOHN GORDON,—I shall be in town
this afternoon, probably by the same train which
will bring this letter, and will do myself the
honour of calling upon you at your club the next
day at twelve.—I am, dear Mr. John Gordon,
faithfully yours,

'WILLIAM WHITTLESTAFF.'

Then there was to be an answer to the appeal
which he had made. Of what nature would be
the answer? As he laid his hand upon his heart,
and felt the violence of the emotion to which he
was subjected, he could not doubt the strength
of his own love.

CHAPTER XIX

Mr. Whittlestaff's Journey discussed*

'I DON'T think that if I were you I would go up to London, Mr. Whittlestaff,' said Mary. This was on the Tuesday morning.

'Why not?'

'I don't think I would.'

'Why should you interfere?'

'I know I ought not to interfere.'

'I don't think you ought. Especially as I have taken the trouble to conceal what I am going about.'

'I can guess,' said Mary.

'You ought not to guess in such a matter. You ought not to have it on your mind at all. I told you that I would not tell you. I shall go. That's all that I have got to say.'

The words with which he spoke were ill-natured and savage. The reader will find them to be so, if he thinks of them. They were such that a father would hardly speak, under any circumstances, to a grown-up daughter,—much less that a lover would address to his mistress. And Mary was at present filling both capacities. She had been taken into his house almost as an adopted daughter, and had, since that time, had all the privileges accorded to her. She had now been promoted still higher, and had become his affianced bride. That the man should have turned upon her thus, in answer to her counsel, was savage, or at least ungracious. But at every word her heart became fuller and more full of

an affection as for something almost divine.
What other man had ever shown such love for
any woman? and this love was shown to her,—
who was nothing to him,—who ate the bread of
charity in his house. And it amounted to this,
that he intended to give her up to another man,
—he who had given such proof of his love,—he,
of whom she knew that this was a question of
almost life and death,—because in looking into
his face she had met there the truth of his heart!
Since that first avowal, made before Gordon had
come,—made at a moment when some such
avowal from her was necessary,—she had spoken
no word as to John Gordon. She had endeavoured
to show no sign. She had given herself up to her
elder lover, and had endeavoured to have it
understood that she had not intended to transfer
herself because the other man had come across
her path again like a flash of lightning. She
had dined in company with her younger lover
without exchanging a word with him. She had
not allowed her eyes to fall upon him more than
she could help, lest some expression of tenderness should be seen there. Not a word of hope
had fallen from her lips when they had first met,
because she had given herself to another. She
was sure of herself in that. No doubt there had
come moments in which she had hoped—nay,
almost expected—that the elder of the two might
give her up; and when she had felt sure that it
was not to be so, her very soul had rebelled
against him. But as she had taken time to think
of it, she had absolved him, and had turned her
anger against herself. Whatever he wanted,—
that she believed it would be her duty to do for

him, as far as its achievement might be in her power.

She came round and put her arm upon him, and looked into his face. 'Don't go to London. I ask you not to go.'

'Why should I not go?'

'To oblige me. You pretend to have a secret, and refuse to say why you are going. Of course I know.'

'I have written a letter to say that I am coming.'

'It is still lying on the hall-table down-stairs. It will not go to the post till you have decided.'

'Who has dared to stop it?'

'I have. I have dared to stop it. I shall dare to put it in the fire and burn it. Don't go! He is entitled to nothing. You are entitled to have, —whatever it is that you may want, though it is but such a trifle.'

'A trifle, Mary!'

'Yes. A woman has a little gleam of prettiness about her,—though here it is but of a common order.'

'Anything so uncommon I never came near before.'

'Let that pass; whether common or uncommon, it matters nothing. It is something soft, which will soon pass away, and of itself can do no good. It is contemptible.'

'You are just Mrs. Baggett over again.'

'Very well; I am quite satisfied. Mrs. Baggett is a good woman. She can do something beyond lying on a sofa and reading novels, while her good looks fade away. It is simply because a woman is pretty and weak that she is made so

much of, and is encouraged to neglect her duties.
By God's help I will not neglect mine. Do not
go to London.'

He seemed as though he hesitated as he sat
there under the spell of her little hand upon his
shoulder. And in truth he did hesitate. Could it
not be that he should be allowed to sit there all
his days, and have her hand about his neck
somewhat after this fashion? Was he bound to
give it all up? What was it that ordinary selfishness allowed? What depth of self-indulgence
amounted to a wickedness which a man could
not permit himself to enjoy without absolutely
hating himself? It would be easy in this case to
have all that he wanted. He need not send the
letter. He need not take this wretched journey to
London. Looking forward, as he thought that
he could look, judging from the girl's character,
he believed that he would have all that he desired,—all that a gracious God could give him,
—if he would make her the recognized partner
of his bed and his board. Then would he be
proud when men should see what sort of a wife
he had got for himself at last in place of Catherine Bailey. And why should she not love him?
Did not all her words tend to show that there
was love?

And then suddenly there came a frown across
his face, as she stood looking at him. She was
getting to know the manner of that frown. Now
she stooped down to kiss it away from his brow.
It was a brave thing to do; but she did it with a
consciousness of her courage. 'Now I may burn
the letter,' she said, as though she were about
to depart upon the errand.

'No, by heaven!' he said. 'Let me have a sandwich and a glass of wine, for I shall start in an hour.'

With a glance of his thoughts he had answered all those questions. He had taught himself what ordinary selfishness allowed. Ordinary selfishness,—such selfishness as that of which he would have permitted himself the indulgence,—must have allowed him to disregard the misery of John Gordon, and to keep the girl to himself. As far as John Gordon was concerned, he would not have cared for his sufferings. He was as much to himself,—or more,—than could be John Gordon. He did not love John Gordon, and could have doomed him to tearing his hair,— not without regret, but at any rate without remorse. He had settled that question. But with Mary Lawrie there must be a never-dying pang of self-accusation, were he to take her to his arms while her love was settled elsewhere. It was not that he feared her for himself, but that he feared himself for her sake. God had filled his heart with love of the girl,—and, if it was love, could it be that he would destroy her future for the gratification of his own feelings? 'I tell you it is no good,' he said, as she crouched down beside him, almost sitting on his knee.

At this moment Mrs. Baggett came into the room, detecting Mary almost in the embrace of her old master. 'He's come back again, sir,' said Mrs. Baggett.

'Who has come back?'

'The Sergeant.'

'Then you may tell him to go about his business. He is not wanted, at any rate. You are to remain here, and have your own way, like an old fool.'

'I am that, sir.'

'There is not any one coming to interfere with you.'

'Sir!'

Then Mary got up, and stood sobbing at the open window. 'At any rate, you'll have to remain here to look after the house, even if I go away. Where is the Sergeant?'

'He's in the stable again.'

'What! drunk?'

'Well, no; he's not drunk. I think his wooden leg is affected sooner than if he had two like mine, or yours, sir. And he did manage to go in of his self, now that he knows the way. He's there among the hay, and I do think it's very unkind of Hayonotes to say as he'll spoil it. But how am I to get him out, unless I goes away with him?'

'Let him stay there and give him some dinner. I don't know what else you've to do.'

'He can't stay always,—in course, sir. As Hayonotes says,—what's he to do with a wooden-legged sergeant in his stable as a permanence? I had come to say I was to go home with him.'

'You're to do nothing of the kind.'

'What is it you mean, then, about my taking care of the house?'

'Never you mind. When I want you to know, I shall tell you.' Then Mrs. Baggett bobbed her head three times in the direction of Mary Lawrie's back, as though to ask some question whether the leaving the house might not be in reference to Mary's marriage. But she feared that it was not made in reference to Mr. Whittlestaff's marriage also. What had her master meant when he had said that there was no one coming to interfere with her, Mrs. Baggett? 'You needn't ask any questions just at present, Mrs. Baggett,' he said.

'You don't mean as you are going up to London just to give her up to that young fellow?'

'I am going about my own business, and I won't be inquired into,' said Mr. Whittlestaff.

'Then you're going to do what no man ought to do.'

'You are an impertinent old woman,' said her master.

'I daresay I am. All the same, it's my duty to tell you my mind. You can't eat me, Mr. Whittlestaff, and it wouldn't much matter if you could. When you've said that you'll do a thing, you ought not to go back for any other man, let him be who it may,—especially not in respect of a female. It's weak, and nobody wouldn't think a straw of you for doing it. It's some idea of being generous that you have got into your head. There ain't no real generosity in it. I say it ain't manly, and that's what a man ought to be.'

Mary, though she was standing at the window, pretending to look out of it, knew that during the whole of this conversation Mrs. Baggett was making signs at her,—as though indicating an opinion that she was the person in fault. It was as though Mrs. Baggett had said that it was for her sake,—to do something to gratify her,—that Mr. Whittlestaff was about to go to London. She knew that she at any rate was not to blame.

She was struggling for the same end as Mrs. Baggett, and did deserve better treatment. 'You oughtn't to bother going up to London, sir, on any such errand, and so I tells you, Mr. Whittlestaff,' said Mrs. Baggett.

'I have told him the same thing myself,' said Mary Lawrie, turning round.

'If you told him as though you meant it, he wouldn't go,' said Mrs. Baggett.

'That's all you know about it,' said Mr. Whittlestaff. 'Now the fact is, I won't stand this kind of thing. If you mean to remain here, you must be less free with your tongue.'

'I don't mean to remain here, Mr. Whittlestaff. It's just that as I'm coming to. There's Timothy Baggett is down there among the hosses, and he says as I am to go with him. So I've come up here to say that if he's allowed to sleep it off to-day, I'll be ready to start to-morrow.'

'I tell you I am not going to make any change at all,' said Mr. Whittlestaff.

'You was saying you was going away,—for the honeymoon, I did suppose.'

'A man may go away if he pleases, without any reason of that kind. Oh dear, oh dear, that letter is not gone! I insist that that letter should go. I suppose I must see about it myself.' Then when he began to move, the women moved also. Mary went to look after the sandwiches, and Mrs. Baggett to despatch the letter. In ten minutes the letter was gone, and half an hour afterwards Mr. Whittlestaff had himself driven down to the station.

'What is it he means, Miss?' said Mrs. Baggett, when the master was gone.

'I do not know,' said Mary, who was in truth very angry with the old woman.

'He wants to make you Mrs. Whittlestaff.'

'In whatever he wants I shall obey him,—if I only knew how.'

'It's what you is bound to do, Miss Mary. Think of what he has done for you.'

'I require no one to tell me that.'

'What did Mr. Gordon come here for, disturbing everybody? Nobody asked him;—at least, I suppose nobody asked him.' There was an insinuation in this which Mary found it hard to bear. But it was better to bear it than to argue on such a point with the servant. 'And he said things which put the master about terribly.'

'It was not my doing.'

'But he's a man as needn't have his own way. Why should Mr. Gordon have everything just as he likes it? I never heard tell of Mr. Gordon till he came here the other day. I don't think so much of Mr. Gordon myself.' To this Mary, of course, made no answer. 'He's no business disturbing people when he's not sent for. I can't abide to see Mr. Whittlestaff put about in this way. I have known him longer than you have.'

'No doubt.'

'He's a man that'll be driven pretty nigh out of his mind if he's disappointed.' Then there was silence, as Mary was determined not to discuss the matter any further. 'If you come to that, you needn't marry no one unless you pleases.' Mary was still silent. 'They shouldn't make me marry them unless I was that way minded. I can't abide such doings,' the old woman again went on after a pause. 'I knows what I knows, and I sees what I sees.'

'What do you know?'* said Mary, driven beyond her powers of silence.

'The meaning is, that Mr. Whittlestaff is to be disappointed after he have received a promise. Didn't he have a promise?' To this Mrs. Baggett got no reply, though she waited for one before she went on with her argument. 'You knows he had; and a promise between a lady and gentleman ought to be as good as the law of the land. You stand there as dumb as grim death, and won't say a word, and yet it all depends upon you. Why is it to go about among everybody, that he's not to get a wife just because a man's come home with his pockets full of diamonds? It's that that people'll say; and they'll say that you went back from your word just because of a few precious stones. I wouldn't like to have it said of me anyhow.'

This was very hard to bear, but Mary found herself compelled to bear it. She had determined not to be led into an argument with Mrs. Baggett on the subject, feeling that even to discuss her conduct would be an impropriety. She was strong in her own conduct, and knew how utterly at variance it had been with all that this woman imputed to her. The glitter of the diamonds had been merely thrown in by Mrs. Baggett in her passion. Mary did not think that any one would be so base as to believe such an accusation as that. It would be said of her that her own young lover had come back suddenly, and that she had preferred him to the gentleman to whom she was tied by so many bonds. It would be said that she had given herself to him and had then taken back the gift, because the young lover had come across her path. And it would be told also that there had been no word of promise given to this young lover. All that would be very bad, without any allusion to a wealth of diamonds. It would not be said that, before she had pledged herself to Mr. Whittlestaff, she had pleaded her affection for her young lover, when she had known nothing even of his present existence. It would not be known that though there had been no lover's vows between her and John Gordon, there had yet been on both sides that unspoken love which could not have been strengthened by any vows. Against all that she must guard herself, without thinking of the diamonds. She had endeavoured to guard herself, and she had thought also of the contentment of the man who had been so good to her. She had declared to herself that of herself she would think not at all. And she had determined also that all the likings, —nay, the affection of John Gordon himself,— should weigh not at all with her. She had to decide between the two men, and she had decided that both honesty and gratitude required her to comply with the wishes of the elder. She had done all that she could with that object, and was it her fault that Mr. Whittlestaff had read the secret of her heart, and had determined to give way before it? This had so touched her that it might almost be said that she knew not to which of her two suitors her heart belonged. All this, if stated in answer to Mrs. Baggett's accusations, would certainly exonerate herself from the stigma thrown upon her, but to Mrs. Baggett she could not repeat the explanation.

'It nigh drives me wild,' said Mrs. Baggett. 'I don't suppose you ever heard of Catherine Bailey?'

'Never.'

'And I ain't a-going to tell you. It's a romance as shall be wrapped inside my own bosom. It was quite a tragedy,—was Catherine Bailey; and one as would stir your heart up if you was to hear it. Catherine Bailey was a young woman. But I'm not going to tell you the story; —only that she was no more fit for Mr. Whittlestaff than any of them stupid young girls that walks about the streets gaping in at the shop-windows in Alresford. I do you the justice, Miss Lawrie, to say as you are such a female as he ought to look after.'

'Thank you, Mrs. Baggett.'

'But she led him into such trouble, because his heart is soft, as was dreadful to look at. He is one of them as always wants a wife. Why didn't he get one before? you'll say. Because till you came in the way he was always thinking of Catherine Bailey. Mrs. Compas she become, "Drat her and her babies!" I often said to myself. What was Compas? No more than an Old Bailey lawyer;—not fit to be looked at alongside of our Mr. Whittlestaff. No more ain't Mr. John Gordon, to my thinking. You think of all that, Miss Mary, and make up your mind whether you'll break his heart after giving a promise. Heart-breaking ain't to him what it is to John Gordon and the likes of him.'

CHAPTER XX

Mr. Whittlestaff takes his Journey

MR. WHITTLESTAFF did at last get into the train and had himself carried up to London. And he ate his sandwiches and drank his sherry with an air of supreme satisfaction,—as though he had carried his point. And so he had. He had made up his mind on a certain matter; and, with the object of doing a certain piece of work, he had escaped from the two dominant women of his household, who had done their best to intercept him. So far his triumph was complete. But as he sat silent in the corner of the carriage, his mind reverted to the purpose of his journey, and he cannot be said to have been triumphant. He knew it all as well as did Mrs. Baggett. And he knew too that, except Mrs. Baggett and the girl herself, all the world was against him. That ass Montagu Blake every time he opened his mouth as to his own bride let out the idea that John Gordon should have his bride because John Gordon was young and lusty, and because he, Whittlestaff, might be regarded as an old man. The Miss Halls were altogether of the same opinion, and were not slow to express it. All Alresford would know it, and would sympathise with John Gordon. And as it came to be known that he himself had given up the girl whom he loved, he could read the ridicule which would be conveyed by the smiles of his neighbours.

To tell the truth of Mr. Whittlestaff, he was a man very open to such shafts of ridicule. The '*robur et æs triplex*'* which fortified his heart went only to the doing of a good and unselfish action, and did not extend to providing him with that adamantine shield which virtue should of itself supply. He was as pervious to these stings as a man might be who had not strength to act in opposition to them. He could screw himself up to the doing of a great deed for the benefit of another, and could as he was doing so deplore with inward tears the punishment which the world would accord to him for the deed. As he sat there in the corner of his carriage, he was thinking of the punishment rather than of the glory. And the punishment must certainly come now. It would be a punishment lasting for the remainder of his life, and so bitter in its kind as to make any further living almost impossible to him. It was not that he would kill himself. He did not meditate any such step as that. He was a man who considered that by doing an outrage to God's work an offence would be committed against God which admitted of no repentance. He must live through it to the last. But he must live as a man who was degraded. He had made his effort, but his effort would be known to all Alresford. Mr. Montagu Blake would take care of that.

The evil done to him would be one which would admit of no complaint from his own mouth. He would be left alone, living with Mrs. Baggett,—who of course knew all the facts. The idea of Mrs. Baggett going away with her husband was of course not to be thought of. That was another nuisance, a small evil in comparison with the great misfortune of his life.

He had brought this girl home to his house to
be the companion of his days, and she had come
to have in his mouth a flavour, as it were, and
sweetness beyond all other sweetnesses. She had
lent a grace to his days of which for many years
he had not believed them to be capable. He was
a man who had thought much of love, reading
about it in all the poets with whose lines he was
conversant. He was one who, in all that he read,
would take the gist of it home to himself, and ask
himself how it was with him in that matter. His
favourite Horace had had a fresh love for every
day;* but he had told himself that Horace knew
nothing of love. Of Petrarch and Laura* he had
thought; but even to Petrarch Laura had been
a subject for expression rather than for passion.
Prince Arthur, in his love for Guinevere,* went
nearer to the mark which he had fancied for
himself. Imogen, in her love for Posthumus,*
gave to him a picture of all that love should be.
It was thus that he had thought of himself in all
his readings; and as years had gone by, he had
told himself that for him there was to be nothing
better than reading. But yet his mind had been
full, and he had still thought to himself that, in
spite of his mistake in reference to Catherine
Bailey, there was still room for a strong passion.

Then Mary Lawrie had come upon him, and
the sun seemed to shine nowhere but in her eyes
and in the expression of her face. He had told
himself distinctly that he was now in love, and
that his life had not gone so far forward as to
leave him stranded on the dry sandhills. She
was there living in his house, subject to his orders,
affectionate and docile; but, as far as he could

judge, a perfect woman. And, as far as he could judge, there was no other man whom she loved. Then, with many doubtings, he asked her the question, and he soon learned the truth,—but not the whole truth.

There had been a man, but he was one who seemed to have passed by and left his mark, and then to have gone on altogether out of sight. She had told him that she could not but think of John Gordon, but that that was all. She would, if he asked it, plight her troth to him and become his wife, although she must think of John Gordon. This thinking would last but for a while, he told himself; and he at his age—what right had he to expect aught better than that? She was of such a nature that, when she had given herself up in marriage, she would surely learn to love her husband. So he had accepted her promise, and allowed himself for one hour to be a happy man.

Then John Gordon had come to his house, falling upon it like the blast of a storm. He had come at once—instantly—as though fate had intended to punish him, Whittlestaff, utterly and instantly. Mary had told him that she could not promise not to think of him who had once loved her, when, lo and behold! the man himself was there. Who ever suffered a blow so severe as this? He had left them together. He had felt himself compelled to do so by the exigencies of the moment. It was impossible that he should give either one or the other to understand that they would not be allowed to meet in his house. They had met, and Mary had been very firm. For a few hours there had existed in his bosom the feeling that even yet he might be preferred.

But gradually that feeling had disappeared, and the truth had come home to him. She was as much in love with John Gordon as could any girl be with the man whom she adored. And the other rock on which he had depended was gradually shivered beneath his feet. He had fancied at first that the man had come back, as do so many adventurers, without the means of making a woman happy. It was not for John Gordon that he was solicitous, but for Mary Lawrie. If John Gordon were a pauper, or so nearly so as to be able to offer Mary no home, then it would clearly be his duty not to allow the marriage. In such case the result to him would be, if not heavenly, sweet enough at any rate to satisfy his longings. She would come to him, and John Gordon would depart to London, and to the world beyond, and there would be an end of him. But it became palpable to his senses generally that the man's fortunes had not been such as this. And then there came home to him a feeling that were they so, it would be his duty to make up for Mary's sake what was wanting,— since he had discovered of what calibre was the man himself.

It was at Mr. Hall's house that the idea had first presented itself to him with all the firmness of a settled project. It would be, he had said to himself, a great thing for a man to do. What, after all, is the meaning of love, but that a man should do his best to serve the woman he loves? 'Who cares a straw for him?' he said to himself, as though to exempt himself from any idea of general charity, and to prove that all the good which he intended to do was to be done for love alone. 'Not a straw; whether he shall stay at home here and have all that is sweetest in the world, or be sent out alone to find fresh diamonds amidst the dirt and misery of that horrid place, is as nothing, as far as he is concerned. I am, at any rate, more to myself than John Gordon. I do not believe in doing a kindness of such a nature as that to such a one. But for her——! And I could not hold her to my bosom, knowing that she would so much rather be in the arms of another man.' All this he said to himself; but he said it in words fully formed, and with the thoughts, on which the words were based, clearly established.

When he came to the end of his journey, he had himself driven to the hotel, and ordered his dinner, and ate it in solitude, still supported by the ecstasy of his thoughts. He knew that there was before him a sharp cruel punishment, and then a weary lonely life. There could be no happiness, no satisfaction, in store for him. He was aware that it must be so; but still for the present there was a joy to him in thinking that he would make her happy, and in that he was determined to take what immediate delight it would give him. He asked himself how long that delight could last; and he told himself that when John Gordon should have once taken her by the hand and claimed her as his own, the time of his misery would have come.

There had hung about him a dream, clinging to him up to the moment of his hotel dinner, by which he had thought it possible that he might yet escape from the misery of Pandemonium and be carried into the light and joy of Paradise. But as he sat with his beef-steak before him, and ate his accustomed potato, with apparently as good a gusto as any of his neighbours, the dream departed. He told himself that under no circumstances should the dream be allowed to become a reality. The dream had been of this wise. With all the best intentions in his power he would offer the girl to John Gordon, and then, not doubting Gordon's acceptance of her, would make the same offer to the girl herself. But what if the girl refused to accept the offer? What if the girl should stubbornly adhere to her original promise? Was he to refuse to marry her when she should insist that such was her right? Was he to decline to enter in upon the joys of Paradise when Paradise should be thus opened to him? He would do his best, loyally and sincerely, with his whole heart. But he could not force her to make him a wretch, miserable for the rest of his life!

In fact it was she who might choose to make the sacrifice, and thus save him from the unhappiness in store for him. Such had been the nature of his dream. As he was eating his beef-steak and potatoes, he told himself that it could not be so, and that the dream must be flung to the winds. A certain amount of strength was now demanded of him, and he thought that he would be able to use it. 'No, my dear, not me; it may not be that you should become my wife, though all the promises under heaven had been given. Though you say that you wish it, it is a lie which may not be ratified. Though you

implore it of me, it cannot be granted. It is he
that is your love, and it is he that must have you.
I love you too, God in his wisdom knows, but it
cannot be so. Go and be his wife, for mine you
shall never become. I have meant well, but have
been unfortunate. Now you know the state of
my mind, than which nothing is more fixed on
this earth.' It was thus that he would speak to
her, and then he would turn away; and the
term of his misery would have commenced.

On the next morning he got up and prepared
for his interview with John Gordon. He walked
up and down the sward of the Green Park,
thinking to himself of the language which he
would use. If he could only tell the man that he
hated him while he surrendered to him the girl
whom he loved so dearly, it would be well. For
in truth there was nothing of Christian charity
in his heart towards John Gordon. But he
thought at last that it would be better that he
should announce his purpose in the simplest
language. He could hate the man in his own
heart as thoroughly as he desired. But it would
not be becoming in him, were he on such an
occasion to attempt to rise to the romance of
tragedy. 'It will be all the same a thousand years
hence,' he said to himself as he walked in at
the club door.

CHAPTER XXI

The Green Park

HE asked whether Mr. John Gordon was with-in, and in two minutes found himself standing in the hall with that hero of romance. Mr. Whittlestaff told himself, as he looked at the man, that he was such a hero as ought to be happy in his love. Whereas of himself, he was conscious of a personal appearance which no girl could be expected to adore. He thought too much of his personal appearance generally, complaining to himself that it was mean; whereas in regard to Mary Lawrie, it may be said that no such idea had ever entered her mind. 'It was just because he had come first,' she would have said if asked. And the 'he' alluded to would have been John Gordon. 'He had come first, and therefore I had learned to love him.' It was thus that Mary Lawrie would have spoken. But Mr. Whittlestaff, as he looked up into John Gordon's face, felt that he himself was mean.

'You got my letter, Mr. Gordon?'

'Yes; I got it last night.'

'I have come up to London, because there is something that I want to say to you. It is something that I can't very well put up into a letter, and therefore I have taken the trouble to come to town.' As he said this he endeavoured, no doubt, to assert his own dignity by the look which he assumed. Nor did he intend that Mr. Gordon should know anything of the struggle which he had endured.

But Mr. Gordon knew as well what Mr. Whittlestaff had to say as did Mr. Whittlestaff himself. He had turned the matter over in his own mind since the letter had reached him, and was aware that there could be no other cause for seeing him which could bring Mr. Whittlestaff up to London. But a few days since he had made an appeal to Mr. Whittlestaff—an appeal which certainly might require much thought for its answer—and here was Mr. Whittlestaff with his reply. It could not have been made quicker. It was thus that John Gordon had thought of it as he had turned Mr. Whittlestaff's letter over in his mind. The appeal had been made readily enough. The making of it had been easy; the words to be spoken had come quickly, and without the necessity for a moment's premeditation. He had known it all, and from a full heart the mouth speaks. But was it to have been expected that a man so placed as had been Mr. Whittlestaff, should be able to give his reply with equal celerity? He, John Gordon, had seen at once on reaching Croker's Hall the state in which things were. Almost hopelessly he had made his appeal to the man who had her promise. Then he had met the man at Mr. Hall's house, and hardly a word had passed between them. What word could have been expected? Montagu Blake, with all his folly, had judged rightly in bringing them together. When he received the letter, John Gordon had remembered that last word which Mr. Whittlestaff had spoken to him in the squire's hall. He had thought of the appeal, and had resolved to give an answer to it. It was an appeal which required an answer. He had turned it over in his mind, and had at last told himself what the answer should be. John Gordon had discovered all that when he received the letter, and it need hardly be said that his feelings in regard to Mr. Whittlestaff were very much kinder than those of Mr. Whittlestaff to him.

'Perhaps you wouldn't mind coming out into the street,' said Mr. Whittlestaff. 'I can't say very well what I've got to say in here.'

'Certainly,' said Gordon; 'I will go anywhere.'

'Let us go into the Park. It is green there, and there is some shade among the trees.' Then they went out of the club into Pall Mall, and Mr. Whittlestaff walked on ahead without a word. 'No; we will not go down there,' he said, as he passed the entrance into St. James's Park by Marlborough House, and led the way through St. James's Palace into the Green Park. 'We'll go on till we come to the trees; there are seats there, unless the people have occupied them all. One can't talk here under the blazing sun;—at least I can't.' Then he walked on at a rapid pace, wiping his brow as he did so. 'Yes, there's a seat. I'll be hanged if that man isn't going to sit down upon it! What a beast he is! No, I can't sit down on a seat that another man is occupying. I don't want any one to hear what I've got to say. There! Two women have gone a little farther on.' Then he hurried to the vacant bench and took possession of it. It was placed among the thick trees which give a perfect shade on the north side of the Park, and had Mr. Whittlestaff searched all London through, he could not have found a more pleasant spot in which to make his communication. 'This will do,' said he.

'Very nicely indeed,' said John Gordon.

'I couldn't talk about absolutely private business in the hall of the club, you know.'

'I could have taken you into a private room, Mr. Whittlestaff, had you wished it.'

'With everybody coming in and out, just as they pleased. I don't believe in private rooms in London clubs. What I've got to say can be said better *sub dio*.* I suppose you know what it is that I've got to talk about.'

'Hardly,' said John Gordon. 'But that is not exactly true. I think I know, but I am not quite sure of it. On such a subject I should not like to make a surmise unless I were confident.'

'It's about Miss Lawrie.'

'I suppose so.'

'What makes you suppose that?' said Whittlestaff, sharply.

'You told me that you were sure I should know.'

'So I am, quite sure. You came all the way down to Alresford to see her. If you spoke the truth, you came all the way home from the diamond-fields with the same object.'

'I certainly spoke the truth, Mr. Whittlestaff.'

'Then what's the good of your pretending not to know?'

'I have not pretended. I merely said that I could not presume to put the young lady's name into your mouth until you had uttered it yourself. There could be no other subject of conversation between you and me of which I was aware.'

'You had spoken to me about her,' said Mr. Whittlestaff.

'No doubt I had. When I found that you had

given her a home, and had made yourself, as it were, a father to her——'

'I had not made myself her father,—nor yet her mother. I had loved her, as you profess to do.'

'My profession is at any rate true.'

'I daresay. You may or you mayn't; I at any rate know nothing about it.'

'Why otherwise should I have come home and left my business in South Africa? I think you may take it for granted that I love her.'

'I don't care twopence whether you do or don't,' said Mr. Whittlestaff. 'It's nothing to me whom you love. I should have been inclined to say at first sight that a man groping in the dirt for diamonds wouldn't love any one. And even if you did, though you might break your heart and die, it would be nothing to me. Had you done so, I should not have heard of you, nor should I have wished to hear of you.'

There was an incivility in all this of which John Gordon felt that he was obliged to take some notice. There was a want of courtesy in the man's manner rather than his words, which he could not quite pass by, although he was most anxious to do so. 'I daresay not,' said he; 'but here I am and here also is Miss Lawrie. I had said what I had to say down at Alresford, and of course it is for you now to decide what is to be done. I have never supposed that you would care personally for me.'

'You needn't be so conceited about yourself.'

'I don't know that I am,' said Gordon;—'except that a man cannot but be a little conceited who has won the love of Mary Lawrie.'

'You think it impossible that I should have done so.'

'At any rate I did it before you had seen her. Though I may be conceited, I am not more conceited for myself than you are for yourself. Had I not known her, you would probably have engaged her affections. I had known her, and you are aware of the result. But it is for you to decide. Miss Lawrie thinks that she owes you a debt which she is bound to pay if you exact it.'

'Exact it!' exclaimed Mr. Whittlestaff. 'There is no question of exacting!' John Gordon shrugged his shoulders. 'I say there is no question of exacting. The words should not have been used. She has my full permission to choose as she may think fit, and she knows that she has it. What right have you to speak to me of exacting?'

Mr. Whittlestaff had now talked himself into such a passion, and was apparently so angry at the word which his companion had used, that John Gordon began to doubt whether he did in truth know the purpose for which the man had come to London. Could it be that he had made the journey merely with the object of asserting that he had the power of making this girl his wife, and of proving his power by marrying her. 'What is it that you wish, Mr. Whittlestaff?' he asked.

'Wish! What business have you to ask after my wishes? But you know what my wishes are very well. I will not pretend to keep them in the dark. She came to my house, and I soon learned to desire that she should be my wife. If I know what love is, I loved her. If I know what love is, I do love her still. She is all the world to me. I have no diamonds to care for; I have no rich mines to occupy my heart; I am not eager in the pursuit of wealth. I had lived a melancholy, lonely life till this young woman had come to my table,—till I had felt her sweet hand upon mine, —till she had hovered around me, covering everything with bright sunshine. Then I asked her to be my wife;—and she told me of you.'

'She told you of me?'

'Yes; she told me of you—of you who might then have been dead, for aught she knew. And when I pressed her, she said that she would think of you always.'

'She said so?'

'Yes; that she would think of you always. But she did not say that she would always love you. And in the same breath she promised to be my wife. I was contented,—and yet not quite contented. Why should she think of you always? But I believed that it would not be so. I thought that if I were good to her, I should overcome her. I knew that I should be better to her than you would be.'

'Why should I not be good to her?'

'There is an old saying of a young man's slave and an old man's darling. She would at any rate have been my darling. It might be that she would have been your slave.'

'My fellow-workman in all things.'

'You think so now; but the man always becomes the master. If you grovelled in the earth for diamonds, she would have to look for them amidst the mud and slime.'

'I have never dreamed of taking her to the diamond-fields.'

'It would have been so in all other pursuits.'

'She would have had none that she had not chosen,' said John Gordon.

'How am I to know that? How am I to rest assured that the world would be smooth to her if she were your creature? I am not assured— I do not know.'

'Who can tell, as you say? Can I promise her a succession of joys if she be my wife? She is not one who will be likely to look for such a life as that. She will know that she must take the rough and smooth together.'

'There would have been no rough with me,' said Mr. Whittlestaff.

'I do not believe in such a life,' said John Gordon. 'A woman should not wear a stuff gown always; but the silk finery and the stuff gown should follow each other. To my taste, the more there may be of the stuff gown and the less of the finery, the more it will be to my wishes.'

'I am not speaking of her gowns. It is not of such things as those that I am thinking.' Here Mr. Whittlestaff got up from the bench, and began walking rapidly backwards and forwards under the imperfect shade on the path. 'You will beat her.'

'I think not.'

'Beat her in the spirit. You will domineer over her, and desire to have your own way. When she is toiling for you, you will frown at her. Because you have business on hand, or perhaps pleasure, you will leave her in solitude. There may a time come when the diamonds shall have all gone.'

'If she is to be mine, that time will have come already. The diamonds will be sold. Did you ever see a diamond in my possession? Why do you twit me with diamonds? If I had been a coal-owner, should I have been expected to keep my coals?'

'These things stick to the very soul of a man. They are a poison of which he cannot rid himself. They are like gambling. They make everything cheap that should be dear, and everything dear that should be cheap. I trust them not at all,—and I do not trust you, because you deal in them.'

'I tell you that I shall not deal in them. But, Mr. Whittlestaff, I must tell you that you are unreasonable.'

'No doubt. I am a poor miserable man who does not know the world. I have never been to the diamond-fields. Of course I understand nothing of the charms of speculation. A quiet life with my book is all that I care for;—with just one other thing, one other thing. You begrudge me that.'

'Mr. Whittlestaff, it does not signify a straw what I begrudge you.' Mr. Whittlestaff had now come close to him, and was listening to him. 'Nor, as I take it, what you begrudge me. Before I left England she and I had learned to love each other. It is so still. For the sake of her happiness, do you mean to let me have her?'

'I do.'

'You do?'

'Of course I do. You have known it all along. Of course I do. Do you think I would make her miserable? Would it be in my bosom to make her come and live with a stupid, silly old man, to potter on from day to day without any excitement? Would I force her into a groove in which her days would be wretched to her? Had she come to me and wanted bread, and have seen before her all the misery of poverty, the stone-coldness of a governess's life; had she been left to earn her bread without any one to love her, it might then have been different. She would have looked out into another world, and have seen another prospect. A comfortable home with kindness, and her needs supplied, would have sufficed. She would then have thought herself happy in becoming my wife. There would then have been no cruelty. But she had seen you, and though it was but a dream, she thought that she could endure to wait. Better that than surrender all the delight of loving. So she told me that she would think of you. Poor dear! I can understand now the struggle which she intended to make. Then in the very nick of time, in the absolute moment of the day—so that you might have everything and I nothing—you came. You came, and were allowed to see her, and told her all your story. You filled her heart full with joy, but only to be crushed when she thought that the fatal promise had been given to me. I saw it all, I knew it. I thought to myself for a few hours that it might be so. But it cannot be so.'

'Oh, Mr. Whittlestaff!'

'It cannot be so,' he said, with a firm determined voice, as though asserting a fact which admitted no doubt.

'Mr. Whittlestaff, what am I to say to you?'

'You! What are you to say? Nothing. What should you say? Why should you speak? It is not for love of you that I would do this thing; nor yet altogether from love of her. Not that I would not do much for her sake. I almost think that I would do it entirely for her sake, if there were no other reason. But to shame myself by taking that which belongs to another, as though it were my own property! To live a coward in mine own esteem! Though I may be the laughing stock and the butt of all those around me, I would still be a man to myself. I ought to have felt that it was sufficient when she told me that some of her thoughts must still be given to you. She is yours, Mr. Gordon; but I doubt much whether you care for the possession.'

'Not care for her! Up to the moment when I received your note, I was about to start again for South Africa. South Africa is no place for her,— nor for me either, with such a wife. Mr. Whittle-staff, will you not allow me to say one word to you in friendship?'

'Not a word.'

'How am I to come and take her out of your house?'

'She must manage it as best she can. But no; I would not turn her from my door for all the world could do for me. This, too, will be part of the punishment that I must bear. You can settle the day between you, I suppose, and then you can come down; and, after the accustomed fashion, you can meet her at the church-door. Then you can come to my house, and eat your breakfast there if you will. You will see fine things prepared for you,—such as a woman wants on those occasions,—and then you can carry her off wherever you please. I need know nothing of your whereabouts. Good morning now. Do not say anything further, but let me go my way.'

CHAPTER XXII

John Gordon writes a Letter

WHEN they parted in the park, Mr. Whittlestaff trudged off to his own hotel, through the heat and sunshine. He walked quickly, and never looked behind him, and went as though he had fully accomplished his object in one direction, and must hurry to get it done in another. To Gordon he had left no directions whatever. Was he to be allowed to go down to Mary, or even to write her a letter? He did not know whether Mary had ever been told of this wonderful sacrifice which had been made on her behalf. He understood that he was to have his own way, and was to be permitted to regard himself as betrothed to her, but he did not at all understand what steps he was to take in the matter, except that he was not to go again to the diamond-fields. But Mr. Whittlestaff hurried himself off to his hotel, and shut himself up in his own bedroom,—and when there, he sobbed, alas! like a child.

The wife whom he had won for himself was probably more valuable to him than if he had simply found her disengaged and ready to jump into his arms. She, at any rate, had behaved well. Mr. Whittlestaff had no doubt proved himself to be an angel, perfect all round,—such a man as you shall not meet perhaps once in your life. But Mary, too, had so behaved as to enhance the love of any man who had been already engaged to her. As he thought of the whole story of the past week, the first idea that occurred to him was that he certainly had been present to her mind during the whole period of his absence. Though not a word had passed between them, and though no word of absolute love for each other had even been spoken before, she had been steady to him, with no actual basis on which to found her love. He had known, and she had been sure, and therefore she had been true to him. Of course, being a true man himself, he worshipped her all the more. Mr. Whittlestaff was absolutely, undoubtedly perfect; but in Gordon's estimation Mary was not far off perfection. But what was he to do now, so that he might approach her?

He had pledged himself to one thing, and he must at once go to work and busy himself in accomplishing it. He had promised not to return to Africa; and he must at once see Mr. Tookey, and learn whether that gentleman's friends would be allowed to go on with the purchase as arranged. He knew Poker & Hodge to be moneyed men, or to be men, at any rate, in command of money. If they would not pay him at once, he must look elsewhere for buyers; but the matter must be settled. Tookey had promised to come to his club this day, and there he would go and await his coming.

He went to his club, but the first person who came to him was Mr. Whittlestaff. Mr. Whittlestaff when he had left the park had determined never to see John Gordon again, or to see him only during that ceremony of the marriage, which it might be that he would even yet escape. All that was still in the distant future. Dim ideas as to some means of avoiding it flitted through his brain. But even though he might see Gordon on that terrible occasion, he need not speak to him. And it would have to be done then, and then only. But now another idea, certainly very vague, had found its way into his mind, and with the object of carrying it out, Mr. Whittlestaff had come to the club. 'Oh, Mr. Whittlestaff, how do you do again?'

'I'm much the same as I was before, thank you. There hasn't happened anything to improve my health.'

'I hope nothing may happen to injure it.'

'It doesn't much matter. You said something about some property you've got in diamonds, and you said once that you must go out to look after it.'

'But I'm not going now. I shall sell my share in the mines. I am going to see a Mr. Tookey about it immediately.'

'Can't you sell them to me?'

'The diamond shares,—to you!'

'Why not to me? If the thing has to be done at once, of course you and I must trust each other. I suppose you can trust me?'

'Certainly I can.'

'As I don't care much about it, whether I get what I buy or not, it does not much matter for me. But in truth, in such an affair as this I would trust you. Why should not I go in your place?'

'I don't think you are the man who ought to go there.'

'I am too old? I'm not a cripple, if you mean that. I don't see why I shouldn't go to the diamond-fields as well as a younger man.'

'It is not about your age, Mr. Whittlestaff; but I do not think you would be happy there.'

'Happy! I do not know that my state of bliss here is very great. If I had bought your shares, as you call them, and paid money for them, I don't see why my happiness need stand in the way.'

'You are a gentleman, Mr. Whittlestaff.'

'Well; I hope so.'

'And of that kind that you would have your eyes picked out of your head before you had been there a week. Don't go. Take my word for it, that life will be pleasanter to you here than there, and that for you the venture would be altogether dangerous. Here is Mr. Tookey.' At this point of the conversation, Mr. Tookey entered the hall-door, and some fashion of introduction took place between the two strangers. John Gordon led the way into a private room, and the two others followed him. 'Here's a gentleman anxious to buy my shares, Tookey,' said Gordon.

'What! the whole lot of the old Stick-in-the-Mud? He'll have to shell down* some money in order to do that! If I were to be asked my opinion, I should say that the transaction was hardly one in the gentleman's way of business.'

'I suppose an honest man may work at it,' said Mr. Whittlestaff.

'It's the honestest business I know out,' said Fitzwalker Tookey; 'but it does require a gentleman to have his eyes about him.'

'Haven't I got my eyes?'

'Oh certainly, certainly,' said Tookey; 'I never knew a gentleman have them brighter. But there are eyes and eyes. Here's Mr. Gordon did have a stroke of luck out there;—quite wonderful! But because he tumbled on to a good thing, it's no reason that others should. And he's sold his claim already, if he doesn't go himself,—either to me, or else to Poker & Hodge.'

'I'm afraid it is so,' said John Gordon.

'There's my darling wife, who is going out with me, and who means to stand all the hardship of the hard work amidst those scenes of constant labour,—a lady who is dying to see her babies there. I am sure, sir, that Mr. Gordon won't forget his promises to me and my wife.'

'If you have the money ready.'

'There is Mr. Poker in a hansom cab outside, and ready to go with you to the bank at once, as the matter is rather pressing. If you will come with him, he will explain everything. I will follow in another cab, and then everything can be completed.' John Gordon did make an appointment to meet Mr. Poker in the city later on in the day, and then was left together with Mr. Whittlestaff at the club.

It was soon decided that Mr. Whittlestaff should give up all idea of the diamond-fields, and in so doing he allowed himself to be brought back to a state of semi-courteous conversation with his happy rival. 'Well, yes; you may write to her, I suppose. Indeed I don't know what right I have to say that you may, or you mayn't. She's more yours than mine, I suppose.' 'Turn her out! I don't know what makes you take such an idea as that in your head.' John Gordon had not suggested that Mr. Whittlestaff would turn Mary Lawrie out,—though he had spoken of the steps he would have to take were he to find Mary left without a home. 'She shall have my house as her own till she can find another. As she will not be my wife, she shall be my daughter,—till she is somebody else's wife.' 'I told you before that you may come and marry her. Indeed I can't help myself. Of course you may go on as you would with some other girl;—only I wish it were some other girl. You can go and stay with Montagu Blake, if you please. It is nothing to me. Everybody knows it now.' Then he did say good-bye, though he could not be persuaded to shake hands with John Gordon.

Mr. Whittlestaff did not go home that day, but on the next, remaining in town till he was driven out of it by twenty-four hours of absolute misery. He had said to himself that he would remain till he could think of some future plan of life that should have in it some better promise of success for him than his sudden scheme of going to the diamond-fields. But there was no other plan which became practicable in his eyes. On the afternoon of the very next day London was no longer bearable to him; and as there was no other place but Croker's Hall to which he could take himself with any prospect of meeting friends who would know anything of his ways of life, he did go down on the following day. One consequence of this was, that Mary had received from her lover the letter which he had written almost as soon as he had received Mr. Whittle-staff's permission to write. The letter was as follows:—

'DEAR MARY,—I do not know whether you

are surprised by what Mr. Whittlestaff has done;
but I am,—so much so that I hardly know how
to write to you on the matter. If you will think
of it, I have never written to you, and have never
been in a position in which writing seemed to be
possible. Nor do I know as yet whether you are
aware of the business which has brought Mr.
Whittlestaff to town.

'I suppose I am to take it for granted that all
that he tells me is true; though when I think what
it is that I have to accept,—and that on the word
of a man who is not your father, and who is a
perfect stranger to me,—it does seem as though
I were assuming a great deal. And yet it is no
more than I asked him to do for me when I saw
him at his own house.

'I had no time then to ask for your permission;
nor, had I asked for it, would you have granted
it to me. You had pledged yourself, and would
not have broken your pledge. If I asked for
your hand at all, it was from him that I had to
ask. How will it be with me if you shall refuse
to come to me at his bidding?

'I have never told you that I loved you, nor
have you expressed your willingness to receive
my love. Dear Mary, how shall it be? No doubt
I do count upon you in my very heart as being
my own. After this week of troubles it seems as
though I can look back upon a former time in
which you and I had talked to one another as
though we had been lovers. May I not think
that it was so? May it not be so? May I not
call you my Mary?

'And indeed between man and man, as I
would say, only that you are not a man, have

I not a right to assume that it is so? I told him that it was so down at Croker's Hall, and he did not contradict me. And now he has been the most indiscreet of men, and has allowed all your secrets to escape from his breast. He has told me that you love me, and has bade me do as seems good to me in speaking to you of my love.

'But, Mary, why should there be any mock modesty or pretence between us? When a man and woman mean to become husband and wife, they should at any rate be earnest in their profession. I am sure of my love for you, and of my earnest longing to make you my wife. Tell me;—am I not right in counting upon you for wishing the same thing?

'What shall I say in writing to you of Mr. Whittlestaff? To me personally he assumes the language of an enemy. But he contrives to do so in such a way that I can take it only as the expression of his regret that I should be found to be standing in his way. His devotion to you is the most beautiful expression of self-abnegation that I have ever met. He tells me that nothing is done for me; but it is only that I may understand how much more is done for you. Next to me,—yes, Mary, next to myself, he should be the dearest to you of human beings. I am jealous already, almost jealous of his goodness. Would that I could look forward to a life in which I would be regarded as his friend.

'Let me have a line from you to say that it is as I would wish it, and name a day in which I may come to visit you. I shall now remain in London only to obey your behests. As to my future life, I can settle nothing till I can discuss it with you, as it will be your life also. God bless you, my own one.—Yours affectionately,

JOHN GORDON.'

'We are not to return to the diamond-fields. I have promised Mr. Whittlestaff that it shall be so.'

Mary, when she received this letter, retired into her own room to read it. For indeed her life in public,—her life, that is, to which Mrs. Baggett had access,—had been in some degree disturbed since the departure of the master of the house. Mrs. Baggett certainly proved herself to be a most unreasonable old woman. She praised Mary Lawrie up to the sky as being the only woman fitted to be her master's wife, at the same time abusing Mary for driving her out of the house were the marriage to take place; and then abusing her also because Mr. Whittlestaff had gone to town to look up another lover on Mary's behalf. 'It isn't my fault; I did not send him,' said Mary.

'You could make his going of no account. You needn't have the young man when he comes back. He has come here, disturbing us all with his diamonds, in a most objectionable manner.'

'You would be able to remain here and not have to go away with that dreadfully drunken old man.' This Mary had said, because there had been rather a violent scene with the one-legged hero in the stable.

'What's that to do with it? Baggett ain't the worst man in the world by any means. If he was a little cross last night, he ain't so always. You'd be cross yourself, Miss, if you didn't get straw enough under you to take off the hardness of the stones.'

'But you would go and live with him.'

'Ain't he my husband! Why shouldn't a woman live with her husband? And what does it matter where I live, or how. You ain't going to marry John Gordon, I know, to save me from Timothy Baggett!' Then the letter had come— the letter from Mary's lover; and Mary retired to her own room to read it. The letter she thought was perfect, but not so perfect as was Mr. Whittlestaff. When she had read the letter, although she had pressed it to her bosom and kissed it a score of times, although she had declared that it was the letter of one who was from head to foot a man, still there was room for that jealousy of which John Gordon had spoken. When Mary had said to herself that he was of all human beings surely the best, it was to Mr. Whittlestaff and not to John Gordon that she made allusion.

CHAPTER XXIII

Again at Croker's Hall

ABOUT three o'clock on that day Mr. Whittle-staff came home. The pony-carriage had gone to meet him, but Mary remained purposely out of the way. She could not rush out to greet him, as she would have done had his absence been occasioned by any other cause. But he had no sooner taken his place in the library than he sent for her. He had been thinking about it all the way down from London, and had in some sort prepared his words. During the next half hour he did promise himself some pleasure, after that his life was to be altogether a blank to him. He would go. To that only had he made up his mind. He would tell Mary that she should be happy. He would make Mrs. Baggett under-stand that for the sake of his property she must remain at Croker's Hall for some period to which he would decline to name an end. And then he would go.

'Well, Mary,' he said, smiling, 'so I have got back safe.'

'Yes; I see you have got back.'

'I saw a friend of yours when I was up in London.'

'I have had a letter, you know, from Mr. Gordon.'

'He has written, has he? Then he has been very sudden.'

'He said he had your leave to write.'

'That is true. He had. I thought that, perhaps,

he would have taken more time to think about it.'

'I suppose he knew what he had to say,' said Mary. And then she blushed, as though fearing that she had appeared to have been quite sure that her lover would not have been so dull.

'I daresay.'

'I didn't quite mean that I knew.'

'But you did.'

'Oh, Mr. Whittlestaff! But I will not attempt to deceive you. If you left it to him, he would know what to say,—immediately.'

'No doubt! No doubt!'

'When he had come here all the way from South Africa on purpose to see me, as he said, of course he would know. Why should there be any pretence on my part?'

'Why, indeed?'

'But I have not answered him;—not as yet.'

'There need be no delay.'

'I would not do it till you had come. I may have known what he would say to me, but I may be much in doubt what I should say to him.'

'You may say what you like.' He answered her crossly, and she heard the tone. But he was aware of it also, and felt that he was disgracing himself. There was none of the half-hour of joy which he had promised himself. He had struggled so hard to give her everything, and he might, at any rate, have perfected his gift with good humour. 'You know you have my full permission,' he said, with a smile. But he was aware that this smile was not pleasant,—was not such a smile as would make her happy. But it did not signify. When he was gone away, utterly abolished, then she would be happy.

'I do not know that I want your permission.'

'No, no; I daresay not.'

'You asked me to be your wife.'

'Yes; I did.'

'And I accepted you. The matter was settled then.'

'But you told me of him,—even at first. And you said that you would always think of him.'

'Yes; I told you what I knew to be true. But I accepted you; and I determined to love you with all my heart,—with all my heart.'

'And you knew that you would love him without any determination.'

'I think that I have myself under more control. I think that in time,—in a little time,—I would have done my duty by you perfectly.'

'As how?'

'Loving you with all my heart.'

'And now?' It was a hard question to put to her, and so unnecessary! 'And now?'

'You have distrusted me somewhat. I begged you not to go to London. I begged you not to go.'

'You cannot love two men.' She looked into his face, as though imploring him to spare her. For though she did know what was coming,— though had she asked herself, she would have said that she knew,—yet she felt herself bound to disown Mr. Gordon as her very own while Mr. Whittlestaff thus tantalised her. 'No; you cannot love two men. You would have tried to love me and have failed. You would have tried not to love him, and have failed then also.'

'Then I would not have failed. Had you remained here, and have taken me, I should certainly not have failed then.'*

'I have made it easy for you, my dear;—very easy. Write your letter. Make it as loving as you please. Write as I would have had you write to me, could it have been possible. O, Mary! that ought to have been my own! O, Mary! that would have made beautiful for me my future downward steps! But it is not for such a purpose that a young life such as yours should be given. Though he should be unkind to you, though money should be scarce with you, though the ordinary troubles of the world should come upon you, they will be better for you than the ease I might have prepared for you. It will be nearer to human nature. I, at any rate, shall be here if troubles come; or if I am gone, that will remain which relieves troubles. You can go now and write your letter.'

She could not speak a word as she left the room. It was not only that her throat was full of sobs, but that her heart was laden with mingled joy and sorrow, so that she could not find a word to express herself. She went to her bedroom and took out her letter-case to do as he had bidden her;—but she found that she could not write. This letter should be one so framed as to make John Gordon joyful; but it would be impossible to bring her joy so to the surface as to satisfy him even with contentment. She could only think how far it might yet be possible to sacrifice herself and him. She sat thus an hour, and then went back, and, hearing voices, descended to the drawing-room. There she found Mr. Blake and Kattie Forrester and Evelina Hall. They had come to call upon Mr. Whittlestaff and herself, and were full of their own news. 'Oh, Miss Lawrie, what do you think?' said Mr. Blake. Miss Lawrie, however, could not think, nor could Mr. Whittlestaff. 'Think of whatever is the greatest joy in the world,' said Mr. Blake.

'Don't make yourself such a goose,' said Kattie Forrester.

'Oh, but I am in earnest. The greatest joy in all the world.'

'I suppose you mean you're going to be married,' said Mr. Whittlestaff.

'Exactly. How good you are at guessing! Kattie has named the day. This day fortnight. Oh dear, isn't it near?'

'If you think so, it shall be this day fortnight next year,' said Kattie.

'Oh dear no! I didn't mean that at all. It can't be too near. And you couldn't put it off now, you know, because the Dean has been bespoke. It is a good thing to have the Dean to fasten the knot. Don't you think so, Miss Lawrie?'

'I suppose one clergyman is just the same as another,' said Mary.

'So I tell him. It will all be one twenty years hence. After all, the Dean is an old frump, and papa does not care a bit about him.'

'But how are you to manage with Mr. Newface?' asked Mr. Whittlestaff.

'That's the best part of it all. Mr. Hall is such a brick, that when we come back from the Isle of Wight he is going to take us all in.'

'If that's the best of it, you can be taken in without me,' said Kattie.

'But it is good; is it not? We two, and her maid. She's to be promoted to nurse one of these days.'

'If you're such a fool, I never will have you. It's not too late yet, remember that.' All which rebukes—and there were many of them—Mr. Montagu Blake received with loud demonstrations of joy. 'And so, Miss Lawrie, you're to be in the same boat too,' said Mr. Blake. 'I know all about it.'

Mary blushed, and looked at Mr. Whittlestaff. But he took upon himself the task of answering the clergyman's remarks. 'But how do you know anything about Miss Lawrie?'

'You think that no one can go up to London but yourself, Mr. Whittlestaff. I was up there myself yesterday;—as soon as ever this great question of the day was positively settled, I had to look after my own *trousseau*. I don't see why a gentleman isn't to have a *trousseau* as well as a lady. At any rate, I wanted a new black suit, fit for the hymeneal altar. And when there I made out John Gordon, and soon wormed the truth out of him. At least he did not tell me downright, but he let the cat so far out of the bag that I soon guessed the remainder. I always knew how it would be, Miss Lawrie.'

'You didn't know anything at all about it,' said Mr. Whittlestaff. 'It would be very much more becoming if you would learn sometimes to hold your tongue.'

Then Miss Evelina Hall struck in. Would Miss Lawrie come over to Little Alresford Park, and stay there for a few days previous to the wedding? Kattie Forrester meant to bring down a

sister with her as a bridesmaid. Two of the Miss
Halls were to officiate also, and it would be taken
as a great favour if Miss Lawrie would make a
fourth. A great deal was said to press upon her
this view of the case, to which, however, she
made many objections. There was, indeed, a
tragedy connected with her own matrimonial
circumstances, which did not make her well inclined to join such a party. Her heart was not
at ease within her as to her desertion of Mr.
Whittlestaff. Whatever the future might bring
forth, the present could not be a period of joy
But in the middle of the argument, Mr. Whittlestaff spoke with the voice of authority. 'Accept
Mr. Hall's kindness,' he said, 'and go over for a
while to Little Alresford.'

'And leave you all alone?'

'I'm sure Mr. Hall will be delighted if you will
come too,' said Mr. Blake, ready at the moment
to answer for the extent of his patron's house and
good-nature.

'Quite out of the question,' said Mr. Whittlestaff, in a tone of voice intended to put an end
to that matter. 'But I can manage to live alone
for a few days, seeing that I shall be compelled
to do so before long, by Miss Lawrie's marriage.'
Again Mary looked up into his face. 'It is so,
my dear. This young gentleman has managed to
ferret out the truth, while looking for his wedding
garments. Will you tell your papa, Miss Evelina,
that Mary will be delighted to accept his kindness?'

'And Gordon can come down to me,' said
Blake, uproariously, rubbing his hands; 'and we
can have three or four final days together, like
two jolly young bachelors.'

'Speaking for yourself alone,' said Kattie,— 'you'll have to remain a jolly young bachelor a considerable time still, if you don't mend your manners.'

'I needn't mend my manners till after I'm married, I suppose.' But they who knew Mr. Blake well were wont to declare that in the matter of what Miss Forrester called his manners, there would not be much to make his wife afraid.

The affair was settled as far as it could be settled in Mr. Gordon's absence. Miss Lawrie was to go over and spend a fortnight at Little Alresford just previous to Kattie Forrester's marriage, and Gordon was to come down to the marriage, so as to be near to Mary, if he could be persuaded to do so. Of this Mr. Blake spoke with great certainty. 'Why shouldn't he come and spoon a bit, seeing that he never did so yet in his life? Now I have had a lot of it.'

'Not such a lot by any means,' said Miss Forrester.

'According to all accounts he's got to begin it. He told me that he hadn't even proposed regular. Doesn't that seem odd to you, Kattie?'

'It seemed very odd when you did it.' Then the three of them went away, and Mary was left to discuss the prospects of her future life with Mr. Whittlestaff. 'You had better both of you come and live here,' he said. 'There would be room enough.' Mary thought probably of the chance there might be of newcomers, but she said nothing. 'I should go away, of course,' said Mr. Whittlestaff.

'Turn you out of your own house!'

'Why not? I shan't stay here any way. I am tired of the place, and though I shan't care to sell it, I shall make a move. A man ought to make a move every now and again. I should like to go to Italy, and live at one of those charming little towns.'

'Without a soul to speak to.'

'I shan't want anybody to speak to. I shall take with me just a few books to read. I wonder whether Mrs. Baggett would go with me. She can't have much more to keep her in England than I have.' But this plan had not been absolutely fixed when Mary retired for the night, with the intention of writing her letter to John Gordon before she went to bed. Her letter took her long to write. The thinking of it rather took too long. She sat leaning with her face on her hands, and with a tear occasionally on her cheek, into the late night, meditating rather on the sweet goodness of Mr. Whittlestaff than on the words of the letter. It had at last been determined that John Gordon should be her husband. That the fates seem to have decided, and she did acknowledge that in doing so the fates had been altogether propitious. It would have been very difficult,—now at last she owned that truth to herself,—it would have been very difficult for her to have been true to the promise she had made, altogether to eradicate John Gordon from her heart, and to fill up the place left with a wife's true affection for Mr. Whittlestaff. To the performance of such a task as that she would not be subjected. But on the other hand, John Gordon must permit her to entertain and to evince a regard for Mr. Whittlestaff, not similar at all to the regard which she would feel for her husband, but almost equal in its depth.

At last she took the paper and did write her letter, as follows:—

'DEAR MR. GORDON,—I am not surprised at anything that Mr. Whittlestaff should do which shows the goodness of his disposition and the tenderness of his heart. He is, I think, the most unselfish of mankind. I believe you to be so thoroughly sincere in the affection which you express for me, that you must acknowledge that he is so. If you love me well enough to make me your wife, what must you think of him who has loved me well enough to surrender me to one whom I had known before he had taken me under his fostering care?

'You know that I love you, and am willing to become your wife. What can I say to you now, except that it is so. It is so. And in saying that, I have told you everything as to myself. Of him I can only say, that his regard for me has been more tender even than that of a father. —Yours always most lovingly,

'MARY LAWRIE.'

CHAPTER XXIV

Conclusion*

THE day came at last on which Mary's visit to Little Alresford was to commence. Two days later John Gordon was to arrive at the Parsonage, and Mary's period of being 'spooned' was to be commenced,—according to Mr. Blake's phraseology. 'No, my dear; I don't think I need go with you,' said Mr. Whittlestaff, when the very day was there.

'Why not come and call?'

'I don't much care about calling,' said Mr. Whittlestaff. This was exactly the state of mind to which Mary did not wish to see her friend reduced,—that of feeling it to be necessary to avoid his fellow-creatures.

'You think Mr. Blake is silly. He is a silly young man, I allow; but Mr. Hall has been very civil. As I am to go there for a week, you might as well take me.' As she spoke she put her arm around him, caressing him.

'I don't care particularly for Mr. Blake; but I don't think I'll go to Little Alresford.' Mary understood, when he said this the second time, that the thing was fixed as fate. He would not go to Little Alresford. Then, in about a quarter of an hour, he began again—'I think you'll find me gone when you come back again.'

'Gone! where shall you have gone?'

'I'm not quite comfortable here. Don't look so sad, you dear, dear girl.' Then he crossed the room and kissed her tenderly. 'I have a nervous irritable feeling which will not let me remain quiet. Of course, I shall come for your marriage, whenever that may be fixed.'

'Oh, Mr. Whittlestaff, do not talk in that way! That will be a year to come, or perhaps two or three. Do not let it disturb you in that way, or I shall swear that I will not be married at all. Why should I be married if you are to be miserable?'

'It has been all settled, my dear. Mr. Gordon is to be the lord of all that. And though you will be supposed to have fixed the day, it is he that will really fix it;—he, or the circumstances of his life. When a young lady has promised a young gentleman, the marriage may be delayed to suit the young gentleman's convenience, but never to suit hers. To tell the truth, it will always be felt convenient that she shall be married as soon as may be after the promise has been given. You will see Mr. Gordon in a day or two, and will find out then what are his wishes.'

'Do you think that I shall not consult your wishes?'

'Not in the least, my dear. I, at any rate, shall have no wishes,—except what may be best for your welfare. Of course I must see him, and settle some matters that will have to be settled. There will be money matters.'

'I have no money,' said Mary,—'not a shilling! He knows that.'

'Nevertheless there will be money matters, which you will have the goodness to leave to me. Are you not my daughter, Mary, my only child? Don't trouble yourself about such matters as these, but do as you're bid. Now it is time for you to start, and Hayonotes will be ready to go with you.' Having so spoken, Mr. Whittlestaff put her into the carriage, and she was driven away to Little Alresford.

It then wanted a week to the Blake-cum-Forrester marriage, and the young clergyman was beginning to mix a little serious timidity with his usual garrulous high spirits. 'Upon my word, you know I'm not at all sure that they are going to do it right,' he said with much emphasis to Miss Lawrie. 'The marriage is to be on Tuesday. She's to go home on the Saturday. I insist upon being there on the Monday. It would make a fellow so awfully nervous travelling on the same day. But the other girls—and you're one of them, Miss Lawrie—are to go into Winchester by train on Tuesday morning, under the charge of John Gordon. If any thing were to happen to any of you, only think, where should I be?'

'Where should we be?' said Miss Lawrie.

'It isn't your marriage, you know. But I suppose the wedding could go on even if one of you didn't come. It would be such an awful thing not to have it done when the Dean is coming.' But Mary comforted him, assuring him that the Halls were very punctual in all their comings and goings when any event was in hand.

Then John Gordon came, and, to tell the truth, Mary was subjected for the first time to the ceremony of spooning. When he walked up to the door across from the Parsonage, Mary Lawrie took care not to be in the way. She took herself to her own bedroom, and there remained, with feverish, palpitating heart, till she was summoned by Miss Hall. 'You must come down and bid him welcome, you know.'

'I suppose so; but——'

'Of course you must come. It must be sooner or later. He is looking so different from what he was when he was here before. And so he ought, when one considers all things.'

'He has not got another journey before him to South Africa.'

'Without having got what he came for,' said Miss Hall. Then when they went down, Mary was told that John Gordon had passed through the house into the shrubbery, and was invited to follow him. Mary, declaring that she would go alone, took up her hat and boldly went after him. As she passed on, across the lawn, she saw his figure disappearing among the trees. 'I don't think it very civil for a young lady's young man to vanish in that way,' said Miss Hall. But Mary boldly and quickly followed him, without another word.

'Mary,' he said, turning round upon her as soon as they were both out of sight among the trees. 'Mary, you have come at last.'

'Yes; I have come.'

'And yet, when I first showed myself at your house, you would hardly receive me.' But this he said holding her by the hand, and looking into her face with his brightest smile. 'I had postponed my coming almost too late.'

'Yes, indeed. Was it my fault?'

'No;—nor mine. When I was told that I was doing no good about the house, and reminded that I was penniless, what could I do but go away?'

'But why go so far?'

'I had to go where money could be earned. Considering all things, I think I was quick enough. Where else could I have found diamonds but at the diamond-fields? And I have been perhaps the luckiest fellow that has gone and returned.'

'So nearly too late!'

'But not too late.'

'But you were too late,—only for the inexpressible goodness of another. Have you thought what I owe—what you and I owe—to Mr. Whittlestaff?'

'My darling!'

'But I am his darling. Only it sounds so conceited in any girl to say so. Why should he care so much about me?—or why should you, for the matter of that?'

'Mary, Mary, come to me now.' And he held out both his hands. She looked round, fearing intrusive eyes, but seeing none, she allowed him to embrace her. 'My own,—at last my own. How well you understood me in those old days. And yet it was all without a word,—almost without a sign.' She bowed her head before she had escaped from his arms. 'Now I am a happy man.'

'It is he that has done it for you.'

'Am I not thankful?'

'How can I be thankful as I ought? Think of the gratitude that I owe him,—think of all the love! What man has loved as he has done? Who has brought himself so to abandon to another the reward he had thought it worth his while to wish for? You must not count the value of the thing.'

'But I do.'

'But the price he had set upon it! I was to be the comfort of his life to come. And it would have been so, had he not seen and had he not believed. Because another has loved, he has given up that which he has loved himself.'

'It was not for my sake.'

'But it was for mine. You had come first, and had won my poor heart. I was not worth the winning to either of you.'

'It was for me to judge of that.'

'Just so. But you do not know his heart. How prone he is to hold by that which he knows he has made his own. I was his own.'

'You told him the truth when he came to you.'

'I was his own,' said Mary, firmly. 'Had he bade me never to see you again, I should never have seen you. Had he not gone after you himself, you would never have come back.'

'I do not know how that might be.'

'It would have been to no good. Having consented to take everything from his hands, I could never have been untrue to him. I tell you that I should as certainly have become his wife, as that girl will become the wife of that young clergyman. Of course I was unhappy.'

'Were you, dear?'

'Yes. I was very unhappy. When you flashed upon me there at Croker's Hall, I knew at once all the joy that had fallen within my reach. You were there, and you had come for me! All the way from Kimberley, just for me to smile upon you! Did you not?'

'Indeed I did.'

'When you had found your diamonds, you thought of me,—was it not so?'

'Of you only.'

'You flatterer! You dear, bonny lover. You whom I had always loved and prayed for, when I knew not where you were! You who had not left me to be like Mariana, but had hurried home at once for me when your man's work was done,— doing just what a girl would think that a man should do for her sake. But it had been all destroyed by the necessity of the case. I take no blame to myself.'

'No; none.'

'Looking back at it all, I was right. He had chosen to want me, and had a right to me. I had taken his gifts, given with a full hand. And where were you, my own one? Had I a right to think that you were thinking of me?'

'I was thinking of you.'

'Yes; because you have turned out to be one in a hundred: but I was not to have known that. Then he asked me, and I thought it best that he should know the truth and take his choice. He did take his choice before he knew the truth,— that you were so far on your way to seek my hand.'

'I was at that very moment almost within reach of it.'

'But still it had become his. He did not toss it from him then as a thing that was valueless. With the truest, noblest observance, he made me understand how much it might be to him, and then surrendered it without a word of ill humour, because he told himself that in truth my heart was within your keeping. If you will keep it well, you must find a place for his also.' It was thus that Mary Lawrie suffered the spooning that was inflicted upon her by John Gordon.

.   .   .   .

The most important part of our narrative still remains. When the day came, the Reverend Montagu Blake was duly married to Miss Catherine Forrester in Winchester Cathedral, by the Very Reverend the Dean, assisted by the young lady's father; and it is pleasant to think that on that occasion the two clergymen behaved to each other with extreme civility. Mr. Blake at once took his wife over to the Isle of Wight, and came back at the end of a month to enjoy the hospitality of Mr. Hall. And with them came the lady's maid, of whose promotion to a higher sphere in life we shall expect soon to hear. Then came a period of thorough enjoyment for Mr. Blake in superintending the work of Mr. Newface.

'What a pity it is that the house should ever be finished!' said the bride to Augusta Hall; 'because as things are now, Montagu is supremely happy: he will never be so happy again.'

'Unless when the baby comes,' said Augusta.

'I don't think he'll care a bit about the baby,' said the bride.

The writer, however, is of a different opinion, as he is inclined to think that the Reverend Montagu Blake will be a pattern for all fathers. One word more we must add of Mr. Whittlestaff and his future life,—and one word of Mrs. Baggett. Mr. Whittlestaff did not leave Croker's Hall. When October had come round, he was present at Mary's marriage, and certainly did not carry himself then with any show of outward joy. He was moody and silent, and, as some said, almost uncourteous to John Gordon. But before Mary went down to the train, in preparation of her long wedding-tour, he took her up to his bedroom, and there said a final word to her. 'Give him my love.'

'Oh, my darling! you have made me so happy.'

'You will find me better when you come back, though I shall never cease to regret all that I have lost.'

Mrs. Baggett accepted her destiny, and remained in supreme dominion over all womenkind at Croker's Hall. But there was private pecuniary arrangement between her and her master, of which I could never learn the details. It resulted, however, in the sending of a money-order every Saturday morning to an old woman in whose custody the Sergeant was left.

APPENDIX 1

Trollope's Autograph Composition of *An Old Man's Love*

TROLLOPE wrote about a third of the manuscript of *An Old Man's Love*. This seems to have been all that his stiffened hand could manage. The remaining two-thirds was written to his dictation by his niece Florence Bland. Trollope evidently liked to kick off chapters. Otherwise, he wrote occasional short passages. There are, however, a few longer stretches in his hand perhaps indicating that he was feeling unusually well. There also seems to me some evidence that Trollope took over at points of narrative complexity (e.g. pages 40–61, 190–215). The reader may perhaps be interested in comparing those passages Trollope wrote by hand with those Miss Bland took down. Page references that follow are to this World's Classics edition. I am grateful to Princeton University Library (Robert H. Taylor Collection) for letting me examine the manuscript.

Page 3, 'Two years ago' to page 4, 'I don't care one straw for Mrs. Baggett'

Page 12, 'Mr. Whittlestaff had not been a fortunate man' to page 12, 'the necessity of saving a shilling'

Page 16, 'The same idea had occurred to him as to Mrs. Baggett' to page 16, 'there was room for infinite joy'

Page 19, 'And so it went on' to page 20, 'Mrs. Baggett could not bring herself to understand it'

Page 24, 'There is nothing more difficult' to page 24, 'such as the words have painted it'

Page 28, 'An incident must now be told' to page 28, 'to man, woman, or child'

Page 36, 'She sat listening to all that he had to say to her' to page 37, 'must be resolved in so short a time?'

Page 40, 'But you will never repeat what you now hear' to page 61, 'I shouldn't 've minded it'

Page 67, 'She was bound to say something' to page 68, 'at work among the diamond-fields for two years'

Page 74, 'He said he had come from Kimberley' to page 74, 'said Gordon, looking'

Page 75, 'There had been no promise' to page 76, 'holding himself somewhat more erect as he spoke'

Page 80, 'The door was closed' to page 80, 'the wife of another man'

Page 84, 'She could not tell him of that second meeting' to page 85, ' "It matters not at all," she said'

Page 94, 'The Rev. Montagu Blake was curate' to page 94, '£300 a-year perhaps, and,—'

Page 98, 'Well; I don't know. He is old' to page 99, 'whether old Whittlestaff will think of marrying'

Page 103, 'All this happened just as John Gordon came up' to page 104, 'under all the circumstances, it was better not'

Page 108, 'I own, sir, that it is singular' to page 109, 'should be considered as over'

Page 117, 'Such a man must maunder' to page 117, 'cannot be stern and cruel for that occasion only'

Page 122, 'And so he stalked on' to page 123, 'deposited the man in an empty stall'

Page 127, 'It was clear that the young lady intended him to understand' to page 127, 'the good things of matrimony and the living'

Page 131, 'But that was all' to page 133, 'I have heard your name—that's all'

Page 137, 'And Mr. Blake would certainly have been unable to keep such a secret' to page 139, 'the gentlemen followed them half an hour afterwards'

Page 146, 'There's an invitation come' to page 147, 'instead of that precious stone?'

Page 150, 'in the neighbourhood. Nothing but trouble' to page 151, 'because she well understood that Mr. Gordon was'

Page 156, 'This would be her last opportunity' to page 156, 'the chance of changing her mind was still in her power'

Page 160, 'He was an unfortunate man' to page 166, 'she said, plucking up herself suddenly'

Page 169, 'The next day was Saturday' to page 169, 'her own affairs,—as far as'

Page 174, 'Not to him' to page 175, 'Drat them fine feelings'

Page 180, 'The next day was Sunday' to page 181, 'he said to himself, or so vain as that an old man'

Page 184, 'I should like John Gordon to be present' to page 186, 'Where are you going?'

Page 190, 'On the day arranged' to page 215, 'the old woman again went on after a pause'

Page 219, 'And the punishment must certainly come' to page 219, 'who of course knew all the facts'

Page 233, 'Who can tell, as you say?' to page 234, 'Of course I do. You have known it'

Page 237, 'When they parted in the park' to page 237, 'As he thought of the whole'

Page 241, 'If you will come with him' to page 242, 'he did go down on the following day'

Page 247, 'About three o'clock on that day' to page 252, 'She's to be promoted to nurse one of these days'

Page 254, 'I needn't mend my manners' to page 255, 'Without a soul to speak to'

Page 257, 'The day came at last' to page 258, 'let me remain quiet'

Page 260, 'Yes; I have come' to page 263, 'Had I a right to think'

APPENDIX 2
John Gordon and Kimberley

IN describing John Gordon's South African experiences (particularly in Chapters 6 and 18) Trollope recycled much of his own experience visiting the colony in 1877, which he wrote up in his travel book *South Africa*.[1] Trollope's description of Kimberley, given below, closely matches that of John Gordon, as given on page 68 of *An Old Man's Love*:

I cannot say that Kimberley is in other respects an alluring town;—perhaps as little so as any town that I have ever visited. There are places to which men are attracted by the desire of gain which seem to be so repulsive that no gain can compensate the miseries incidental to such an habitation. I have seen more than one such place and have wondered that under any inducement men should submit themselves, their wives and children to such an existence. I remember well my impressions on reaching Charles Dickens' Eden at the junction of the Ohio and Mississippi rivers and my surprise that any human being should have pitched his tent in a place so unwholesome and so hideous. I have found Englishmen collected on the Musquito Coast, a wretched crew; and having been called on by untoward Fate and a cruel Government to remain a week at Suez have been driven to consider whether life could have been possible there for a month. During my sojourn at Kimberley, though I was the recipient of the kindest hospitality and met two or three whom I shall ever remember among the

[1] 2 vols. (London, 1878).

pleasant acquaintances of my life,—yet the place itself was distasteful to me in the extreme. When I was there the heat was very great, the thermometer registering 160 in the sun, and 97 in the shade. I was not absolutely ill, but I was so nearly ill that I was in fear the whole time. Perhaps having been in such personal discomfort, I am not a fair judge of the place. But an atmosphere composed of dust and flies cannot be pleasant,—of dust so thick that the sufferer fears to remove it lest the raising of it may aggravate the evil, and of flies so numerous that one hardly dares to slaughter them by the ordinary means lest their dead bodies should be noisome. When a gust of wind would bring the dust in a cloud hiding everything, a cloud so thick that it would seem that the solid surface of the earth had risen diluted into the air, and when flies had rendered occupation altogether impossible. I would be told, when complaining, that I ought to be there, in December say, or February,—at some other time of the year than that the present,—if I really wanted to see what flies and dust could do. I sometimes thought that the people of Kimberley were proud of their flies and their dust.

And the meat was bad, the butter uneatable, vegetables a rarity,—supplied indeed at the table at which I sat but supplied at a great cost. Milk and potatoes were luxuries so costly that one sinned almost in using them. A man walking about with his pocket full of diamonds would not perhaps care for this; but even at Kimberley there are those who have fixed incomes,—an unfortunate Deputy Governor or the like,—to whom sugar at 2s. 6d. a pound and other equally necessary articles in the same proportion, must detract much from the honour and glory of the position. When I was there 'transport', no doubt, was unusually high. Indeed, as I arrived, there were muttered threats that 'transport' would be discontinued altogether unless rain would come. For the understanding of this it must be known that almost everything consumed at Kimberley has to be carried up from the coast, five hundred miles, by ox-waggons, and that the oxen have to feed themselves on the grasses along the road. When there has been a period of drought there are no grasses, and when there are no grasses the oxen will die instead of making progress. Periods of drought are by no means uncommon in South Africa. When I was at Kimberley there had been a period of drought for many months. There had, indeed, been no rain to speak of for more than a year. As one consequence of this the grocers were charging 2s. 6d. a pound for brown sugar. Even the chance of such a state of things militates very much against the comfort of a residence.

I do not think that there is a tree to be seen within five miles of the town. When I was there I doubt whether there was a blade of grass within twenty miles, unless what might be found on the very marge of the low water of the Vaal river. Everything was brown, as though the dusty dry uncovered ugly earth never knew the blessing of verdure. To ascertain that the roots of grass were remaining one had to search the ground. There is to be a park; and irrigation has been proposed so that the park may become green;— but the park had not as yet progressed beyond the customary brown. In all Kimberley and its surroundings there was nothing pretty to meet the eye;— except, indeed, women's faces which were as bright there as elsewhere. It was a matter of infinite regret to me that faces so bright should be made to look out on a world so ugly.

The town is built of corrugated iron. My general readers will probably not have seen many edifices so constructed. But even in England corrugated iron churches have been erected, when the means necessary for stone buildings have been temporarily wanting; and I think I have seen the studios of photographers made of the same material. It is probably the most hideous that has yet come to man's hands;—but it is the most portable and therefore in many localities the cheapest,—and in some localities the only material possible. It is difficult to conceive the existence of a town in which every plank used has had to be dragged five hundred miles by oxen; but such has been the case at Kimberley. Nor can bricks be made which will stand the weather because bricks require to be burned and cannot well be burned without fuel. Fuel at Kimberley is so expensive a luxury that two thoughts have to be given to the boiling of a kettle. Sun-burned bricks are used and form the walls of which the corrugated iron is the inside casing; but sun-burned bricks will not stand the weather and can only be used when they are cased. Lath and plaster for ceilings there is little or none. The rooms are generally covered with canvas which can be easily carried. But a canvas ceiling does not remain long clean, or even rectilinear. The invincible dust settles upon it and bulges it, and the stain of the dust comes through it. Wooden floors are absolutely necessary for comfort and cleanliness; but at Kimberley it will cost £40 to floor a moderate room. The consequence is that even people who are doing well with their diamonds live in comfortless houses, always meaning to pack up and run after this year, or next year, or perhaps the year after next. But if they have done ill with their diamonds they remain till they may do better; and if they have done well then there falls upon them the Auri sacra fames. When £30,000 have been so easily heaped together why not have £60,000;—and when

£60,000 why not £100,000? And when they spend money largely in this state of trial, in a condition which is not intended to be prolonged,—but which is prolonged from year to year by the desire for more? Why try to enjoy life here, this wretched life, when so soon there is a life coming which is to be so infinitely better? Such is often the theory of the enthusiastic Christian,—not however often carried out to its logical conclusions. At such a place as Kimberley the theory becomes more lively; but the good time is postponed till the capacity for enjoying it is too probably lost.

The town of Kimberley is chiefly notable for a large square,—as large perhaps as Russell Square. One or two of the inhabitants asked me whether I was not impressed by the grandeur of its dimensions so as to feel that there was something of sublimity attached to it! 'I thought it very ugly at first,' said one lady who had been brought out from England to make her residence among the diamonds;—'but I have looked at it now till I have to own its magnificence.' I could not but say that corrugated iron would never become magnificent in my eyes. In Kimberley there are two buildings with a storey above the ground, and one of these is in the square. This is its only magnificence. There is no pavement. The roadway is all dust and holes. There is a market place in the midst which certainly is not magnificent. Around are the corrugated iron shops of the ordinary dealers in provisions. An uglier place I do not know how to imagine. When I was called upon to admire it, I was lost in wonder; but acknowledged that it was well that necessity should produce such results.

EXPLANATORY NOTES

IN the *Times Literary Supplement* for 25 January 1941
R. W. Chapman raised some queries about the World's
Classics text of *An Old Man's Love* (which this edition
reproduces). Chapman noted that the production of the
novel (which he thought 'not one of Trollope's best')
was supervised by Trollope's son Henry, who was not a
good proof-reader. Chapman, who was himself eagle-
eyed as a reader of novels, pointed to a number of
oddities in the World's Classics text and suggested
corrections. He did not have access to the manuscript or
to the proofs (which seem not to have survived). Many
of Chapman's guesses prove to be right and even when
he is wrong he usually puts his finger on some anomaly
in the text. I deal with his substantive observations in
the notes that follow. I am grateful to Mac Pigman for
assistance with Trollope's classical allusions and quota-
tions in the text.

1   *his country seat in Hampshire*: R. H. Super (*The
Chronicler of Barsetshire* (Ann Arbor, Mich., 1988),
427) notes that the action is set 'at Alresford in the
Hampshire downs, only ten or fifteen miles from
Harting'. Trollope moved to his house at Harting,
on the Sussex–Hampshire border near Petersfield,
in July 1880. It is unusual for him to use a real
place-name for the action of his fiction, as he does
in *An Old Man's Love*.

3   *But that expression, which*: Chapman thinks that the
'which' here may not be in the manuscript. It is
(Florence Bland was writing at this point).

    *whether he could or would not bring into his own
house*: Chapman thinks that 'would' is an error for

'could'. The manuscript does, indeed, have 'could or could not'.

12 *does not write down a man his good luck*: Chapman is dubious about this phrase and thinks that Trollope (who was indeed writing at this point) wrote 'a man's good luck'. He is half right. Trollope got into rather a muddle with crossings out in the sentence. He originally wrote 'mans', did not correct it by adding the apostrophe and carelessly inserted 'his' before 'good luck' as an afterthought. The printer had a choice of bad readings, and chose 'his good luck', changing 'mans' to 'man'.

he was recommended to drink whisky: see Trollope's letter to his brother Tom at this period: 'I drink no wine, I may drink whisky, thus I sustain myself', (*The Letters of Anthony Trollope*, ed. N. John Hall, 2 vols. (Stanford, Calif., 1983), II. 936).

15 *had he been a shoemaker*: Trollope liked to compare his writing novels with the lowly but useful trade of the shoemaker. The most famous instance is in *An Autobiography* (1883), although R. H. Super has traced the comparison back as far as April 1860.

Cicero's de Natura Deorum: Marcus Tullius Cicero (106–43 BC), orator and philosopher. Cicero's 'Of the Nature of the Gods' is a dialogue addressed to Brutus in which the teachings on divinity of the Epicurean, Stoic, and Academic schools are discussed. Trollope published a life of Cicero in 1880, a couple of years before *An Old Man's Love*. His last chapter is devoted to Cicero's views on the gods. Trollope writes: 'I should have hardly thought it necessary to devote a chapter of my book to the religion of a pagan had I not, while studying Cicero's life, found that I was not dealing with a pagan's mind.' Cicero, Trollope concludes, was 'almost a Christian, even before Christ'. In the context, it is interesting to note that Trollope turned to private study of the classics to console himself for giving up his beloved hunting, in 1878.

knew probably well the whole story: Chapman surmises this must be 'knew perfectly well'. But Florence Bland wrote 'probably'. Perhaps she misheard Trollope.

18 *But with her gratitude . . . the reserve of a grown-up child*: Chapman is very unhappy with this sentence. He is right to be. It was dictated by Trollope to Florence Bland, and later corrected in his hand so as to produce nonsense. It reads in the manuscript: 'She treated him at first almost as a servant,—at any rate with none of the familiarity of a child ['child' crossed out, 'friend' inserted], and hardly with the reserve of a grown young woman ['young woman' crossed out, '-up child' inserted].' Had Trollope left the sentence as it originally stood it would have been fine.

19 *the young lady's marriage*: Trollope originally dictated 'his own marriage' which makes more sense than 'the young lady's marriage'. But he obviously changed it because of the ambiguity whether 'his own marriage' means Whittlestaff's or that of Whittlestaff's unnamed friend.

21 *as beards go now*: Trollope had—for twenty-five years at least—sported a remarkably full and bushy beard. He was proud of his facial hair, writing in his travel book *The West Indies and the Spanish Main* (1859) 'If I have any personal vanity, it is wrapped up in my beard. It is a fine, manly article' (see Super, *The Chronicler of Barsetshire*, 104).

22 *chimney-pot*: i.e. a black, elongated, silk top hat.

The article was still widely worn in the 1880s, though evidently not by the fashion conscious.

24 *Southey's Lodore is supposed to have been effective*: the Lodore falls are in Cumberland, at the foot of Derwentwater, near Keswick. Robert Southey wrote a charming poem, 'The Cataract of Lodore, described in Rhyme for the Nursery' in 1820. The poem is a *tour de force* of rhyme ('Collecting, projecting, | Receding and speeding, | And shocking and rocking, | And darting and parting, | And threading and spreading', etc.).

of Amelia Booth, of Clarissa, of Di Vernon, and of Maggie Tulliver: the heroines of famous novels: Henry Fielding's *Amelia* (1752), Samuel Richardson's *Clarissa* (1748–9), Walter Scott's *Rob Roy* (1817), and George Eliot's *The Mill on the Floss* (1860).

Of Thackeray's Beatrix I have a vivid idea, because she was drawn for him by an artist under his own eye: Trollope, who was writing not dictating, got into rather a muddle here. He first wrote 'Of Thackeray's Beatrix, I have a vivid idea, because Thackeray absolutely drew her portrait as well as painted her character.' Then, having written this, he suddenly remembered that *The History of Henry Esmond* was a novel that Thackeray had *not* in fact illustrated. It was published in 1852 in three unillustrated volumes and reprinted in 1858 also without pictures. Rather than check, Trollope then hazarded a guess that the pictorial *Esmond* which he remembered seeing—with its handsome illustrations by George du Maurier—had been done under Thackeray's supervision (as he had supervised Richard Doyle on *The Newcomes* and Fred Walker on *Philip*). In fact, du Maurier's pictures were done after Thackeray's death in 1863 for the 'Library Edition' of the author's works in 1867–9. There was, I believe, no illustrated edition of *Esmond* during Thackeray's lifetime and certainly none that he superintended.

29   *as her master displayed them*: Trollope, who was dictating, first said 'as her husband displayed them'. It's an interesting slip.

46   *without putting in e'er a drop of brandy*: to keep the preserved fruit from going mouldy.

48   *service is no heritance*: although 'heritance' is an archaic word, Chapman thinks it must be wrong here. He is right. Trollope wrote 'service is no 'heritance'—Mrs Baggett's mutilation of 'inheritance'.

54   *you can hardly go on loving him as you have done*: Chapman thinks this is odd and proposes 'living here' for 'loving him'. Trollope was writing at this point in the manuscript, and his hand is extremely hard to read. But 'loving him' does look more likely to me, as it evidently did to Blackwood's compositor.

60   *I mustn't demean me to say*: Trollope first wrote 'It must demean me', which makes sense, even if it sounds too lofty for Mrs Baggett. He changed it to 'It mustn't demean me' evidently intending to create a comic double negative. This was further corrected by the compositor or Henry Trollope to the very awkward 'I mustn't demean me'.

     ou'd make: Chapman proposes 'as'd make'. He is right, 'as'd' is what Trollope wrote in the manuscript. By 'anchor' Mrs Baggett presumably means 'anchorite'.

64   *more shandy*: a rare word, although one that

Trollope liked to use. Dialect in origin it means 'wild' and 'irrational'.

66 *such as had dwelt*: Chapman proposes 'such as he had dwelt'. Florence Bland, however, wrote 'such as had dwelt'.

68 *I know no spot more odious in every way*: for Trollope's jaundiced view of Kimberley, see Appendix 2.

72 *She was still, at heart, Mary Lawrie*: Chapman proposes 'at least'. This is indeed what Trollope wrote and inserted interlineally into the passage, which was otherwise written in Florence Bland's hand.

74 *If Miss Lawrie will tell me that I may go away*: Chapman proposes 'must go away', but Trollope wrote 'may'.

85 *set his mind*: Chapman thinks Trollope may have written 'set his heart'. He in fact wrote 'mind'.

86 *the pity of it!*: John Gordon echoes Othello's exclamation to Iago (IV. i. 195–6) on being convinced of Desdemona's supposed adultery: 'But yet the pity of it, Iago! O Iago, the pity of it, Iago!'

93 *should make him too ecstatic in his wish*: Chapman suggests 'spirit' or 'bliss' for 'wish' here. Florence Bland indeed wrote 'bliss'.

94 *one of the prebendaries of Winchester*: a prebend is a cathedral benefice and a prebendary its holder. The term was generally replaced by 'canon' in the nineteenth century. Winchester, with its Cathedral, is some ten miles from Alresford.

95 *Mr. Furnival*: later in the text he is Mr Hall (see page 126). William Coyle notes the error and comments: 'The most interesting possibility is that while completing his last novel Trollope

reverted to *Orley Farm* where Mr Furnival's infatuation with Lady Mason was used as an excuse for a long address to the reader on middle-aged men in love.' (*Nineteenth Century Fiction*, 6:3 (1951), 222).

97 *crescit amor diamonds*: the love of diamonds grows.

see your diamonds turn into slate-stones: evidently Montagu refers to a fable in which the devil bribes a man with diamonds which later change to slate-stones. I cannot locate the author or the title of the story.

98 *Blake is a very good name for whisky*: Montagu seems to allude to a Blake's whisky. I have not encountered the brand.

101 *I shall be off to the diamond-fields again by the first mail*: i.e. mail-boat. Such vessels, like mail trains, were proverbially fast.

115 *but only in the funds*: consolidated government funds (also called 'consols'), first set up in 1751 to handle the national debt. They paid 3 per cent and were famously safe.

124 *had been looking at somebody taking a glass of gin*: this is what Florence Bland wrote. But clearly what is meant is 'had been looking for somebody to take him a glass of gin'.

128 *straight off the reel*: a Victorian idiom, now obsolete, meaning 'without stopping, in an uninterrupted course or succession' (*OED*).

135 *these bad times*: the 1870s and early 1880s were a period of acute agricultural distress in England. Crop prices and rents fell, there was a series of disastrous summers for harvests (particularly that of 1879). In 1879 a Royal Commission was set up to investigate this crisis in British agriculture. It

reported in 1882, as Trollope was writing *An Old Man's Love*.

138 *What does spem gregis mean?*: it means 'hope of the flock', a quotation from Virgil, *Eclogues*, 1. i. 15.

and Mr. Gordon the possibility of changing his: Chapman suggests that 'Gordon' is a printer's error for 'Blake', due to anticipation of 'Gordon' in the next line. He adds, 'if the text is sound, Miss Hall's bad manners are almost beyond belief'. This may be so, but none the less Trollope wrote 'Gordon'.

139 *a clergyman's throat*: a common term for laryngitis, to which clergymen were peculiarly prone.

his resurgam sung: 'I shall arise [at the Resurrection]'. Mr Hall means that as Mrs Blake Kattie would not want the Revd Harbottle to come back to life and reclaim his parish.

155 *Percontatorem fugito nam garrulus idem est*: Horace, *Epistles*, 1. xviii. 69. The sense is: 'Flee from a story-teller, for such a person cannot hold his tongue'.

158 *Have you seen diamonds, Miss Lawrie?*: Chapman suggests this should be 'his diamonds', which is indeed what Florence Bland wrote in the manuscript.

161 *Stanley crossed the continent*: Henry (later Sir Henry) Morton Stanley (1840–1904) discovered David Livingstone in Africa in 1871. But the reference here is to Stanley's great Anglo-American expedition of 1874–7, in which he started from the east coast and eventually reached the ocean at the mouth of the Congo in West Africa. The expedition is described in Stanley's *Through the Dark Continent* (1878).

162 *when prepared for another wish*: it is not clear to me

what this means. Trollope (whose writing is almost indecipherable here) may have written 'proposed'.

165 *The 'Oxford and Cambridge' in Pall Mall*: not one of Trollope's clubs, since he had not attended either of the two great universities. Founded in 1830, the club's Pall Mall premises were erected in 1837.

171 *to fit himself for Botany Bay*: in New South Wales, Australia. Mrs Baggett is comically out of date. Transportation of convicts to New South Wales had stopped years before.

177 *Gemmas, marmor, ebur . . . Sunt qui non habeant; est qui non curat habere*: Horace, *Epistles*, II. ii. 180–2. The sense is: 'Jewels, marble, ivory . . . there are those who do not have them, and there is the man who does not want them'.

178 *Me lentus Glycerae torret amor meæ*: Horace, *Odes*, III. xix. 28. The sense is: 'tenacious love for Glycera consumes me'.

run smoothly with those of Jesus Christ?: Trollope originally dictated 'run on all fours with those of Jesus Christ'. Henry Trollope or Blackwood's compositor obviously thought the horsy idiom rather blasphemous and sanitized it.

180 *Mr. Whittlestaff meditates a Journey*: in the manuscript and the proof which Blackwood's sent Henry Trollope the title is 'Mr. Whittlestaff intends to see a man upon Business'. Evidently someone other than the novelist—probably Henry Trollope—changed it.

181 *the Rev. Mr. Lowlad*: evidently a young and evangelical ('low') clergyman.

Intermissa, Venus, diu rursus bella moves? Parce, precor, precor: *Odes*, IV. i, opening lines. The 50-year-old

Horace's request that Venus should leave him in peace and not afflict him with love (in this case, for a young male).

Non sum qualis eram: I am not that which I once was. Horace, *Odes*, IV. i. 13.

183 *It is something about Augustus, I think*: Augustus was the first Roman emperor, 43 BC–AD 14. The month of August is so named in his honour.

184 *Black Gang Chine or Ventnor*: Blackgang Chine is a chasm on the Isle of Wight, some five miles west of the town of Ventnor.

186 *for more than two months*: in the light of Mary's next remark, Chapman thinks Trollope may have written 'two years', since she has been at Croker's Hall about that length of time. In fact Florence wrote and Trollope presumably dictated 'two months', illogical though it is.

189 *must at any rate be prevented*: Chapman notes 'that here, as occasionally elsewhere in Trollope, "at any rate" means "at any price" '.

192 *the great basin*: Trollope describes the gigantic pit which contained the hundreds of Kimberley diamond mine workings in *South Africa* (1878), vol. ii, chapter 8, 'The Story of the Diamond Fields':

You stand upon the marge and there, suddenly, beneath your feet lies the entirety of the Kimberley mine, so open, so manifest, and so uncovered that if your eyes were good enough you might examine the separate operations of each of the three or four thousand human beings who are at work there. It looks to be so steep down that there can be no way to the bottom other than the aerial contrivances which I will presently endeavour to explain. It is as though you were looking into a vast bowl, the sides of which are smooth as should be the sides of a bowl, while round the bottom are

various marvellous incrustations among which ants are
working with all the usual energy of the ant-tribe. And
these incrustations are not simply at the bottom, but
come up the curves and slopes of the bowl irregularly,—
half-way up perhaps in one place, while on another side
they are confined quite to the lower deep. The pit is 230
feet deep, nearly circular, though after awhile the eye
becomes aware of the fact that it is oblong. At the top
the diameter is about 300 yards of which 250 cover what
is technically called 'blue',—meaning diamondiferous
soil.

198 *I haven't touched a B. and S.*: brandy and soda.

200 *without a red cent*: Tookey uses American slang,
meaning 'without a penny'. The redness of the
cent alludes to its being made of copper.

201 *Poker & Hodge*: Chapman thinks 'Hedge' more
likely, as Trollope liked meaningful names. But he
definitely wrote 'Hodge'.

202 *Never be conscious of anything within your own bosom*:
Tookey apparently paraphrases the first half of
Horace's 'nil conscire sibi; nulla pallescere culpa',
Epistles, i. i. 61. The sense is: 'Have nothing on
your conscience; turn pale at no guilt'.

204 *I may kill beasts in Buenos Ayres, or take a tea-farm in
Thibet, or join the colonists in Tennessee*: John Gordon
is very desperate. At this time, Tibet was largely
unexplored, and no place for a European to grow
tea. Buenos Aires was the centre of a bloody civil
war. Since 1870, Tennessee had indeed been
attracting immigrants but was still in a *post-bellum*
slump. Trollope may, perhaps, have been thinking
of his mother, Frances Trollope, in the American
reference. In 1827, with the family fortunes at a
low ebb, Mrs Trollope went to western Tennessee
to become a member of the Nashoba slave

emancipation colony. She did not take to the colonist life, and soon left.

206 *Mr. Whittlestaff's Journey discussed*: this chapter, up to the top of page 215, is written by Trollope on Athenaeum Club notepaper.

215 *What do you know?*: Chapman thinks this question would make more sense if 'know' was 'mean'. Florence Bland wrote 'know', but the sentence occurs just as Trollope was switching from writing to dictating and it may be he was momentarily confused.

219 *robur et æs triplex*: Horace, *Odes*, I. iii. 9 'His breast must have been protected all round *with oak and three-ply bronze*, who first launched his frail boat on the rough sea'.

220 *His favourite Horace had had a fresh love for every day*: Trollope alludes to the large number of pseudonymous lovers, male and femalë whom Horace addresses in his *Odes*.

Of Petrarch and Laura: Petrarch (Francesco Petrarca, 1304–74) was the Italian poet who wrote love poems to the pseudonymous Laura.

Prince Arthur, in his love for Guinevere: Guinevere was the faithless wife of King Arthur in the Arthurian legend. Trollope was evidently fond of Tennyson's *Idylls of the King*; 'Guinevere', one of the earliest, was published in 1859. The whole twelve-part sequence was not published until 1891.

Imogen, in her love for Posthumus: Imogen is the heroine of Shakespeare's *Cymbeline*. A princess, she marries the poor but worthy Posthumus. Great complications ensue when he is banished.

224 *Though you say that you wish it, it is a lie which may not be ratified*: this sentence does not 'ring true' to

Chapman, who suggests that 'lie' may be a mistake for 'wish'. Florence Bland definitely wrote 'lie'.

229   *sub dio*: in the open air.

238   *though no word of absolute love for each other had even been spoken before*: Chapman thinks that 'there is something wrong here. The facts were that they were not engaged, and that there had been no overt love-making. Perhaps the text is the result of some change made *currente calamo*. Perhaps Trollope wrote something like "not a word of marriage".' In fact, this sentence occurs just on a change from Trollope's writing to Florence Bland's taking down his dictation. She definitely wrote 'no word of absolute love', but Trollope's concentration may have momentarily lapsed as he changed creative gears and adjusted to dictation.

240   *shell down*: in Trollope's day, as in ours, 'shell out' was the commoner usage, although 'down' was occasionally used.

249–50   *and have failed then also.' 'Then I would not have failed . . . I should certainly not have failed then'*: Chapman remarks that 'the confusion of "then" and "there" is very common in Trollope' given his ambiguous way of writing these words. Chapman thinks he wrote 'there', 'There', and 'there' in this exchange. Either is possible from the words Trollope scrawled in the manuscript; 'there' certainly sounds better.

257   *Conclusion*: the opening of this chapter up to 'remain quiet' on the second line of page 258 was written on Athenaeum club notepaper.